TRAPPED IN A WORLD NOT THEIR OWN . . .

Harold, Archbishop of York, had never planned to cause trouble for anyone. But when he used the Time Projector to flee his totalitarian twenty-first-century Earth, he created a disturbance in time which caught in its ripples many an unwilling twentieth-century American, including Bass Foster.

Bass had never wanted to become a lord or a leader of men, but cast back in time, to this world where war was the only way of life, it was fight and conquer—or die. . . .

Yet what neither Harold nor Bass could have foreseen was that they would soon be followed by other travelers in time—travelers intent on putting an end to them both!

CASTAWAYS IN TIME #3

ROBERT ADAMS
—✦OF✦—
QUESTS AND KINGS

Ⓢ

A SIGNET BOOK

NEW AMERICAN LIBRARY

PUBLISHED BY
THE NEW AMERICAN LIBRARY
OF CANADA LIMITED

NAL BOOKS ARE AVAILABLE AT QUANTITY DISCOUNTS WHEN USED
TO PROMOTE PRODUCTS OR SERVICES. FOR INFORMATION PLEASE
WRITE TO PREMIUM MARKETING DIVISION, NEW AMERICAN LIBRARY,
1633 BROADWAY, NEW YORK, NEW YORK 10019.

Copyright © 1986 by Robert Adams

First Printing, November, 1986

2 3 4 5 6 7 8 9

SIGNET TRADEMARK REG. U.S. PAT. OFF. AND FOREIGN COUNTRIES
REGISTERED TRADEMARK — MARCA REGISTRADA
HECHO EN WINNIPEG, CANADA

SIGNET, SIGNET CLASSIC, MENTOR, ONYX, PLUME, MERIDIAN
AND NAL BOOKS are published in Canada by The New American
Library of Canada, Limited, 81 Mack Avenue, Scarborough,
Ontario, Canada M1L 1M8
PRINTED IN CANADA
COVER PRINTED IN U.S.A.

The big, burly man in half-armor and plumed, open-faced bascinet strolled, seemingly aimlessly, along the top of the outer wall of the city, glancing from time to time at the massive bombards ranged at odd intervals. Each of the archaic pieces was covered with waxed tarpaulins against the frequent misty drizzles, and under them, thick, tarred tompions sealed the gaping muzzles, while waxed plugs stopped the touchholes atop the breeches. Wooden sheds thrown up on either side of each bombard held the multitudinous items of supplies and equipment needed to maintain, serve, and clean the antique weapons. Beyond range of the bombards' hellacious recoils stood stacks of four to five of the granite balls which were the heaviest things that the weak-walled tubes would throw, even charged with the weak serpentine powder that had to be mixed on the spot to the individual requirements of each bombard.

The big armored man, Captain Timoteo, *il Duce* di Bolgia, could not imagine just what had gone through the brain—admittedly, a quite often addled brain—of King Tàmhas FitzGerald, his erstwhile employer. The man had had the foresight to mount decent, modern guns that were cast strong enough to be charged with corned powder and would accurately throw iron ball and shell, grape, langrage, or what-have-you farther than all but the very largest of the bombards, could be reloaded in much less time, and could be easily moved about the walls to the spots of most immediate need; but these guns all were mounted on the landward approaches of the fortified city of Tàmhas'burh— the walls and other strong points overlooking the river and anchorages were armed with nothing of any size better or newer than these abominations of world-heavy, barely manageable relics.

Now true, a single massive stone ball from any one of them would go far to crack like a pigeon egg the oaken ribs of even the biggest and best-found ship, but in order for that to take place, the ship would have to be in just the right place at just the right time, a happenstance that was seen very, very infrequently in warfare. Had the ancient tubes been more maneuverable and faster to clean and recharge, they might have been some bare protection against a river packed with ships as thickly as a barrel with Lenten herrings.

But such was not the case. There was no slightest degree of uniformity to these guns—each of them took a different size of stone ball, a different charge of powdery serpentine mixed especially for it, on the spot, by a gunmaster who knew no other gun but the one and was responsible for no other, and each had its own particular and often peculiar quirks with regard to cleaning or charging, recharging or laying. Moreover, the old bombards could be more dangerous to their crews and to those round about than they were to those at whom they chanced to be aimed. Twice, now, since the siege had commenced, bombards still mounted on landward walls had burst, killing their entire crews, setting off mixed powder and maiming men standing far down the stretches of walls with shards or chunks of bronze or iron. Timoteo was of the firm opinion that all of the bombards should long since have been rendered into something useful, such as bells, plowshares, or brass pisspots.

But *Righ* Tàmhas would not hear of gracefully retiring even a single bombard for stupidly emotional reasons. He frequently pointed out that such and such a gun—he had

pet names for each of more than twoscore of the things—
had had a part in such and such a "great triumph" over
such and such foes during the "illustrious reign" of his
great-great-grandfather and gave such inanities as the firm
reasons why the venerable piece could not be replaced
with a new tube that would throw iron safely for a much
greater distance, use less powder, foul less thickly and
frequently, be traversed when need be, fire faster than a
couple of shots per hour, and imperil less the lives and
well-being of those who served it and served around it.

Pragmatic and more than a little cynical, *il Duce* di
Bolgia had never been able to fathom or relate to the
thinking processes of those who allowed their emotions to
make their decisions for them. His brother, Robert, was
and had always been far the better at doing any necessary
handling of such types; moreover, the *Righ* had taken a
liking to the younger of the brothers, and so Timoteo had
left the management of the none-too-bright, self-deluded
kinglet to Roberto and to Sir Ugo D'Orsini, who had
traveled with the di Bolgia condotta from Palermo.

Aside from his ongoing difficulties with the tempera-
mental, often childish, but powerful and unbelievably arrogant pocket king, *Righ* Tàmhas de FitzGerald—whose
"kingdom," even at the most far-flung boundaries claimed
by him and his cousin-advisers, was not quite so large as
the Duchy of Bolgia, and less than half the size of the
Duchy of D'Este—Timoteo thought that he could almost
come to like this kind of warfare, this variety of investment and siege.

He had lost a bare handful of men from his own condotta,
and there had been perhaps that many more lost from the
Ifriqan condotta of Sir Alariq al-Iswid, and almost all of
them had fallen in the sally that had convinced the *Ard-
righ*, Brian VIII, that another frontal assault against
Tàmhas'burh would cost more than he cared to pay. After
that, with other fish to fry, the *Ard-Righ* had wisely marched
his army off, leaving his trains to continue a passive
investment of Tàmhas'burh.

Upon the withdrawal of the *Ard-Righ*'s main force, *Righ*

Tàmhas had been hot to lead a sally-forth against the siege
lines to capture all the guns and engines, butcher the
gunners and engineers, and sack the camps, but after a few
nights of quiet, professional reconnaissances led by Timoteo
and Sir Alariq, Sir Roberto and Sir Ugo had had to convince the hot-blooded, thick-headed monarch that Brian
the Burly had left behind more than enough quality soldiers to make any sally a risky to bloody business, beyond
any safe capability of the much-shrunken Royal Army of
Munster.

Tàmhas had railed and shouted and stomped up and
down the length of the audience chamber, thrown a cathedra chair through a window, snapped the etched and inletted
blade of a gold-hilted dress dagger by trying to drive it into
the top of a polished oaken table. As he stared at the
broken bauble, the big, muscular man began to cry and
moan of how the Holy See and its chosen captain, di
Bolgia, had ruined him and Munster, driving loyal *bonaghts*
and *galloglaiches* and even noble FitzGerald kinsmen away
from their loving sovran, leaving him and Munster now
defenseless except for craven, money-grubbing oversea
mercenaries, with no true loyalty of bravery in them not
reckoned in grams of gold and ounces of silver. On hearing this last, it was only Sir Ugo's firm grip on his thick,
solid upper arm that kept Sir Roberto from stalking out
unbidden.

But at length, while the *Righ* moaned and sobbed on
with his litany of his totally undeserved abuses at the
hands of those he had trusted and those who had been sent
to aid him, Sir Roberto regained enough self-control to
step forward and say, "Your majesty, the di Bolgia condotta
and that of Sir Alariq al-Iswid were sent here to hold this
city, to try to make a modern army of the Munster forces,
also, but first and foremost to keep open this port. My
illustrious brother, Sir Alariq, and Le Chevalier Marc have
unanimously agreed that the city cannot be held, the port
cannot be kept open, if the best of the now available forces
are frittered away in open assault on entrenched foemen

for the possible capture of a few guns, trebuchets, and catapults and a bit of common camp loot.

"However, these strictures apply only to the companies not to noble-born individuals. If your majesty and his councillors and his gentlemen-at-arms wish to ride out against the siege lines, both Sir Ugo and I will ride behind your banner."

Righ Tàmhas, after using his long fingers to blow mucus from his nostrils onto the Persian carpet, snuffled and looked up. "And your brother and that blackamoor, what will they do, Sir Roberto?"

The younger di Bolgia shrugged. "Most likely they will bar the city gates behind us, observe the combat from the walls, let any survivors back in and haggle with the victors for the return of any wounded, work out ransoms, and buy noble bodies back for honorable, Christian interments."

The *Righ* snuffled once again, used a silken sleeve to wipe his nose, and nodded profoundly. "I knew that I had chosen aright, Sir Robert, Sir Ugo, I knew from first meeting that you two, alone of all the pack of new-model cravens who fight what little they do only for specie, were both good old-fashioned knights who valued your honor above all else in this world. I will be most happy to have you both ride out in my warband, but first I must meet with my full council. You will be summoned. You have my leave to now depart. May our Savior bless and keep you both."

Once some hundreds of yards distant from the palace, Sir Ugo laid hold to Sir Roberto's bridle arm and nearly jerked the stocky man out of the saddle. "What the bloody hell do you think you're up to, man? *You* may be as deluded as that so-called king is into thinking that you're still living two or three hundred years ago, but not me, not the third son of Geraldo D'Orsini. I've got far better things to do with my life than toss it away in the most senseless of a harebrained pocket king's schemes. Ride out to your death with those mad FitzGeralds if that is your desire, but ride without me!"

Roberto just grinned. "Simmer down, Ugo, simmer

down. Nobody's going to ride anywhere. Haven't you yet taken the true measure of that precious pack of FitzGerald cousins who were introduced to us as the Royal Council? Oh, yes, they every one talk and rant just as bloodthirstily as does their royal relative, but one and all, their hands are every bit as soft as my mistress's bottom. I have no doubt that they'd make good poisoners, and one or two of them might even be able to screw up the gumption to thrust a dagger in a man's back, but no one of them is in any manner of means a soldier. Recall, if you will, the exact way in which I phrased my offer of military service to Sniffing Tàmhas: 'If your majesty *and his concillors* and his gentlemen-at-arms wish to ride out . . .' and so on. Did you note the suddenly milk-pale faces on those three mothers' mistakes, Ugo? I did, and I also saw the 'secret signal' that they gave Tàmhas just before he dismissed us and announced an urgent meeting of the full council.''

Sir Ugo dropped his hand from Roberto's arm and sat back in his saddle. ''By the dusty pecker of Christ's ass-colt, di Bolgia, you're as devious as a cardinal. With any luck, you'll split that royal dolt away from his council as cleanly as . . . God's Wounds, if you and your brother had chosen the church instead of war . . . who knows?

''But once they're all sacked or worse, what then, Roberto? That man is about as capable of dealing with the affairs of what little is now left of his kingdom as is this gelding I ride today, and what noblemen are there about who are not related to him some way or anoth—? But . . . but, of course! And just who dreamed all this up, you or *il Duce?*''

''Actually,'' drawled Roberto, ''the germ of the plan came from *Le Chevalier*. He is a shrewd judge of the weak he descended, a sleekly groomed and richly accoutered seem. It was either somehow get firm control of this easily swayed kinglet . . . or do away with him entirely, only to see him succeeded by yet another of his ilk who might have been even more difficult and intransigient.

''This way, we two are just now the very jewels of Tàmhas's bloodshot eye; while, shortly, he will have damned all his councillors for cowards and be very much in need of solace and sage counsel by men he feels are alike to him and so can be implicitly trusted to lead him in the pursuit of old-fashioned honor.''

Sir Ugo slapped the reins languidly on his mount's neck and tapped his heels gently against the barrel to get moving once more, then he chuckled and shook his head. ''So, Tàmhas will rule the city, we will rule Tàmhas, and . . . who will rule us, Roberto? Does His Grace di Rezzi, the legate, know anything concerning any of this?''

Sir Roberto shrugged. ''*I* didn't tell him. I've only seen the man once, after all. Whether others have or will or haven't or won't is none of my purely personal affair, Ugo. As to who will rule us, I don't know about you, but my loyalties will lie just where they always have lain: with His Grace my brother, and the welfare of his company. You will find as has many another that we di Bolgias cleave closely one to the other, for there are but the two of us against a hard and often a cruel world.''

After his early-morning wall-walk, the Duce di Bolgia returned to his small but comfortable mansion, where his serving men helped him to disarm and redress in less military and far more ornate clothing. In the courtyard, as he descended, a sleekly groomed and richly accoutered barb awaited him, stamping and prancing and tossing her small, neat head. At a brisk walk, trailed closely by his bannerman, his squires, and some of the axmen of his personal guard, the eldest of the di Bolgias wound his way through the already bustling streets of the city to the mansion of the Papal Legate, Giosué di Rezzi, acting Archbishop of Munster.

Il Duce could not say that he liked di Rezzi—his employer in residence and in fact. The rigid old man was flinty of nature, and the irreverent, thoroughly practical, outspoken, and not overly moral di Bolgia steel right often struck sparks off that flint. For all of that, the condottiere thoroughly respected the legate, for the man—unlike many another representative of the clergy di Bolgia had met on occasions too numerous to count—said just what he thought, said it out in words any man could understand, and never, so far, had tried to honey-coat criticisms of di Bolgia or anyone else. So, having this degree of marked respect for the cleric, *il Duce* felt an obligation to apprise him of just what he and his brother and the other military leaders were about with regard to their figurehead employer, King Tàmhas di FitzGerald.

He was ushered into the legate's bedchamber, where the air was hot and thickly cloyed with the competing scents of burning incense and herbs piled upon coals of the half-dozen braziers near the huge bed. When he once had dropped to one knee and kissed the ring, the legate signed a servant to bring a chair for him, signing another to bring wine for the noble guest.

His eyes swollen and wet-looking, speaking nasally, while sneezing and coughing often, the old man got directly to a point. "Your grace di Bolgia, yesterday afternoon, King Tàmhas saw fit to dissolve his Royal Council, having three of his closest advisers hustled into an inner courtyard and there beheaded by members of the FitzGerald Guards. Two others of them were hanged last night, and it is my understanding that the rest currently languish in the warren of cells and foul dens under the royal residence.

"Now, while a spate of interfamilial violence is far from uncommon among these primitives here in *Irland*, I think me that I detect the fine Italian touch in all of this barbarity just past. The proper and more usual pattern would have been for the king to chose new advisers from among others of his kin. Instead, he has named his latest councillors to be none other than Sir Roberto di Bolgia, Sir Ugo d'Orsini, Your Grace, himself, le Chevalier Marc Marcel de Montjoie de Vires, and one solitary FitzGerald, a guardsman named Sean something or other, who will be about as outclassed on such a council as a lapdog among as many boarhounds.

"Your Grace di Bolgia, I demand to know just what chicanery you and your brother and the rest are perpetrating here against the King and the Kingdom of Munster."

The servant padded in with a ewer of wine, a goblet, and a small legged silver tray. When he had poured and tasted and departed, di Bolgia took a long draught, smiled, and said, "Your Grace di Rezzi, to tell you of these things was the very reason I called upon you so early. I should have known that such information would already have been imparted to you by others, of course, for Your Grace is ever a well-informed man."

"Your Grace di Bolgia should be aware by now that flattery will accomplish him nothing but suspicion from me," snapped di Rezzi. "Now get on with it man. Just what are you up to?"

Timoteo shook his head. "No flattery was intended, Your Grace di Rezzi, I but stated established fact. Under the circumstances, with the city and port besieged—albeit mildly so—the king dimwitted and most ill-reded, but a true, old-time fire-eater to suicidal extremes, I was afforded but three options, namely: to take you and your people aboard with me and mine and sail away, forfeiting the city and port and all to the *Ard-Righ* (whenever he got back to take it); to arrange the quiet demise of King Tàmhas and maybe still be saddled with a royal FitzGerald nincompoop in his successor; or to arrange to get rid of that sycophantic so-called Royal Council and give the poor royal ninny advisers who could and would cool down his hot head and help him to keep the city and port, which seems so important to the Holy See. This lastmost option we have now accomplished, Your Grace di Rezzi."

Di Rezzi stared at Timoteo over slender, steepled fingers and asked, "And had this . . . this scheme not blossomed as it did, what would Your Grace then have done, pray tell?"

Timoteo spoke bluntly. "Then Tàmhas would have been dead inside a week, of course, Your Grace. And had we drawn yet another of his ilk for the new Righ of Munster, then I would have advised total withdrawal from the city, port, and land."

"*Hmmph!*" grunted the ailing old man. "You're candid enough, aren't you, Your Grace di Bolgia? And your morality leaves much to be desired—you cheerfully admit to planning that has resulted in the deaths of at least five noble *Irlandesi* already, with who knows how many more yet to be done to death, and to contemplating regicide and/or desertion of your trusting allies in their time of direst need. What other dark sins lie upon your soul, eh? Besides corrupting a child-mistress, as you have been doing for some time, that is?''

Timoteo laughed good-naturedly. ''Your Grace di Rezzi, the lady Rosaleen is no child—she is a full fourteen years old and a widow.''

''Do you intend marriage . . . or merely sinful lust and dalliance with this poor, bereaved young woman, then?'' demanded the legate, his tones now that of a stern priest.

Timoteo laughed even more heartily. ''Marry Rosaleen? Hardly, Your Grace. Bigamy is not one of my vices, and I still have a wife living in Bolgia. Nor does Rosaleen want marriage, only . . . ahhh, variety, shall we say, a lover who is neither an *Irlandesi* nor yet a distant relative. Our relationship is purely physical, lustful, sinful, and enjoyable as all hell, Your Grace di Rezzi, and I will be the first to admit to those unvarnished facts.''

Dropping his hands to his lap, the old man pursed his lips and glared at his visitor in helpless rage. ''Is Your Grace aware that I have petitioned His Grace D'Este no less than three times to have a certain intemperate, blasphemous, insubordinate, and unabashedly sinful condottiere recalled and replaced with one who might be easier to control and might offer a better example to his soldiers?''

Timoteo arched his eyebrows. ''Really? And His Grace D'Este made reply?''

Looking as if he had but just bitten into something rotten, the Legate replied sourly, ''I was advised that said insubordinate sinner was, with all of his glaring faults, still the best of the best for this work at hand and that I should temper my care for the good of his immortal soul with the knowledge that just now Holy Mother the Church owns more need for the proven expertise of his mind and the strength of his body.''

Timoteo nodded once. "Yes, I had thought that I had proper measure of the man. His Grace D'Este and I are much alike, when push comes to shove . . . as, too, are Your Grace and I, would Your Grace care to admit that which I am certain he knows aloud."

"I humbly beseech our Savior that that not be so, Your Grace di Bolgia. Like all mortal men, I harbor many faults, but I would hope that adultery, fornication, a mind freely set to cold-blooded murder, debauchery, frequent blasphemy of the very crudest water, I would pray that these not be included amongst them.

"I would suppose that were I to inform King Tàmhas of the cruel trick you have played against him, it would scarcely improve matters, so I shall keep my peace . . . for now. But I warn Your Grace, do not make the cardinal error of pressing my forbearance too far.

"Now, leave me. I am ill, as Your Grace can see, and I own but little energy to do all that I must do every day, ill or well. The very sight and sound of Your Grace sorely angers me, and that fire of rage consumes energy better put to creative uses."

Timoteo, *il Duce* di Bolgia, felt a twinge of shame as he left his most recent "conference" with the Papal Legate. The man was both old and infirm, and he had disliked that which he had had to do—calculatedly enrage him, bait him, really—but it had all been very necessary; now, at least, he knew for certain that di Rezzi knew no more of the di Bolgia schemes than Timoteo wanted him to know and so would be able to transmit no more than that to Palermo or Rome, and *il Duce* thought it best for the nonce that only his version of the roiled, muddy politics of Munster and *Irland* reach the eyes of D'Este and his co-conspirators. Nor must anyone of power in the Church harbor, for a while, even the barest flicker of suspicion that their hired great captain was most assiduously frying some of his own fish on the same griddle as theirs.

Sir Sean FitzRobert of Desmonde sat across an elaborate chessboard of white and black marble squares set in enameled bronze from his opponent, *Le Chevalier* Marc. Sir Sean was, like all of the nobility and not a few of the commoners of Munster, a blood relation of *Righ* Tàmhas Fitzgerald. Careful scrutiny of many genealogical tables had affirmed to the di Bolgias, Marc, and Sir Ugo that FitzRobert owned as much clear title to the blood-splattered throne of Munster as did any living man other than the reigning monarch, and should it prove a necessity—as it very well might, all things considered—to send King Tàmhas to hell suddenly, a quick replacement of the water of Sir Sean would be a most handy asset.

Unlike his cousin, the king, and far too many of their other male relatives, Sir Sean was more than a muscular, dimwitted fire-eater. Not that he was not an accomplished warrior, too; he had had some years as a mercenary in Europe, some more in Great *Irland*, across the Western Sea, and had invaded England with the Irish contingent of Crusaders against King Arthur III Tudor, most recently, being one of the few of that ill-starred lot who had come home with more than his life, his sword, and his shirt.

For his class, country, and upbringing, he was not ill-educated. He spoke his native Irish, the bastard dialect of antique Norman French of his cousin's court, modern French, Low German, Spanish, Roman Italian, English, Latin, and a couple of Skraeling tongues from Great Irland. Also, although he could write little more than his name, he could read Latin, French, and Irish well and Roman and Spanish after a fashion; like all widely traveled mercenaries, he had a few words or phrases in a vast diversity of other languages or dialects, but nothing approaching fluency in most of them.

Nor was the thirtyish knight any more like to his sovran than survival in that royal figure's court had made necessary. Even before he had been taken under the collective wing of the one French and three Italian noblemen, he had washed once monthly without fail, be the season summer or winter, spring or autumn. His squires brushed his shoulder-length, wavy, russet hair daily and combed his beard and mustachios and dense eyebrows; moreover, and sometimes as often as twice the week, he submitted to their minstrations with fine-comb, sitting near a smoking brazier so that the lice and nits might more easily be cast to a certain death upon the coals.

He used scent, of course, as they all did, but his four new foreign mentors had convinced him that he would not need nearly as much of the hellishly expensive stuff did he have his squires and servants commence to regularly shake out and brush off his clothing and hang the garments in a sunny, well-ventilated chamber, rather than in the close, noisome confines of a garderobe.

They could only make over FitzRobert to a certain extent, however; if they ground off too much of the Munster-Irish barbarity, made him too clearly the mirror image of a civilized gentleman, there might well be insurmountable difficulty in getting him crowned when the time came upon them, as Timoteo and the others were certain it would, soon or late. Sir Sean was already considered to be somewhat eccentric by the most of the Munster court, but as he owned his regard of *Righ* Tàmhas, it was generally excused as peculiarities acquired during his years of selling his sword in foreign lands.

Of course, Sir Sean had been kept completely in the dark regarding his almost certain royal destiny, for like all his kin he owned a loud, flapping tongue and an often indulged habit of boasting. He was allowed to know only that he had been picked for membership on the Royal Council because of his proven valor, his relatively open mind, his linguistic abilities, his reading talents, and his possession of a reasoning mind. And he was bright; he knew enough to keep his mouth firmly shut during council meetings unless pointedly asked for an opinion or comment.

Timoteo was very glad that the man had been on hand when needed, but still was of the opinion that he could have been a great captain had he remained in Europe as a mercenary officer rather than returning to Munster. At the Game of Battles, for instance, FitzRobert had but to see a new tactic or strategy once to adapt it to his own play, right often with surprising improvements, too. It was the same with swordwork, also; within bare minutes of first using a personal attack or defense movement, he or his brother, Sir Ugo or *Le Chevalier*, right often found themselves fed back the identical maneuver by Sir Sean. And as the new-made commander of the FitzGerald Guard, he did that which even the military experts from Italy had been unable to attain—he subjected the troop of noble Irish bodyguards to and maintained them under firm discipline . . . with not one desertion from their ranks to show for his efforts.

During their initial and exceedingly secret meeting in a tiny port at the foot of the Slieve Mish Mountains (to Timoteo, who had seen real mountains, those called such in Irland were laughable little molehills), *Ard-Righ* Brian, called "the Burly," had wrinkled his brows and opined, "We suppose that since the addlepated Munsterians will no doubt insist on yet another Norman bastard of the same FitzGerald ilk, with all that house's inbred faults, this FitzRobert is as good choice as any of them; at least he has the reputation for being a gentleman of honor and martial prowess. We must insist, however, that his predecessor be not just set aside but slain. The new-crowned *righ* must immediately forgo claims to the disputed lands along the marches of Munster and send the Star of Munster to Tara. Then and only then will we recognize him as *Righ* Sean, lift our siege, and march our armies out of those undisputed parts of Munster that we now occupy.

"As regards this other matter, *Dux* di Bolgia, we will have to see a *fait accompli* in Rome before we even contemplate changing our present course in here in *Eireann*. Can Sicola, D'Este, and the rest unseat these Spaniards and Moors and bring a sense of sanity and rightness back to the Roman Papacy, with long-overdue redress and justice extended to us and to our sorely tried cousin King Arthur of England, then . . . perhaps. We can just now give you no firmer answer to send to your employers, we fear.

"Understand, *Dux* di Bolgia, and see to it that those who employ your services understand that we would really prefer to see a Papacy in England, at York, or even, God willing, at Tara, here in *Eireann*. Should this occur—and plans for it are jelling fast—Rome could but watch herself lose hegemony over the most of northern and coastal Europe, Iceland, Greenland, and probably eke all of the lands to the west north of the Spanish holdings.

"In such a case, a vastly weakened and impoverished Rome might well find its few remaining assets taken over by either the newer, northern Papacy or Constantinople or both together—the precedent is there; it has happened before; remember the Alexandrine Papacy of old.

"In point of fact, *Dux* di Bolgia, the plans of your employers may already have become a case of too little and far too late to save the Roman Papacy to which we all were born. Rome has played favorites with a callous intensity for at least two hundred years now, alienating and deeply angering whole kingdoms, not just their kings. Norway, Gottland, England, and now *Eireann* have been slighted as if they were ill-favored and illegal offspring; while certain other kingdoms have enjoyed the feast, others have been obliged to crouch in the rushes and snap at scraps and offal.

"The lands to the west make an excellent case in point, *Dux* di Bolgia. Certain men of Connachta, Breifne, and Ui Neill were settled in parts of the northern continent there eight hundred years ago; the Norse and Goths have been farther north on the same continent for at least six hundred years, as have also small colonies of Scotti, Breton fishermen, and Welsh. Yet when the Genoan, Columbo, and that Florentine, Vespucci, made landfall on certain southerly islands, to whom did the Spanish-born Roman Pope give all rights to the lands he called new? Why to Spain, of course. And of course also with the proviso that hefty chunks of all profits accrue to Rome. And those profits have been healthy enough, God knows, and will be even more so if the next in the seemingly endless stream of Spanish madmen ever is successful in conquering the Aztec Empire, as the Incas on the southern continent were finally ground down, fifty years ago.

"It all might have been understood and forgiven had matters to the west been set aright when there no longer sat a Spanish or Moorish Pope on St. Peter's seat, but no, Rome seems fundamentally unable to, incapable of admitting publicly to any mistake or misjudgment, ever. To this very day, any man not directly in the service of Spain or Portugal who dares to set foot upon any part of the western lands is automatically excommunicated until he leaves, confesses, and does his penance. This is not fair, *Dux* di Bolgia, it was not fair to begin, especially in the light of clear evidence that Spanish claims were predated by five to six hundred years by other Christian peoples, many of whom have done far more, incidentally, to win souls for Christ than have the Spaniards, who seem mostly concerned with gaining bodies for servitude.

"If they succeed in their aims, we think that a good place for your employers to begin—after they have fairly settled matters with us and with England, of course—would be to make meaningful rhyme and reason out of the ownership of the western lands, admitting that others own earlier and better claim to certain parts of them than do Spain and Portugal."

CHAPTER
THE FIRST

Sir Bass Foster, by the grace of God, Duke of Norfolk, Earl of Rutland, Markgraf von Velegrad, Baron of Strathtyne, Knight of the Garter (England), Knight of the Order of the *Roten Adler* (Holy Roman Empire), and Lord Commander of the Horse of Arthur III Tudor, King of England and Wales, sat a gentle, easy-gaited bay rounsey at the edge of an exercise field near the sprawling cavalry camp near Norwich Castle, his seat, and watched his squadron of *galloglaiches* put through drill procedures by their mostly Irish officers. The most of the *galloglaiches* themselves were not of Irish antecedents, but rather hailed from the Western Isles of Scotland, and how these examples of the long-renowned and thoroughly fearsome fighters of the ilk had come to be the devoted personal squadron of Bass Foster (who was, at heart, a gentle, peace-loving man) was a story in itself.*

Clad in his long-skirted buffcoat, trousers of doeskin and canvas, lawn shirt and jackboots, with his tanned, scarred face shaded by the wide brim of a plumed hat, Sir Bass looked much like any of his attending gentlemen, save only that he was a bit taller and heftier than the most

*See *Castaways in Time*, Robert Adams, (Signet Books, 1982) and *The Seven Magical Jewels of Ireland* (Signet Books, 1985).

of them; but appearances can be deceiving, for Bass Foster was not a seventeenth-century English nobleman or gentleman, as were they all. He was not even of their universe, much less of their world or time.

Years before that day on the drill field, a device spawned of a future technology had propelled Bass and certain others of his world and time into this one, and their arrival had set in motion currents that had wreaked significant changes in this world and would certainly continue to do so for untold centuries yet to come. Mostly a misfit and seldom truly happy in the world of his origin, Bass had, despite himself, fitted into this one like hand into gauntlet or sword into sheath; depths almost unplumbed in his other-world life had been sounded and he was become a consummate leader of fighting men, a very gifted cavalry tactician, and, more recently, a naval figure of some note, as well. His private fleet of warships, with the unofficial aid of a few royal ships and Lord Admiral Sir Paul Bigod, had raided a certain northern Spanish port and there burned, sunk, or otherwise destroyed the bulk of a fleet being there assembled to bear an invasion force of Crusaders against England. The sack of the place had been thorough and far more rewarding than any had expected, and so even after all shares had been allotted, Bass Foster found himself to have become an exceedingly wealthy man by any standards.

"And it's just not right, none of it," thought His Grace of Norfolk, while he watched the squadron wheel and turn, draw pistols, present and fire, then gallop off to repeat the exercise. "For most of my life before I . . . we came here, I seemed to utterly lack luck; anything and everything I wanted or needed or loved was snatched away from me. It seemed, nonetheless, I tried to hold up my head and play the poor hand that life continued to deal me as best I could.

"Here, on the other hand, I do nothing from the very start except try to keep myself and the others alive and I draw ace after ace after ace. Hell, the way it is here, if I tripped and fell facedown in a fucking dungheap, I'd

probably come up with a fucking diamond, while the
others. . . .?

"Professor Collier, now, for instance. For all that he's
always denigrated by Hal and Wolfie and the King, these
days, his many contributions helped Arthur and England
far more than did mine, back in the beginning. What did
the Fickle Lady deal out to him? Capture and torture by a
clan of savage border ruffians and, after belated rescue, a
bare monastery cell in which to howl out his insanity for
the rest of his life.

"Then there's Pete Fairley, whose talents set up the
Royal Armory at York. His multishot hackbuts won or all
but won at least two full-scale battles for English arms,
and his large-bore breechloading rifled cannon are on the
way to revolutionizing naval warfare, not to even mention
the advances in other, less warlike, directions that his
endless experiments are turning out, like that light but
sturdy and comfortable springed carriage there, that Buddy
Webster came down here in.

"And how about Bud Webster, too? His stockbreeding
and general agricultural projects will no doubt feed folks
far better in years to come than any of us can now imagine, and he got damned nearly as raw a deal as Bill Collier
did. Yes, he's still got his sanity, but he'll limp stiff-
legged for the rest of his life and never be able to sit a
horse in comfort or real security again. And that means a
great deal in this primitive, preindustrial world where about
the only common means of getting about in peace or war
are on horseback or shank's mare. That fine carriage that
Pete has fabricated for Bud is handy and comfortable, true,
but much use on the rutted, muddy, hole-pocked abominations that pass for roads in this version of England will
soon wreck it, no matter how well and cunningly made,
just as they wreck sutler waggons and even ponderous gun
carriages, time and again.

"Susan Sunshine, or whatever her name really was,
now, that's another one. In life, both in this world and the
one from which she was snatched along with the rest of us,
she was a useless parasite, so strung out on drugs most of

the time that she didn't know which end to wipe. When she and Dave Atkins ran out of drugs and hallucinogens, they started trying to make use of a plethora of what are called 'witch plants,' but after she killed herself with amanita of some variety, Dave snapped out of it. I guess it scared the shit out of him, because he's been straight ever since, so you could say that the crazy little doper accomplished something useful in death.

"Once his mind was clear, Dave turned out to be a very talented, highly intelligent, and most flexible young man, near-genius level, I'd say. Despite the facts that he wasn't yet thirty when he came here and had wasted some years of that on the dope scene, he still had earned two master's degrees, and Pete says that he is marvelous at solving problems up at York, that he couldn't keep the armory going sometimes were it not for Dave and Carey Carr.

"Not that Carey is in York that much of the time. He told me once that he became a trucker because he liked traveling, didn't like being in one place for any length of time, and he's the same man here as he was there. I guess he knows the road from York to Norwich or London better than any other man; summer, winter, spring, or fall, good weather or foul, he's always on the move between York and here or York and the King's camp, bringing new innovations of his and Pete's and Dave's and teaching the recipients how to use them properly and safely.

"Krystal?" Foster sighed to himself. "Despite our son, little Joe, if I had it to do all over again, knowing what I know now, I wouldn't . . . I think. Krystal could've contributed—still could contribute, for that matter—so much to the suffering folks of this world. She's a doctor of medicine, a trained psychiatrist, and, in a pinch, a damned good battlefield surgeon. The surgeons of this world are bloody-handed butchers who know next to nothing of human anatomy or of the causes of infection, while those quacks who call themselves physicians are, when they're not poisoning people with their henbane-and-mummy-dust pills, not one whit better than camp-meeting faith healers.

"With the assured backing of Hal—who, under the

present circumstances, is as good as Pope of England and Wales—she could accomplish true miracles in the fields of medicine, surgery, and the like, but she doesn't; all she does is sit around and get bored and bitch and rail at me in letters about ignoring her. And what the hell does she want me to do? Should I tell the king that I can't do his bidding because my wife is bored and lonely and demands that I be constantly nearby to bitch at in person rather than via post-rider?

"I guess that the kernel of the matter is that Krys just isn't very flexible, as easily adaptable to new and strange situations as the rest of us proved to be when put to the test. To her way of thinking, marriage means togetherness, total togetherness—she said once that her mother and father were never parted for more than a few days at a time in nearly thirty years of marriage—and I just've failed to get through to her that this is not twentieth-century New York or America, even, but roughly England, roughly in the seventeenth century, and in a state of warring and invasions with more invasions threatening.

"One thing, of course, is that she just doesn't have enough to do to occupy her mind and her days. She refused to live at my castle in Rutland because it was too primitive to suit her—I guess she never even thought of having it renovated into a more comfortable residence, she just left and went back to Whyffler Hall. And up there, Sir Geoff and Henny Turnbull and Olly Shaftoe commanding a hundred or more well-trained servants between them keep the place running like oiled clockwork.

"That was why I tried to persuade her to start a training program to impart of her knowledge to the local midwives and maybe help to cut down on the appalling losses of newborn babies and their mothers that are so common in this world. But after only a couple of weeks, she'd come up with every cockamamie reason you could imagine why she couldn't keep it up—the midwives were all stupid slatterns, know-it-alls, impossibly superstitious, religious fanatics, there was too much of a language barrier, they all were filthy and the stench of a roomful of them gagged her, and on and on and on *ad infinitum, ad nauseam.* I guess she'd rather just sit around and feel sorry for herself and bitch at me than try to do something useful or helpful.

"And it's been damned near the same story since I prevailed upon Hal to let her and our son and her retinue live on the episcopal estate with Bud Webster. Bud tried to get her interested in stock-breeding . . . vainly, as it turned out. Hal, God bless him, took time that he didn't really have to spare to patiently explain to her just why it was necessary that I be so often gone for so long on the King's business, and for all the good it did anyone, he might as well've been talking to one of Bud Webster's aurochs bull-calves."

Melchoro Salazar and Don Diego, the Castilian having but just arrived back in York with Hal and his retinue from Whyffler Hall, had lived on the estate for a few weeks and tried to interest the Duchess of Norfolk in the ancient art of falconry, only to have her deride their sport as barbaric, bloodthirsty foolishness. Both had still provided some diversion to Krystal, however, until a chance remark informed her that both of them either did own or had owned some slaves—a practice still quite common outside England, Wales, and Scotland, in this world—whereupon she had made things so unpleasant for the two well-meaning and now confused noblemen that they left the estate, collected the troop of *galloglaiches* lent by Bass to Hal for safety in traversing the still-wild and virtually lawless north country between Whyffler Hall and York, and set out for Norwich. As delicately as possible, *Barón* Melchoro suggested to Bass that his lady-wife was become a bit mad.

"But good old Hal, he doesn't give up," thought Bass. "He said in the letter he sent down with Melchoro that immediately he can spare the man, he means to send Rupen Ademian out there to live on the estate for a while, figuring I guess that a relatively urbane man from the same world and time as Krys can maybe settle her down to the realization that she's going to have to live the rest of her life in this world and among these people so she'd better start making the best of it, maybe doing something to improve conditions in it.

"Damned funny about the rest of that bunch of twentieth-century types that were jerked into this world after the rest of us. Every one of them, male and female, just disappeared with the sole exceptions of Rupen and one woman; and nobody since has seen or found or come across, despite thorough, full-scale searches, airy a thread or trace of any of them. One minute it would seem they were all in a guarded suite of rooms in the palace there on the archepiscopal estate, and the next minute, *poof*, they were gone. I get gooseflesh just thinking of the matter. My house, which was brought here with me, disappeared from here in almost the same way, but it couldn't've been that projector that brought us here and sent the house back and then brought the second bunch here, because by the time they disappeared, that projector was in pieces in Hal's lab in York . . . at least, I don't think it could've." He shuddered. "There's just still so damned much that I—none of us, really—know about this business of projections."

Little did His Grace Sir Bass Foster, Duke of Norfolk, Earl of Rutland, Markgraf von Velegrad, Baron of Strathtyne, Knight of the Garter, Knight of the Order of the *Roten Adler*, and Lord Commander of the Horse know just how right he was—just how little any of them, even Harold, Archbishop of York, knew.

Some weeks previously and many leagues to the north of that Norwich drill field, a wrinkled, white-haired and -bearded old man wearing the garb of a high-ranking churchman sat in converse with an olive-skinned man of middle years in a candle-lit chamber of the archepiscopal palace, Yorkminster.

"Well, we did all we could do, I guess," opined Rupen Ademian. "I just hope it works, because after all you've told me about those people of your time in the world you come from, I sure as hell don't want to run into any living ones in this world and time."

"Oh, it will work, Rupen," Harold, Archbishop of

York, assured him confidently. "I cannot but wish I'd thought of something like this many years ago. Had I, then you and your unfortunate friends and relatives would never have been projected into this world, but would've remained safe where you all belonged."

"What do you think really happened to the others, Hal—to Kogh and John and the rest? Could agents of the Roman Church have gotten into the country palace and gotten them all out without anybody seeing them go? If so, then how?"

The old man sighed and shook his head. "No, Rupen, as I have told you before, I think that the Church had nothing to do with it, and all the rumors that float around and about my palace be damned. No, I think that they were snapped back to where they and you came from by way of some quirk in the new, replacement device that— all unbeknownst to us, then—was at that time squatting in the tower cellar beside the two dead men from my world and time."

"But, Hal," queried Rupen, "in that case, why wasn't I jerked back too, me and Jenny Bostwick, huh?"

The archbishop could only sigh once more and again shake his old head. "Were Emmett O'Malley still extant, Rupen, perhaps he could answer your questions. I cannot. My knowledge of the workings of the projection devices— along with a plethora of others—was always most limited; in the time and place from which I came, knowledge had become very specialized, nor were specialists in one field encouraged to dabble in other fields very often. That poor Emmett was given a measure of training and experience outside his field was a fluke of sorts. An even bigger fluke was that, with his limited knowledge and training and under a great deal of stress, he was able to project us into this world at all and not put us inside the stone foundation of that old tower keep."

"What would've happened if he had done so, Hal?" asked Rupen.

The old man shivered. "Immediate death for both of us and the most hellacious explosion this world has ever seen, short of a volcanic eruption, perhaps. There would have been but precious little left of that tower, Rupen. Understand, these devices are not perfected, by any means. Most of the work is still in the experimental stage, and precise control of projections is still a virtual impossibility, in the majority of cases, which is why I seriously doubt that the ones back in that world and time will make any efforts to change the settings of the projector to escape our diabolical trap. No, they'll lose every human or animal they project until they decide that the hideous expense they will be incurring is just making further attempts unfeasible. The costs had already brought about virtual suspension of the project at the time Emmett and I trespassed into the facility and projected ourselves to here. I think that it was only the unremittingly vindictive nature of the very powerful security establishment that got the project started again even on a limited basis; they must have been determined to get us back for the mind-destroying torture that they label 'reeducation,' and if any group of the twenty-first-century United States of America possesses the power to reactivate suspended projects, it is assuredly them.''

''Pardon me, it is not really my affair, Hal, but I must ask, nonetheless. These security people—your voice conveys such hatred for them. They are the reason you left your world and time, then?'' Rupen's voice was gentle and he added, ''You don't have to tell me if you don't want to, of course.''

The archbishop grimaced. ''I . . . I'll tell you all about it . . . someday, soon, but not tonight. All right? Tonight I want you to tell me the remainder of your own story. What happened with you after you came back to your country and began to run the new business in the new location? What was the name of that city?''

''Richmond, Hal, Richmond, Virginia,'' replied Rupen. ''Confederate States Armaments Associates of Richmond finally set up operations in a building only blocks from the capitol of the Commonwealth of Virginia and only a few blocks farther than that from the once White House of the Confederacy.

"My brother-in-law, Dr. Boghos Panoshian, and some of his real-estate friends had helped me find the place. During the American Civil War, a hundred years before, the area had been a fashionable residential area, but a century is a long time, and by then the area was mostly commercial, light industrial and a few warehouses, with almost all of the old homes having been long since torn down for new construction.

"What I, or rather, we, lucked into was an original forty-odd-room mansion—the main house and one wing, that is, the other wing and all of the outbuildings having been destroyed after the land they sat on was sold many decades before us. Although it was way too much space for us then, in the beginning, the rent was dirt-cheap and I could see where it could save us money to start with. We could use the big, high-ceilinged rooms of the empty, dusty old mansion proper for a warehouse. The front doors were wide and opened right onto the street, and the place was a very short distance from the deepwater port on the James River, too. The agent for the owners readily agreed to do any reasonable amount of strenghtening of the floors and supports so they would safely hold cases of rifles and pistols for us if we'd sign a five-year lease for the property, which sounded good to me and my brother, Bagrat.

"Somebody, within fairly recent times, had more or less modernized the remaining wing and bricked up the doorways leading from it into the main mansion. They had put in electrical wiring, modern plumbing, two baths, and a complete kitchen in the back. I figured we could use this wing for our offices and retail outlet and maybe even put in a small shop for customizing the guns, eventually.

"The agent was a pretty nice fellow, and he leveled with me . . . up to a point. He said that one reason we could get the building so cheap was that there was no parking lot, no loading dock, nor any way to put one in without making more structural changes to the mansion than the owners would countenance. I couldn't see how this would adversely affect our operations, though, because we wouldn't be in need of delivery vehicles on any large scale, we could park our cars at curbside, and as long as that front door was wide enough to pass cases of rifles, the trucks that brought them up from the deepwater terminal could just pull up on the street in front of the mansion. So we signed the lease, paid six months' rent in advance, and leased office furniture and equipment while a contractor did what was necessary to make the first floor of the old house strong enough to take the weight of the guns and all, and by the time the first load of rifles and revolvers and equipment came from Italy, we were about ready for them.''

Rupen and Bagrat, however, ran into problems almost immediately. The cases of arms were stacked in the paint-smelly rooms of the old house. All of the Richmond, Virginia, area is generally damp to one degree or another, and this area, not too far removed from the river, was especially so, and moisture in the air breeds rust on iron and steel, verdigris on copper and brass. He and Bagrat and two newly hired employees spent one entire weekend at the strenuous, exceedingly messy job of opening crates, unpacking rifles and pistols, coating all the metal surfaces with Cosmoline, then repacking them. Another weekend went to shrink-packing smaller items—powder flasks, bullet molds, reproduction brass belt buckles, hat badges and insignia—in plastic with tiny packets of silica gel.

The initial shipment thus protected, Rupen fired off a cable to the manufacturers requesting similar protective packing for all of the shipments yet to come. Advertising of various natures had been commenced as soon as the two brothers had obtained an area post office box and orders were already trickling in even as the arms crates were winched up out of the holds of the ship. In the beginning, these were mostly on the basis of Bagrat Ademian's presidency of the company—he being well known in muzzle-loading circles around the country—but the Italian firms contracted by Rupen were producing a quality product, the weapons were well finished, handsomely fitted, and straight-shooting, so soon they were virtually selling themselves to people who had never before met or heard of Bagrat Ademian.

Slightly less than one year after commencing operations, the two knew that the business was a success, and Bagrat left Rupen in sole charge while he was back north to move his family and effects down and into a house he had rented from Boghos, who had started to dabble in real-estate investments. As soon as he and they were back in Richmond and settled, it was Rupen's turn to leave . . . for Italy, to award new contracts and arrange for the manufacture of additional items to supplement their line of reproduction weapons and accessories. He also took along a want list of certain weapons-related oddities and rarities desired by one or more of his private file of wealthy American collectors, just on the off chance.

"Flintlock?" yelped Bargrat, holding up one of the roughed-out prototype weapons he had just uncrated. "Are you outa your frigging mind, Rupen? They didn't use no flintlocks in the fucking Civil War!"

"How would you know?" asked Rupen mildly. "I would imagine that did we know as much as you seem to think you do, those poor, ill-armed bastards of the Confederate States Army used any damned thing they could lay hands to, especially toward the end of the war. But that's neither here nor there, little brother; that's not why I got that prototype and a firm quotation.

"We're doing very well now, even though the actual Civil War Centennial is fast winding down. Apparently, we and the other arms companies that are in this repro business just happened to tap a market that had been lying dormant and unsuspected for years. But, as the song says, there are even bigger things still ahead.

"Think, Bagrat. In about ten years, the Bicentennial of the American Revolution will be celebrated, and, brother, they *did* use flintlocks in that war. I know—I took the time to read up on it. That's the Brown Bess British musket you're holding there. There's also a Charleville French musket, a Pennsylvania-pattern rifle, and a couple of different flintlock pistols, too."

Bagrat nodded and grinned, saying, "Now who's the devious Yankee-Armenian, huh? This does look like a good piece, too." He drew back the cock of the lock and raised the frizzen to expose the priming pan. "When we got everything uncrated, let's see if we can find us some flints and cast some balls and drive out to the place near the airport and shoot these some."

At the end of their second, record-breaking year of unprecedented sales, brother Kogh Ademian journeyed down to Richmond, hat in hand, visibly eating crow and insisting that it was a familial responsibility for Rupen and Bagrat to keep all the Ademian businesses in the family, not to mention taking advantage of the wealth and influence of his Ademian Enterprises, Incorporated.

So anxious was the family tycoon to get in on Confederate States Armaments that he put his normally knife-sharp brain into neutral and allowed his two brothers to horn-swoggle him ruthlessly. He wound up owning three-twelfths of Confederate States Armaments while Rupen and Bagrat both got back the shares in Rappahannock Arms that they had sold in order to finance Confederate States Armaments in the beginning, plus which the small Richmond firm also got access to the immense amounts of Ademian Enterprises' lines of credit . . . none to soon, either, as it quickly developed early in the third year.

In early February, a section of the first floor of the main mansion collapsed one night, dumping tons of crated weapons into the cellar. A city building inspector gave the brothers the bad news: The contractor—by then bankrupt, out of business, and no longer residing in Virginia—had used substandard materials and done very shoddy work. However, the kind of support that they really needed were they to continue to put the old mansion to the kind of use they had in the past two years would call for such extensive remodeling that they would, should they attempt it at all, run afoul of the Historic Buildings types, which types already had contacted Rupen and Bagrat with complaints and thinly veiled threats relative to their "sacrilege."

As the large, strong, modern reinforced-concrete-and-brick auto-parts warehouse next door (on the spot whereon had once stood the main mansion's other wing) was just then for sale, Bagrat phoned a recital of their difficulties to Kogh, and shortly the warehouse had been acquired by Ademian Enterprises. Immediately all of the stock had been moved out of the mansion and into the new warehouse. Bagrat saw most of the clerical staff moved into the small suite of modern offices built into a front corner of said warehouse, leaving only the showrooms and executive offices in the remaining wing of the mansion.

"What are we going to do with that fucking white-ass elephant next door?" he demanded of Rupen. "I can't see paying what the fuckers we talked to want to repair it just so's it can sit there and collect more dust. You talked to those Historic Buildings snotnoses—what do we have to do to it to get them off our necks?"

Before his brother could frame an answer, Bagrat went on, "I tell you, Rupen, was that warehouse office a little bigger, I'd've moved ever damn thing from here down there. Have you noticed how . . . how weird this place is sometimes . . . 'specially of nights or dark days? Lotsa times I've been working in my office or down here, I've got the feeling somebody's come in and is standing, watching me, but ever time I've turned around, looked around, nobody's been there. Doors seem to open and slam shut for no reason, some of them after they've been locked, too, and I'm not the onliest one who's noticed things like that, either. Ever so often, I get the feeling that there's a . . . a something or somebody here that don't want me or any of the rest of us here."

Recognizing the look in his elder brother's eyes, Bagrat said in a defensive tone, "All right, all right, you can think I'm superstitious and nutty all you want to, Mr. Smartass, but I'll tell you something I never told you before. While you was in Italy last time, I run into a feller trains and sells and rents out guard dogs, lives down in Chesterfield County somewhere, and he offered me a damn good deal on a guard dog to live here on weekends and keep the niggers and all from breaking in. But you know something? He couldn't come up with a single one of his dogs would set foot on the front porch even, Rupen; and when he tried to drag some in, they fought him and whined and howled and damn near bit him, their trainer and handler, a coupla times. He was the first one told me this place is probably haunted. I didn't believe him back then, but I sure Lord do, now. In fact, I'm beginning to wonder if half the places in this whole frigging town aren't haunted, after what me and Rose and the kids went through out there in Boghos's place on River Road.''

When Dr. Boghos Panoshian and family had moved to an estate overlooking the James River in Goochland County, they had not sold the executive brick home from which they moved, but rather had leased it. So well had they done on the lease that when another of the houses in the same neighborhood had come onto the market, Boghos had bought it and leased it, too. This second one had been leased to his brother-in-law, Bagrat, and his family of two teenagers and four younger children.

The oversize, sprawling single-story brick house offered more than enough room for even Bagrat's large family— two master suites, four additional bedrooms and two other full baths, a large, airy parlor, formal dining room, spacious kitchen with breakfast area and half bath, a roofed and screened redwood deck that ran the length of the house in the rear, attached two-car garage and utility room, and a den behind the kitchen with another full bath. Like all the other homes in the affluent area, the house had been custom-built and showed it. Rose fell in love with it on sight, and so Bagrat went ahead and signed the lease, shoving aside his strange presentiments and his questions as to why the house had had six owners in ten years, for nearly three years of which it had just sat vacant despite a burgeoning demand for quality housing in the suburban fringes of the rapidly growing city of Richmond.

He and his family had been living in the house for a month or so when the next-door neighbor, a medium-level executive with Reynolds Metals Company, asked—in what Bagrat took to be a most peculiar tone—if he or his wife or children had found aught to dislike about the new home. However, when Bagrat tried to pin him down to specifics, the man would only mutter something about one of the rooms being hard to heat and quickly changed the subject.

This incident flashed back into his mind when, one night soon after, Rose happened to stumble against a wall getting out of the shower and remarked that that wall— which wall separated the front master suite from the bedroom of their youngest daughter, Karen—was icy cold and wondered aloud if something had gone wrong with the heat register in that room and if the child had enough blankets.

When she and Bagrat entered the child's bedroom, it was definitely colder than the rest of the house by ten or fifteen degrees, for all that the register was faithfully performing its function. Moreover, five-year-old Karen was wide awake, huddled under her covers and shivering. With her usual directness, she explained the phenomenon.

"It's the little pale lady, Mama—every time she comes it gets real cold in here."

Further patient questioning got matter-of-factly yet rather unbelievable answers from the usually truthful child. "She's a grownup lady, Mama, you can tell that because she never has any clothes on, but she's small for a grownup, not much bigger than Auntie Perous, at the church." The old woman of whom she spoke was, Bagrat figured, less than five feet tall by two or three inches. "She never says anything, even when her lips move, but I think she's sad most of the time, she just looks sad, even when she's smiling. She visits me a lot, sometimes in the days, but usually at night."

Bagrat and Rose did not know whether to believe the child's wild, fantastic story or not. Nonetheless, she was brought in to sleep with them in the front master suite the rest of that night, and by the next night, they had made other arrangements, giving their eldest son, Al, the den behind the kitchen as a bedroom and moving Karen into the room thus vacated. Her sometime bedroom was converted into a sewing room for Rose and their eldest daughter, Charlene. This rearrangement worked for almost a week.

CHAPTER
THE SECOND

Rupen and a couple of warehousemen were checking bills of lading against crates of rifles when Bagrat came into the warehouse at a dead run, gripped Rupen's arm in a viselike hold, and gasped, "Come on! We got to get out of my house, right away. Rose just called."

In the car, on the way out, Bagrat talked while Rupen drove. "So after ever'thing that went down, I started asking some questions all around that neighborhood, see. That house was built eleven years ago by one of the best contractors in the whole frigging town for a Jew dentist and his wife, but they hadn't lived in it even a year when they drove their car into Upham Creek one New Year's, coming home drunk, and both of them was killed.

"Seems she, the wife, didn't have no people close, and so ever'thing went to his mother—insurance money, cars, house, furniture, ever'thing—the old lady sold ever'thing but just the house and the furniture, and just before she went over to spend twelve, fourteen months in Israel, she advertised the house and rented it out for a year's lease to a man and what she thought then was his wife and his two servants. But no sooner was she out over the Atlantic on El Al than the man she'd rented to moved in with his mistress and five other guys that sold for him.

"The older neighbors say those bastards threw nonstop

38

parties, real orgies, bringing carloads of booze and beer and women in for 'em.

"They say some of the people was neighbors, back then, took that bunch up on invites and went over to some of the first parties, but after a while, wouldn't none of the neighbors go near the place, what with the fights and the public fucking—one old feller told me about two of them, nekkid as jaybirds, was playing sixty-nine out in the back-yard on a fucking picnic table, oncet! Him and his wife and boy all seen the shameless bastard and his hussy, and that's why to this day they got that old high, thick privet hedge on the property line, he says. And the mean, common things they done to people as passed out at their parties!

"Then, almost to the end of their lease, they had a party one weekend and brought in a bunch of girls from some state civil service picnic. That party was a bloody mess, I hear—coupla guys was hurt real bad in fights, and then one of the girls they'd done brought in was raped, too. The guys done it to her hurt her real bad, then just left her and she bled to death in a bed in that same room we had Karen in! And the old guy I talked to said when the county coroner's guys brought the body out, it could've been a ten- or twelve-year-old kid, that's how small it was."

Rupen sighed. "Bagrat, when did you hear all this gossip?"

"Yesterday afternoon and evening, Rupen. That's when I finally caught the old guy, Harry Conyers, home," Bagrat replied.

"And you hotfooted it right home and told it all to Rose, I'll bet," said Rupen, an edge of sarcasm in his voice.

"No, as a matter of fact, I didn't," answered Bagrat, adding, "I meant to, but when I got back home, Al and Haighie and Arsen were all on the deck and Arsen had his oud and I started playing a dumbeg and we just kept it up until Rose came out and called us in for chow and I sort of forgot it until she was asleep.

"That's part of what threw me so bad when she called

today, Rupen. The old guy said that the little bitty woman
was raped and killed had the prettiest blue-black long hair
he'd ever seen, real shiny-like . . . and that's pretty much
what Rose said, too.''

Rose was at the house two doors from hers, being
alcoholically entertained by Mrs. Ioanna Vitolis, who had
lived in the house for nearly twelve years. But even with a
good quarter of a liter of ouzo in her, Rose would not
consider setting foot back in her own house. Still pale and
trembling, with a look of sick horror in her eyes, she told
her husband and brother-in-law what had happened late
that morning.

''I'd gotten the kids all off to school and cleaned up and
all, and about ten-thirty, I set up the sewing machine and
started hemming a skirt for Charlene. It couldn't have been
more than a few minutes after I'd heard the clock strike
eleven that I heard . . . no, not really heard, just *felt* that
somebody was waiting to speak to me but didn't want to
interrupt me, kind of feeling. And I noticed then that even
with the sunlight streaming into the window, it had gotten
real cold in that room, too.

''I turned around and . . . and *she was just standing
there and staring at me!* She wasn't five feet tall and white
as milk, with black eyes and thick black hair that hung
down below her waist, and she was naked, with blood
smeared on her thighs and more streaks of blood that had
run down from out of terrible bite marks on her tiny
breasts and her shoulders and her throat, and it looked like
one of her nipples had been bitten right off.

''Her face was cut in a couple of places and bruised real
bad, and her lips were moving like she was talking or
trying to, but there was no sound. I just sat there for a
minute, I guess, just staring at her. But when her face and
head all of a sudden turned into a skull with eyes, I just
left the machine running and took off out the room door
and out the front door and I guess I'd still be running if
Ioanna here hadn't seen me and run after me and caught
me and brought me back to here.

''Bagrat, I'm never ever going back in that house again

and neither are my children and I'm never going to speak to your sister or her sonofabitching husband that rented us that place and never told us anything about any of this."

Rupen and Bagrat sat, smoking nervously, in the sewing room in the afternoon of that day, not talking much, wondering whether it all was just Rose's and Karen's imagination, dreading that perhaps it was not. Bagrat had remembered that Rupen had long ago mastered the art of reading lips and had suggested that if there really was a wraith inhabiting the house and if they could find out what she wanted, maybe she could be persuaded to go wherever good ghosts are supposed to go and cease terrifying the living.

After an hour or more, Bagrat was nodding off and Rupen had given to read the business section of the *Times-Dispatch*, the Richmond-area morning newspaper, when he noticed that it was suddenly markedly cool in the room. All his nape hairs aprickle, he looked up to see a misty something across the room.

In a low but penetrating voice, he hissed, "Bagrat! Open your eyes but don't move or speak!"

Slowly, the misty something gained form, lengthened, broadened, to become the small body of a woman, looking very solid in nature. Her pretty, heart-shaped face was very pale, which made the marks of a recent and savage beating stand out very clearly. The flesh was discolored and puffy around both of her dark eyes, and the eyes themselves held infinite sadness.

Beside him, he could hear Bagrat whimpering softly in atavistic terror, and he deliberately reached over without looking to lay a comforting hand on his younger brother's knee.

As the pale body beneath the pale, battered face became clearer, Rupen shuddered strongly. She, whoever she was, or had been, had been cruelly used by her attackers; in the course of two wars he had fought, Rupen had seen some awful things and this thing before him was, he knew then, one of the worst ever.

Raising his glance back up to the face, he could see that

the swollen lips were moving now, and he strove to read the message that the whatever-it-was was trying so hard to convey. She looked so very young and helpless—late teens or early twenties, at best—that Rupen could not imagine how any rational man had been able to bring himself to hurt her, and, vastly experienced big brother and many times uncle that he was, he felt very paternal toward her, phantom or not.

And then, in a blink, the head and face were become a bare skull, the dark, sad eyes, however, still visible in the sockets under the arches of the brows. Bagrat's moaning whimpers loudened and became more intense, and Rupen felt his brother's muscles tense under his hand, so he tenderly patted him as one would a frightened animal. Oddly, he himself felt no fear of the thing that stood tenuously before him, only a soul-deep pity.

Extending his right hand, he spoke slowly, "Let me help, my dear. Is there no way I can help you?"

Then her flesh was back over the bones and the lips were again moving. ". . . is Ross? Please tell me where Ross is. He was so kind, so gentle and tender, and he said he'd be right back. But then the big, bald, mean man came, and the other one, and they . . . they hurt me, they hurt me so bad. Ross will make it well, though. Where is Ross? Please tell me where Ross is."

Compassion welling up inside him, Rupen said, "Child, you are no longer alive. Those two men you mentiond, they not only hurt you, they killed your body. Your body has been dead for more than ten years, now, don't you know that?"

He awaited an answer, but when the split and swollen pale lips moved again, it was only a resumption of her pitiful litany. "Where is Ross? Please tell me where Ross is. . . ."

He reflected to himself that these same thoughts of her absent champion had probably been going through her mind as she had lain dying in this very room so long ago, and he could think of nothing else to do. Perhaps, if he could find someone qualified that wouldn't think he was just a psycho . . .? He felt for her, but his extended hand was only a gesture; he knew he could not reach her.

The old archbishop leaned forward. "You actually spoke with a dead woman's ghost, Rupen? What ever happened in the matter?"

Rupen took a draught of cool ale and shrugged. "I suppose that that poor, confused spirit is still haunting that room in that house, Hal, I was never able to effect any help for her. Boghos thought we all—Rose, little Karen, Bagrat, and me—were nuts and as good as said so when Bagrat, who had been renting by the month after the first year, found and bought a brand-new trilevel and moved into it. I told Boghos that if he didn't believe us, he should go over to that house one night and sit in that room for a while, and he did; he would never afterward admit to having seen anything, but he sold the house within less than a week.

"I took the time to check records and look up the third owner of the house, who still lived in Henrico County, Virginia. Once I'd convinced him that I seriously believed in ghosts, that I'd seen at least one and would admit to it in public and that I was not either a journalist of a book writer, he became candid with me, he and his wife, too.

"At the time he had lived, or rather tried to live, in that house, there had been more than just the one ghost, apparently. He and his wife had no children then, had bought the vastly underpriced house as an investment and didn't use most of the bedrooms for anything but storage, and they didn't even know about the young girl's ghost until I told them.

"It seems that when the old woman—the second owner—who had inherited it from her son and daughter-in-law—the first owners—had come back from Israel and seen what her tenants had done to the house and yard and furnishings in only a year or less, she suffered a heart attack or stroke or both and died right in the middle of the living-room floor. As long as the third owners lived there, the old woman's shade kept stalking the place, shrieking now and then, turning lights on or off and opening or slamming doors and otherwise making her continuing presence known and obnoxious.

"The third owners had bought the place as it stood, seriously in need of certain repairs, a thorough repainting, and a complete recarpeting, but the third owner was and still is a building contractor and was able to do the job up brown despite its magnitude and despite difficulties with the previous owner's unfriendly ghost. He it was who added the rear den and third bath to the place, tacked on the double garage and utility room and built the redwood deck. When he sold the house, he made a handsome but well-deserved profit on the transaction.

"The fourth owner was, by the time I went looking for him, deceased, but his widow, after some little time of consideration and getting to know me, finally confided in me that at first they thought that one or both of them were going insane. But then an uncle, a Jesuit priest, stayed with them overnight in the guest room, the rear master suite. Through his good offices, they had the house exorcised, and they never saw or heard the old woman again after that. But then her husband was transferred, and so they sold the house and moved.

"The fifth owners, who had let the place sit untenanted for almost three years before they sold it to Boghos, wouldn't speak to me at all and threatened to call the police if I again telephoned or tried to call on them.

"Due to that and to a number of other, unrelated, factors, I had to give up at that point, but I have always since regretted not being able to help the troubled spirit of that poor young girl to gain peace. I still do, Hal."

The archbishop nodded. "I know you do, Rupen. You are a truly good man, a caring man. It's too bad you never remarried and sired children—you would have made a wonderful father, I think."

"Oh, but I did remarry, Hal, although it was a very short-lived marriage and no children resulted of it, which was probably just as well, considering what an utter kook my second wife turned out to be."

The archbishop settled himself into his cathedra. "Tell

me about her, your second wife, and of your marriage, Rupen.''

In far-off Anqara, a eunuch named Hyacinth—who just happened to be one of the three most powerful in the Holy Sultanate of Christian Osmanli Turks—bore a recently arrived missive to the desk of his large office, ordered that the door be closed and bolted, then broke the seals and spent a quarter hour rapidly decoding it before he took both the original and the translation in hand and prepared himself to bear them to Sultan Omar III.

A deceptively mild-looking and soft-spoken man, Omar could right often be found, as Hyacinth found him on this day, indulging his passions for history, current world affairs, and geography. The lithe, graceful, graying ruler lounged on a cushioned divan, its rich fabric almost hidden by books and scrolls penned or printed in Latin, Greek, Arabic, Turkic, Italian, Spanish, and Portuguese, all of which languages the highly intelligent monarch read well. Several rolled parchment maps sat ready to hand in brass holder, and a large globe was within his reach.

Admitted to the chamber, Hyacinth prostrated himself and crawled on his flat belly across the thick carpets to the side of the divan. After finishing reading his page, Omar signed the eunuch to arise.

"Correspondence?" He waved a hand at the sheaf of papers.

Hyacinth nodded. "Yes, O Light of Heaven, from the man who calls himself Fahrooq."

Omar then moved with a speed he seldom displayed save in battle or the hunt. In a trice, his sweeping arm had cleared space for the eunuch to sit upon the edge of the divan and the court customs bedamned; after all, he and Hyacinth were old friends, had ridden and fought side by side in battle on more than one occasion, and besides, they and the ever-present, mute body guards were the only humans in the chamber.

The middle-aged ruler never changed expression during the reading of the decoded message, even when he heard of the death in battle of one of his favorite grandsons. But when Hyacinth was done, he began to speak, pausing now and again to think, clearly express himself, and allow the eunuch time to take good notes.

"If a return message can be gotten to him who calls himself Fahrooq, tell him that I bear no ill against him, none but God can tell who will live and who die in battle, and, if die a man must, that is perhaps the best way to do so. At least, I would prefer that kind of death, were I free to choose.

"Tell him, also, that I can understand what happened with the camels'-filth Romans and that I think most kindly of Walid Pasha, that he chose to risk his own life to retain command of my ship rather than surrender it to some Roman by-blow of loathsomely diseased swine and feces-eating bitch-dogs.

"Tell him that I hereby officially authorize him and Walid Pasha to continue to serve the laudable-sounding ends of their erstwhile captor, this Sebastián Bey; for all that the description rendered in the message marks him indisputably as a doughty warrior, it also leaves no doubt that he is a merciful, noble, and intelligent gentleman. Such is a rare combination, and I am certain that he who calls himself Fahrooq can profit through observation and emulation of such an uncommon mentor. Would that I had such a great captain here—I can but wonder if Arthur of England and Wales knows just how well served he is by such a living treasure.

"Anent which, please have him who calls himself Farhrooq to indicate obliquely—whenever and if ever the time is ripe, of course—that I could be most generous to a multitalented paladin who chose to serve me and this sultanate.

"Tell him who calls himself Fahrooq to draw maps of every place he can in England, Wales, and Ireland and any other places they touch. Tell him to tell Walid Pasha and Sebastián Bey that whenever he is ready to release the ship and its crew—for I do not seriously think for one second that as shrewd a man as Arthur is reputed to be will ever let this Sebastián Bey go to serve another permanently—it and they will be handsomely ransomed by me. Where practicable, Walid Pasha is to have soundings made and chart the coastal waters wherever they may sail, but then he knows that, already.

"Our ambassador to the court of King Arthur is to be notified at once that, henceforth, any messages and maps or charts brought or sent to him by him who calls himself Fahrooq are to be immediately dispatched to you. Tell him also that he who calls himself Fahrooq is to henceforth have unlimited resources, available on demand, to provide wages for Walid Pasha and the officers and crew, as well as for upkeep of my fine ship.

"Lastly, tell him who just now calls himself Fahrooq to exercise care and caution and try not to get himself killed. You and I will not live forever, Hyacinth, old comrade, and my chosen successor is going to need a wise adviser whom he can trust, whose counsel and judgment on all matters need not be either weighed or questioned, but may be at once accepted."

As he strode back along the maze of crowded corridors which led eventually to his own section of the huge palace complex, Hyacinth wondered whether, despite Omar's wishes, he who chose to call himself Fahrooq would elect to trade his testicles for a chance to gain almost unbridled power, as had he, long years ago. He often had remarked to himself, to Omar, and to others how difficult it was to guess just which men would do so and which would not.

"Oddly enough," Bass thought, "there was a time when I looked forward to getting a letter from Krys; now I dread seeing one of Hal's or Pete's messengers riding in. In the last year, I don't think she's written one cheerful, positive letter—they're all just piss-moan, piss-moan, bitch, bitch, bitch, just like this one. She doesn't seem to know what she wants anymore, but she's more than willing to raise particular hell and draw blood and throw her weight of rank around to get it."

"Jenny Bostwick," went part of the letter, "is a featherheaded nincompoop who can talk of nothing except fancy sports cars (not one of which she ever owned or drove), belly dancing, and the rich foreigner she was planning to meet and marry to give him a green card and save her from ever having to do an honest day's work again. She was little better than a whore back in the other world, and I told her so, upon which she slapped me, twice, very hard. Of course, your ducal honor could not permit of such insubordination, so I ordered her striped, then sent back to Hal's palace in a coach, which was more than the little slut deserved; she should have gone back tied to the tail of a horse, so my ladies tell me.

"I have no way of knowing, of course, what sort of tale she told Hal, but now he is very cool toward me, though he still lionizes our son and that Armenian of his and even Buddy Webster. Whenever he has come down here since the incident I mentioned, he has had this Rupen Ademian and Webster flanking him at table, placing me, the Duchess of Norfolk, beyond them, and this is in no way proper to do.

"Yet, when I sought him out and tried to remonstrate with him as his peer in rank, he coldly informed me that I was no peer of his, that I was only basking in your reflected glory and achievements and that the only reason he had not long since packed me and my household off to Norwich or Rutland Castle or Whyffler Hall was that he had told you that I might stay here until you returned for me. He added that I was become every bit as arrogant and cruel as William Collier ever had been and wondered aloud if I, like him, was beginning to lose my reason. Then he had one of his guards put me out of the room."

"I've never believed in the practice of wife-beating," thought Bass, "but you, my lady wife, just may change my mind in that regard. If any woman ever was asking for it . . . ." He read on, each succeeding sentence and phrase making him angrier until, unable to take more of her carping, he crumpled the letter and hurled it into a corner in utter disgust. Then he went stalking off in search of one of his Irish officers.

"Sir Calum," he ordered when he found the man, "please send word to Sir Conn, immediately. He is to return posthaste with his two squads of *galloglaiches,* for I will want you all with me when I go to serve *Ard-Righ* Brian, and I doubt that Her Grace my wife could be residing in a more heavily guarded place than on the estates of His Grace Archbishop Harold, unless she were to be at the York palace itself, or at Greenwich, with His Majesty."

"And will Your Grace be wanting the Spanisher knight, as well?" inquired Sir Calum.

Bass shrugged. "Why not? He swings steel hard and true, nor is he a poor shot. Yes, summon Don Diego back to me here, too."

In her present mood and frame of mind, he was bedamned if he was going to leave Krystal Foster née Kent in command of a baker's dozen of the savage, conscienceless *galloglaiches* who would consider her wish to be their commission to wreak any barbarity that came into her head, simply because she happened to be the wife of their chosen warleader, Bass Foster. To do such would be akin to giving an idiot child a brace of loaded horse pistols to play with.

And that brought to mind another troubling thought. Just what kind of pampered, overprotected, arrogant little monster was such a mother going to make of their son, Joe Foster? It would be wise, he thought, before he set sail for Ireland, to arrange for the boy's fosterage. And the sooner the better, for the boy's sake. Krystal would pitch a first-class bitch, without any shred of doubt, but by then he would be at sea or in Ireland and it would be his orders that would be obeyed, not hers.

He also would need to make time to write to Hal, enclosing along with that letter another one addressed to Jenny Bostwick, accompanying a small, expensive gift or perhaps a purse of gold to pay something toward her suffering at Krystal's hands. So much to do already and so little time left in which to do it was he to adhere to King

Arthur's schedule. And Krystal was, as usual now, not helping him one damned bit.

Captain and Sailing Master Edwin Alfshott, Walid Pasha, Fahrooq, Sir Liam Kavanaugh, and some score of senior gun captains from the two galleons and the large caravel that made up the backbone of the private fleet of His Grace Sir Bass, Duke of Norfolk, stood or sat or squatted around a man who stood lounging against a long eighteen-pounder bronze culverin.

The tall, spare, heavily freckled, brown-haired man, but recently knighted and ennobled and still most unsure of himself in those new usages, was the royal gun founder, Sir Peter Fairley. He was come down from York to personally demonstrate a new and much safer method of firing cannon and mortars.

The culverin had, under his supervision, been fully charged with propellant powder and several thick wads, but no shot, for these coastal waters wherein the ships lay at anchor were heavily traveled, and no one wished to chance hulling or demasting some hapless, helpless fisherman by accident.

When the gun captain made to prime the piece, however, Sir Peter waved him away and instead thrust what looked a little like a large key made of brass wire and sheet copper into the touchhole. Next he engaged a small brass hook at the end of a slender cord some four or five yards long to a smaller ring set within the larger ring of the "key," just above the copper cylinder that now plugged the touchhole of the loaded culverin. He laid the loosely coiled cord atop the the lavishly carved and ornamented breech of the French-made piece, just forward of the cascabel, which on this particular tube was in the shape of a stylized gargoyle's head.

Beckoning to Fahrooq, whom he had come to know and to like over the past months, he had him take hold of the end of the cord, play it out to its full length, and then, taking a stance to the side and rear of the culverin, take up the slack and, with his hand at waist level, give the cord a sharp jerk.

All eyes were, of course, on the Turkish officer, so not a few men jumped, startled, when the culverin roared and bucked backward, straining against the recoil ropes and belching a smoking wad from its ornate muzzle on a long stream of fire.

After he had gained more than mere grudging attention from the gun captains, Sir Peter had them gather around closer and, with fingers that were big and work-stained and scarred, but still sure and rock-steady, he rapidly dismantled a brace of the friction primers and showed all of them the very simple works.

"Now, see here boys," he said, "ain't nothing magic to thishere deevice. Thishere big ring of heavy-gauge brass wire don't mean nothing, it's just there to give the gunner a handle and to pertect the little copper ring, is all. If you wants them off for some reason, all you got to do is this." He demonstrated.

"What matters here is the littler ring, the copper one, the tube, and what's inside of it." Peeled open, an unsoldered tube showed within a tightly coiled steel spring held in compression by the shaft of copper that depended from the smaller ring above, the shaft being split near its lower end, then bent up under the lowest coil of the tempered-steel spring.

"You see, fellers," Sir Peter Fairley went on, "this stuff what looks like dried paste inside here is stuff that takes fire real easylike, a whole lot easier then even fine-grain gunpowder does. The outsides of thesehere springs has done been made rough after the tempering by filing, and it's little pieces of flints and pyrites is held hard against the springs by the filling compound, so when the ring and its rod is jerked out and the spring ain't being held tight no more, it strikes sparks and the sparks sets off the compound and that shoots enough fire into the main charge for to fire the gun."

After examining two of the primers for a while, Fahrooq had the gun crew on duty swab and reload the waiting culverin. Once he had probed the touchhole, he inserted one of the primers picked out at random from the box Sir Peter had brought, attached the lanyard hook, took a stance, took in the slack, then gave a sharp jerk.

The copper pin came out, the gun again roared and bucked back, the device itself rose up a couple of inches, then settled back into the touchhole.

"Very nice, Sir Peter," the Turk said. "But the thing is mechanical, and all mechanical objects fail to function on occasion. How often do these fail, and what is a gunner to then do when such a failure occurs?"

Sir Peter nodded. "Of all the testing we done done up to York, Fahrooq—and it's been considerable, too—something less than one and a quarter out'n ever twenny has either not ignited at all or hung fire or not throwed enough fire to set off the gun charge, and we done tested it on ever'thing from cannon-royals to old, antique ribaltikins, too, including some of my breechloading chasers. But hell, man, was one to fail, just pop anothern in, quick. If it ain't anothern to hand, well, the gunners still got their flasks of priming powder and linstocks, ain't they?

"Look, fellers, I ain't saying that thesehere is the best things to come down the pike sincet wheellocks, but used right, they sure oughta make things a mite easier for the crews manning guns down on the main battery decks. Another thing, too—when you gets shorthanded during a fight where each gun is firing point-blank, maybe, and don't gotta be laid individual-like, a rating can have the guns charged, use thesehere primers, and shoot all or half of a broadside, all at the same time, with just one jerk of the lanyards."

On hearing this, Walid Pasha, Edwin Alfshott, and Sir Liam looked at each other and nodded. Win, lose, or draw, this new system seemed at least worth a try.

Sir Peter kept the duty gun crew busy, allowing the assembled gunners and officers to personally use the entire box of primers he had brought along on not just the long eighteen-pounder but on some of the heavier pieces on the gun decks below. Not once during the afternoon did any of the devices fail to produce immediate results of a positive nature.

In a private postprandial conversation with His Grace Sir Bass Foster, Duke of Norfolk, at Norwich Castle, that night, Sir Peter said, "Bass, old buddy, your ship captains and their officers is a whole lot nicer, smarter bunch then the hidebound old assholes runs King Arthur's siege train is. Damn near ever one of the siege gunners liked my primers a whole lot, was looking forward to using 'em, they allowed, seeing that they'd even fire great big old fucking bombards, real old ones, too.

"But then when I showed them off to the fucking officers, they never stopped frowning and all and turned them primers down flat. What they all said, when it was boiled down, was that if portfires was good enough for their great-granddaddies, they was good enough for them and the gunners. Now don't that beat all, Bass?"

Foster smiled humorlessly. "From my own experiences from time to time with functionaries in or attached to the King's camp and court, the greedy bastards probably were expecting you to bribe them to let their gunners use the primers."

"But . . . but that's just crazy, Bass," spluttered Sir Peter, "I . . . ever'thing I do up in York is for the King and the kingdom. I ain't some fucking traveling salesman peddling a new kinda soap powder. Don't they know that?"

Shrugging, Foster replied, "Most likely they do, but if they're of the type of which I'm thinking, the adoption of a military advance matters far less to them than does the weight of their private purses. Probably you could gain instant, official approval of the primers if you were to go back to the King's Camp and slip each of those officers a brace of gold onzas."

"In a pig's asshole!" snorted Sir Peter. "Bass, I'll be fucked if I'll pay a passel of crooks extra to do their goddam jobs right!"

Bass just shook his head. "Pete, I know it goes against the grain with an honest man like you, but that's the way affairs are conducted in this world, I've found, especially in proximity to the King or to other high-ranking nobles and churchmen. I don't like it either, but I'm sure as hell having to learn to adapt to it and to other things I don't like. This world is very different from our world, the time and place from which you and I and Buddy and the others came, but it would appear that we're going to live out the rest of our lives here in this different world, for better or for worse, so we're just going to have to learn to live as do the people who were born here. We have only three options: die, as did Arthur Collier and Susan Sunshine, go mad, as did Bill Collier, or adapt to our surroundings and live. And you strike me as the survival type, Pete.''

Sir Peter Fairley cracked his big, scarred knuckles, his firm jaw set, then he relaxed. ''Well, most likely you're right, Bass, and I'm just too stubborn for my own fucking good. But I couldn't go back and bribe them bastards now, even was I a mind to. I only had a few more then twelve hunnerd of them primers to start with, and I used up some down to the King's Camp and then nearly half a gross more of them today out on that big ship, and the rest of them is all promised now to Walid Pasha and Ed Alfshoot and Sir Lem and it'll take months to make up another big batch of them. My smiths up in York—and it seems like I never can get enough good ones, as many as I need—has got more important things to do, mostly, than make and temper lots of little-bitty steel springs, and then too, Bass, you just wouldn't believe the prices merchants is getting anymore for copper ingots.''

Bass nodded again. ''And, of course, you can't use iron or steel tubing because of the danger of accidental sparking and premature explosions of the gunpowder. But . . . let me think for a minute, yes. Pete, how about using steel tubes faced with tin? To the best of my knowledge, tin is still being mined in Wales and Cornwall, in this world, so it wouldn't have to be imported like most of the copper is. Tin isn't ferrous—it won't spark.''

Fairley slammed a work-hardened palm onto the table-top, a broad smile lighting up his face. ''Now, goddammitall, Bass, that's a first-class idea, one I never would of thought up in a million years. Sure thing, and we can do better than just facing the tubes, too. Buddy and me, 'bout a year ago, we had the batt'ries out our old rigs and out your Jeep pickup, too, brought down to York. We worked out a bicycle recharger for them and I've been doing some electroplating here and there, already. I could tin-plate them tubes. Thanks a whole lot, Bass. Is it anything I can do for you, now?''

Foster squirmed in his chair, then said hesitantly, ''Pete . . . it's Krys, my wife . . . Have you seen her, spoken to her, lately? I . . . her letters get worse and worse, and I . . . I'm worried about her, frankly.''

''You got you a right to be, buddy,'' replied Pete, grimly, '' 'cause it ain't none of it I've seen or heard about good. I think Krys is done flipped her lid.''

THE THIRD

His Holiness Abdul, Pope of Rome, lay dying. Despite the ever present risk of fire, the streets closest to his favorite palace had been buried in straw in order to mute the sounds of shod horse hooves and steel-rimmed wheels. Grim-faced, swarthy Moors of His Holiness's picked guards stalked those streets armed with pikestaves, clubs, and short, thick whips of rhinoceros hide to enforce quiet and quell any outbreak of noise or loud talk that might possibly disturb their master. Their ways were cruel, and they were feared and avoided.

Cardinal Prospero Sicola was summoned, searched, but courteously, for weapons, then ushered into the bedchamber of the dying prelate, where the hot air was thick with the reeks of incense and illness. He thought that Abdul already was beginning to look like a corpse—the dry skin drawn tight over the big bones of the face giving his profile an unmistakable raptorial cast.

Upon hearing Sicola's soft tread, Abdul opened his too-bright eyes but did not otherwise move where he sat half propped against a mound of cushions, with his one hand resting upon his chest and his other beneath the gold-stitched silken coverlet.

"Is Your Holiness awake, then?" asked Sicola softly.

"Yes, Brother Prospero," came the reply in a weaker

voice than Sicola ever before had heard from the often
sickly old man. "We are awake and still extant, though for
how much longer is in the hands of our Lord. That merchant-
banker, D'Este, must have dug really deep this time and
hired on a master poisoner; we have been poked, probed,
poulticed, pilled, purged, bled, even clystered, and none
of it to any salubrious effect upon our holy person. Apparently your latest regicidal plot upon our life has succeeded."

Not until he had knelt and kissed the pontiff's ring did
Sicola make reply, arising to stand beside the high, wide,
intricately carven bedstead. He said sadly, "Your Holiness
should have accepted my terms and, after secretly stepping
down, retired to live out the remainder of his life in
comfort and serenity at that small monastery near Tunis.
But allow me to assure Your Holiness that if your suspi-
cions of poisoning be true—and your very own physicians
seem to think otherwise—neither I nor Cardinal D'Este
had aught to do with it, nor I doubt me did any of our
close associates, else I would surely have heard of it, and I
swear upon my hope of salvation that I have heard no such
thing.

"Consider, Your Holiness, you are a very elderly man,
nor have you been in truly good health for some years
now. Death is the eventual end of all mortal creatures, that
is God's plan and His way, He—"

With a brief flash of his old fire, Abdul snorted. "Don't
preach homilies to *us*, you whey-skinned, snubnosed Frank
bastard! We have thought more and more in recent years
that mayhap the sainted Mahmud al-Qaleefah did err by
helping Islam to be merged with, polluted by, and be-
fouled by the brimming cesspool of baseless superstitions
and myths called Christianity. The Veiled Men of the
Mountains and the other small, persecuted bands of folk
who still cleave unto pure, untainted Islam are, we are
beginning to think, the only remaining True Believers.
Allah is God, Brother Prospero. Jesus called Christ was
but another of the great prophets, only a man, like Moses
or Mohammed, of flesh and blood. But, alas, the pattern is
irrevocably set and we all must go down to Gehenna

together. Who can unscramble an egg? We never were able to conceive of a method to set the thing again right, to undo the well-meaning sins wrought by St. Mahmud and those who succeeded him in his aims.

"You think us a backslider, Brother Prospero—no, don't bother to try to deny it, you do, we know. You look upon us in horror, you see before you an apostate Pope. But fear us not, we are dying. But ere long, you and all of the other pretenders may—nay, will—wish old Abdul still alive.

"You spoke at our last meeting but one of Rome being in need of a 'Wind of Change' to sweep away the host of supposed errors and mistakes wrought by us and our predecessor." The old man gasped a rattling gurgle of laughter, then spoke on. "Well, Brother Prospero, lying here with grim death nibbling at us constantly, we have seen snatches of what the near future holds for Rome and for those who, fit to do so or not, would rule her and hers.

"You and the rest of the malcontents will get your 'Wind of Change,' right enough. You'll all get more wind than you bargained for—a whirlwind of death and destruction looms over you even now, and it will commence its work even before our holy body is cold. You may outlive us, briefly, but we know that we shall enjoy the last laugh, Brother Prospero."

Whilst the dying pontiff was conversing with his declared enemy, up the street beyond the tightly sealed window of the death chamber a Moorish guards sergeant and five of his minions were stalking along, seeking out men or women or children to beat. They did not hear the well-oiled hinges of the shutters covering a window above them, and by the time they heard the contrabasso *thrrruuumm* of the crossbow, its thick, stubby bolt had torn through the back and the front of a mail hauberk and the thickness of the body between them, then sped on to penetrate yet one more layer of mail and lodge finally in the hipbone of that man-at-arms.

Whirling about at the first noise from behind his patrol, the sergeant saw the two men go down, screaming in agony and surprise, even as the shutter was slammed shut.

Roaring his rage, the sergeant led his remaining three Moorish Guards in battering down the strangely unbarred street-level door to the house, then charged in with them, clubs and whips discarded, scimitars and pistols out and ready.

Presently, four gashed, headless, swarthy-skinned bodies, all stripped of anything of value, were thrown out the doorway. Slowly, a gaggle of men and women and children gathered in the street to further mutilate the bodies, revile them, spit upon them, and shower them with bits of dung from beneath the straw. Some followed the man with the bolt in his hip as he crawled away from the site of the ambush. Not a few of these folk bore signs of recent abuse inflicted by whip and club and pikestave, and they took thorough, sickening revenge upon their onetime oppressor before someone finally deigned to grant him the mercy of death.

Neither group dispersed until the *thud-thud-clank-jingle* of armed and running men announced the imminent arrival of approaching troops.

Dying Pope or no dying Pope, loud were the cries of rage and outrage when the new-come Moors saw the bodies—by then, all of them hacked, mutilated, and despoiled. Louder still were their howls when they entered the vacant houses and found the four severed heads, lined up neatly on a bench built into a wall, their slit-off penises jammed into the beard-fringed mouths. After searching and thoroughly wrecking the empty house, the section of Moorish Guards departed, seeking first reinforcements, then men to kill.

True to the dying Abdul's vision, the Roman storm had commenced.

"That I ever met Carolyn at all was the purest coincidence." Rupen continued his tale to the archbishop. "While the guest of a wealthy arms collector at a fashionable downtown-Richmond club, I had happened to meet a man who had been a fellow GI Bill student at the city college twenty-odd years before. When, in the course of our conversation, he learned that I was vice president of Confederate States Armaments, he told me that he was just then teaching history courses at that same city college and asked if I might visit one of more of his classes to show off some of my reproductions and tell of how they were made, loaded, and used. Being, at that point, brandy-jovial, I agreed to do so.

"Since by then we were stocking a wide variety of long guns, and single-shot pistols and more than a dozen different cap-and-ball revolvers, taking examples of every item was out of the question, and I limited my burden on the first such visit to four long guns—one flintlock musket, one caplock rifle-musket, a flintlock fuzzee, and a cap-and-ball revolving carbine—and four handguns—a flintlock horse pistol, a caplock derringer, a Colt-type dragoon revolver, and a Remington-type Army-caliber revolver, along with a big briefcase full of accessories.

"So well received was my demonstration that day, so warm was my reception by both students and faculty, that when I was asked to return and do it again, I agreed to do so. My initial demonstration and talk had been in a classroom to about thirty students and a few stray faculty members; for my second appearance, I was requested to bring a larger selection of weapons and to be prepared to do a two-hour demonstration. Not until I arrived on campus did I find out that this one was to be in the largest lecture hall and that my audience was to number in hundreds and include not only students and faculty but also quite a few alumni and plain citizens.

"By the conclusion of that one, I had given out all of my business cards and, actually, sold many of the demonstration weapons on the spot, along with most of the accessories, so when the college offered me an honorarium, I politely declined to accept it . . . and this raised my stock with them through the roof.

"When I arrived at the lecture hall for my third demonstration, this time with Bagrat and two of my nephews, Al and Haigh, it was to find the hall and all of its approaches being picketed by a long-haired, scruffy, ragged, very smelly agglomeration of a type of scum peculiar to that period—'hippies,' they were called. This particular batch were bearing signs and shouting slogans and singing off-key songs protesting the then-ongoing war in Southeast Asia. Although I could not imagine just what a demonstration of eighteenth- and nineteenth-century reproduction weapons and tools had to do with the protracted modern war clear on the other side of the globe, it was clear that the only way I would get the station wagon into the parking lot under the lecture hall would be to run its three-plus tons over some of the unwashed young lunatics who were stretched full-length, in several ranks, across the width of the driveway ramp. Bagrat, Al, and Haigh were in favor of doing just that, but I drove instead, to the administration building, and we ended up carrying everything into the lecture hall through a tunnel connecting the two buildings, thus avoiding any confrontation with the mob of protestors entirely.

"When I asked just what the hell was going on outside the lecture hall, my old friend and sometime fellow student, Paul Czernik, just shook his head. "These peacenik hippies and pseudo-hippies and out-and-out bums, alkies and dopers mostly, will protest at the drop of a frigging hat, Rupen, you know that. What set this off? Me, probably. Your demonstrations have been such a big hit that a reporter from the student newspaper interviewed me and asked about your background. I told him you were a retired infantry officer, a major, that your late father had been an important defense contractor and that your brother, Kogh Ademian, was president and chairman of the board of Ademian Enterprises, the international arms dealers."

Rupen groaned. "And that was all published in the college paper? Hell, Paul, I'm lucky the little bastards didn't drag me out of the car and lynch me."

Professor Czernik looked rueful. "Open mouth, insert foot, leg, thigh, and asshole. I'm sorry, Rupen, I should've realized this bunch of freaks we have for students these days would blow it up out of all proportion. The way the published article read, you were either here recruiting for the Green Berets, preaching the joys of high explosives and napalm, or both at once.''

"Well, Hal," Rupen went on to the archbishop, "when the protesters realized that we'd bypassed them and gotten into the lecture hall, along with a fair portion of our audience, despite them, they went wild, turned so ugly that the security guards who had been outside all came inside, secured all of the doors, shuttered all of the ground-level or easily accessible windows, and rang up the city police.

"By the time the first city cops arrived on the scene, the so-called protest was well on the way to becoming a full-blown riot. And while that mess was in process of being cooled down, a bunch of real revolutionaries occupied most of the administration building, barred and barricaded all the entries and exits, then threatened to set fire to it unless some score of 'nonnegotiable demands' were met at once. The long list of demands was delivered via bullhorn, and most of them were ridiculous to begin; not the college administration, not the city mayor, not the state governor, not even the president could have fulfilled those demands, especially not in the short time which the revolutionaries were allotting . . . and those fledgling Marxists knew the facts of the matter as well as did anyone else.''

Rupen approached Czernik and a gaggle of faculty members huddled together in whispered consultation. "Paul, I've got to get my stationwagon out of that administration building parking facility, *at once.*''

"Mr. Ademian," said the dean of students, Bancroft, "the college has full insurance—any damages to your vehicle will be fully covered, never you fear.''

Rupen shook his head. "You don't understand, sir. I don't give a damn about the car itself; it's insured, too, and it's a company car, anyway, not mine. But I don't think that you, I, any of us want that gang of hoodlums in there to get their grubby hands on a certain wooden box that's in the back of the wagon, covered by an old GI blanket. We were going out to my brother's home from here today to make ready for a shooting match this weekend coming, so within that box are a dozen one-pound canisters of black powder and six or seven tins of percussion caps."

Bancroft stared, open-mouthed, at Rupen for a long moment, then sank into a nearby chair, moaning, his face in his hands. "Oh, my sweet Jesus God! Do you know what you've done, Mr. Ademian? That group in there are most of them foaming fanatics—they're perfectly capable of blowing up the building, just to prove a point!"

"Mr. Bancroft," said Rupen wryly, "don't worry about your precious building, hear? A measly ten pounds of black powder wouldn't put much of a dent in reinforced concrete, steel girders, and brick. But the danger is that they just might have along someone who knows how to make antipersonnel bombs, and I don't want to load down my conscience with that responsibility."

He, Bagrat, the two nephews, and Paul Czernik, along with two of the security guards—unarmed, save for billy clubs and transceivers—arrived before the vertically sliding fire door to the tunnel that connected directly to the underground parking facility for the now-occupied administration building.

Before helping his partner raise the door, one of the guards said, "Mr. Ademian, sir, the little fuckers prob'ly done closed the door leads out onto the street by now, but if it ain't too big and wide a car you got, you could just drive 'er straight through this tunnel here. We does it at night with two-wheelers and jeeps all the time."

In the opened doorway, Rupen told his pudgy, out-of-shape younger brother, "Bagrat, you stay here, you and Al. If Haigh and I can't get our wagon and get it out of there, four wouldn't be able to do any better."

Bagrat opened his mouth to protest, but the tone of his elder brother's voice, the look in his eyes, told him that it would do him no good to say anything. He just watched Rupen and Haigh walk away through the short, wide, brightly lit tunnel

As they came out into the somewhat less well-lit parking area, the two were confronted by a pack of some half-

dozen young men—bearded (most of them, those old enough
or sufficiently masculine to grow a decent crop of facial
hair), shaggy, and grubby, dressed in a rare collection of
military-surplus clothing, beads, rawhide, and either boots
or homemade-looking sandals. Two of them hefted police-
type billies, one bore a sawn-off pool cue, and the foremost held an elegant-looking walking stick that Rupen was
dead certain concealed a steel blade.

"Man," crowed the scruffy blond boy with the cane,
"don't they look pretty, like they just fell out of a bathtub.
Not just coats and ties, three-piece suits, by damn. How
fucking establishment can you get, huh?" Then, in a hard,
cold voice to Rupen, "Whatta you two fuckers want over
here? This building's been took over for the people by the
Revolutionary Peace Committee. It and nothing in it be-
longs to you cocksuckers anymore, see?"

Rupen slowed, stopped, stood stock-still, his system
pumping with adrenaline, but not one trace of excitement
in his stance, his demeanor, or his voice. Quietly, but
firmly, he said, "I am not in any way connected with this
college, young man. I am a visitor on this campus, and I
have come to get my car, that dark-grey Mercury station
wagon, over there behind you."

The blond boy snarled. "Who the hell you think you
are, you old faggot, with this 'young man' shit? My
fucking daddy? You two get your ass back into that fucking tunnel or I'll spill your chitlins all over the floor!"
With a sibilant *zzweep*, he withdrew the blade from the
mahogany cane and shook it at Rupen.

He did not even have time to show shock at the sight of
the PPK coming out of the shoulder holster in Rupen's
hand before a noise so loud that it stunned him and all his
pack and a spurt of flame from the muzzle of the pistol
sped a lead slug that left a silvery smear on the concrete
between his feet, then caromed off, whining like a banshee
until the crashing of glass announced that it had found a
lodgment somewhere among the parked automobiles.

Both blade and cane dropping from his suddenly weak
and nerveless grasp, the blond boy held both hands out

toward Rupen and backed away on unsteady legs, shaking his head and stuttering, a damp satin spreading from his crotch and down the left leg of his baggy, filthy suntan slacks. Bypassing the elevator completely, the pack poured up the fire stairs at a speed of knots, leaving their billies and the pool cue on the floor of the parking facility along with the sword-cane.

When he had negotiated the tunnel and come to a stop in the basement of the lecture hall, Paul Czernik remarked, "Company car or not, Rupen, you'd better get a good mechanic to look at that engine. That backfire over there was as loud as a gunshot. Did you have any trouble getting to the car?"

Both hands on the wheel, Rupen shook his head. "There was a small reception committee, Paul. But they were all just posturing kids—I outbluffed them."

Young Haigh Panoshian knew the truth of the matter, of course, but Uncle Rupen's stock had gone up a thousand percent during those few moments and only a quiet word was required to gain his instant silence on the matter, except among family members, naturally.

"Would you have really shot the boy, Rupen?" asked the archbishop.

"Him or any or all of them, had I felt I had to, Hal," replied Rupen, adding. "But I knew I wouldn't have to, that one, possibly two warning shots would assuredly do the trick with them. A hideaway weapon like that sword-cane is not designed or intended as a threat, it's to be drawn and immediately used. I could tell from the way he held and flourished it that he'd never really applied it to its true purpose before; he was making to slash at me with a stabbing weapon, one that didn't even have a true edge, so I knew I was confronting, at best, a thoroughly inexperienced amateur whose closest exposures to that kind of violence previously had most likely been watching movies or television."

The Archbishop of York nodded. "You'll work out very well in this world, Rupen. You're truly a gentleman and gentle—which two do not always come in one package—

but you can be as hard as tempered steel, without qualms
or regret. You're a true survivor type."

A smile flitted briefly across Rupen Ademian's olive-
hued face. "I am pure Armenian, *Der* Hal, so what else
could I be but a survivor? But back to how I met the
woman who became my second wife.

"After that hellish afternoon, Bagrat and I became very
popular with the administration, the most of the faculty,
and a fair number of the students of that college; we all
had—to use a Civil War term—'seen the elephant together.' A few months later, when Ademian Enterprises
found itself in dire need of a hefty income tax deduction,
Bagrat and I persuaded Kogh to donate it, or most of it, to
the city college building fund, whereupon we all were in
like Flynn, and that following June, they had Kogh speak
at their commencement ceremony, then conferred honorary
degrees on all three of us.

"At the faculty-administration-alumni cocktail party that
followed, that evening, Carolyn Foote Carter was introduced to me by someone or other. I don't know to this day
exactly how the hell she got into that party, for she wasn't
faculty or an alumna, just a graduate student in the Master
of Social Work program offered by that college.

"At twenty-six, Carolyn was a most attractive young
woman, really far too young for me by the standards of
that time and place, but she gave the impression of being
much taken by me . . . and I fell for her wiles, too, there
being no fool like an old fool, as the song says. I rational-
ized it all out to where it made good sense, of course. I'd
refused, over the sixteen years since Marge's murder, to
allow myself to become deeply involved or committed to
any woman, so I had right often been very lonely, when I
wasn't too busy to notice it. I was, by then, almost forty-
eight years old and financially not too bad off for a
foreign-born immigrant with not a hell of a lot of formal
education, and I figured that if anybody had earned a few
years of happiness, it was me.

"Far from being an immigrant, Caroly was come of the
old Tidewater aristocracy—known as the FFV or First

Families of Virginia. Some of her people still were holders of inherited land and wealth, but her parents seemed to have blown most of their own—they only owned the names, a modest home, and an inordinate amount of arrogance and pride of ancestry. Carolyn's father was a middling attorney connected with a prestigious Richmond law firm and most likely could have lived far more comfortably than he actually did, had he and his wife not felt obligated to maintain for themselves and their children a societal niche far above their existing means.

"Neither of them nor Carolyn's siblings nor any of their relatives ever really liked me, but they all realized just why Carolyn was so intent on staking out a claim on me. I didn't, not for a good while. Even at the wedding reception—it and the wedding itself paid for by Carolyn's father, with money 'borrowed' from me—when I happened to overhear a brace of her aunts remarking that yes, it was nauscating to think of the poor little thing and a dirty foreigner, but that as I was well-to-do, it would be a good first marriage and the resultant alimony would allow her to live well long enough to find a man of her own class, I didn't manage to put two and two together properly."

When *il Duce*, Timoteo di Bolgia, strode into the presence of His Grace Giosué di Rezzi, Archbishop of Munster, he already knew the news that he assumed he had been summoned to the archepiscopal palace to hear; one of his spies had sent word almost as soon as the swift ship had docked and the seals on the documents had been broken.

When he had knelt, kissed the archbishop's ring, then arisen, the frail-looking clergyman said solemnly, "Your Grace di Bolgia, I have just received word from Cardinal D'Este. His Holiness Abdul II al-Zaman died three weeks agone. Due to certain administrative problems, no election has as yet been held or even scheduled, but it would seem that a committee chaired by His Grace Cardinal Prospero Sicola has the reins firmly in hand.

"The message goes on to say that I should board the vessel that brought the message and sail to Palermo, at once. But dare I leave *Irland* and Munster, Your Grace? Should I do so, will His Highness Tàmhas of Munster still be alive when I return?"

Timoteo shrugged. "Your Grace, the life or the death of any man, regardless his rank or calling, is finally in the hands of God."

The slight man's eyes blazed. "Don't dare to fence with me, you godless heathen adulterer! I posed an understandable question and I'll have a straight answer of you, at least as straight and as truthful an answer as such a one as you could give."

Timoteo nodded, his face looking grim. "All right, Your Grace, here it all is in a nutshell: *I* presently have no designs upon the life of *Righ* Tàmhas; he has proved almost completely cooperative with his new council. As to just how long he will live, however, that is contingent upon how successful I and the other councillors are in restraining his perennial impulses to lead his FitzGerald Guards and his wild Rus-Goths in a suicidal daylight mounted charge against the fortifications of the *Ard-Righ*'s siege forces. As well planned, laid-out, and defended as are those fortifications, the *Righ* and his minion's desire to attack them makes about as much sense as would the plans of a troop of bullfrogs to mount assault on a nest of vipers. In his redundant Irish way, the *Righ* continues to babble about the requirements of his honor, the need to drive the trespassing Meathians from the Sacred Soil of Munster, and some of his blatherings even make a sort of sense, in a silly, old-fashioned way. But as I pointed out to the royal ass on the last occasion he swore he would do it on the next morning, what matters satisfied honor or reclaimed land to a cold, well-hacked corpse?

"No, Your Grace, if you want a reasonably firm assurance that *Righ* Tàmhas will be alive when you return from Palermo, should you choose to go, wring a vow out of the *Righ* that he will not, for any reason, leave the confines of the city walls."

*   *   *

The speedy but virtually unarmed lugger conveying di Rezzi, his secretary, their servants, four bodyguards, Sir Ugo, and his two squires sailed directly to the island of Majorca. In the port of Palmas, the archepiscopal party and their baggage were all transshipped to a waiting Genoan galleass, *Spaventoso*, all bristling with cannon.

When he had formally welcomed di Rezzi aboard, the commander of the warship, one Sir Giorgio Predone, said bluntly, almost rudely, "Your Grace, this may not be either an easy or a pleasant voyage. The battling between Roman factions has spilled over, out of the city itself, you see. The triple-damned Moorish bastards have never needed much excuse to sail out and prey on honest shipping, and the mere unsupported rumor, without a single grain of truth to it, that old Abdul might have been poisoned has got them all—from Sidi Barani to Beni Saf—armed and at sea after gold and slaves and anything else they can lay hands on.

"If it happens to us, it may well happen suddenly, so when I tell Your Grace to repair to his cabin and bar the door, I pray he does just that immediately, for his life is in my keeping on board this ship."

Turning from di Rezzi, Predone demanded, "D'Orsini, is it, Sir Ugo? The Roman D'Orsinis? Then I take it you're a Knight of the Church, eh?" There was a barely discernible tinge of disgust and condescension in the Genoan's voice, for Papal knights quite often in the last hundred and fifty years had been nothing of the sort, their swords and gilded spurs mere baubles akin to their rings and bracelets and neck chains.

Nodding his answers silently, Sir Ugo feigned to not notice the slighting tone, but one of his squires, himself a noble-born Roman, was not so temperate in nature.

"My lord Predone," he burst out unbidden, "you should know that my puissant lord, Sir Ugo D'Orsini, is on loan to His Grace from the staff of the famous condottiere *il Duce*, Sir Timoteo di Bolgia."

"Is it so?" drawled Sir Giorgio. Smiling warmly, he

said, "Your pardon, please, for my rudeness, Sir Ugo, but these be harder times than usual, and every nonfighter aboard makes for a bigger risk at sea. May I say that it is indeed an honor to have a man of your water aboard my ship. I have long admired, greatly respected, and avidly followed the career of the illustrious *Duce* di Bolgia. His exploits are bringing respect back to Italian arms and men-of-arms. When you are established in your place below, come back to the bridge here, pray. I would have you tour *Spaventoso*."

Despite the dire warnings, however, the voyage was uneventful, though slow as compared to the lugger they had quitted at Palmas, until Sicily was already a dim smudge on the horizon. Then it was that three small, fast, maneuverable feluccas bore down upon them, the bow-chasers firing long before they had achieved even maximum range.

Awakened by the nearby pealing of bugles and thunder-roll of a drum directly overhead, Sir Ugo was hardly on his feet when a staccato pounding on his door commenced. Throwing open the portal to the small, cramped sleeping space, the knight confronted a ten- or twelve-year-old officer trainee, who bobbed a short, hurried bow and gasped out his message.

"M'Lord D'Orsini, if it pleases m'lord, Sir Giorgio urges that m'lord arm with haste, with haste, m'lord. Moorish pirates be coming up fast on the starboard, three of them, as fast as sail and oars can drive them." The white-faced youngster gulped and added, "There will be a sea fight . . . and soon."

Once buckled and laced into three-quarter armor, with his preferred battle rapier and a brace of wheellock pistols at his waist, a dagger in each of his boot tops, and his helmet under his left arm, the tall, slender but wiry noble-man paced down the narrow corridor and tapped at the door to the larger cabin which housed the archbishop and most of his party.

"Your Grace, the ship is about to be attacked by no less than three Moorish ships. If the *Spaventoso* be sunk or taken, your four guards will not do you much good, but up above, adding their weights and strength to the defending forces, who can say what prodigies they might wreak with me and my two squires?''

After flourishing a salute and resheathing his rapier, Sir Ugo said, ''Sir Giorgio, I am come with two squires and four men-at-arms, these last courtesy of His Grace di Rezzi. Also Monsignor Tedeschi, His Grace's secretary, will be up shortly, and he claims some degree of skill with a fowling piece.''

Captain Predone nodded, the still-unbuckled cheek plates of his open-faced helm rattling to either side of his grin. ''Is it so, Sir Ugo? Then the monsignor could do equally well, I trow, with a port piece—those swivels are all mostly nothing but oversized fowlers.''

Turning his head, he bawled, ''Master gun captain, there'll be a priest up on deck shortly. Place him as gunner on a port or a base.''

To Ugo, he said, ''You and your lot stay by me, and don't fret or go running off to the first fight you see. I fear me there'll be action and blood enough for us all, ere this engagement ends. I . . . will you look at that bugger, the middlemost one out there, pulling ahead of the other two? Why, I think he is going to try ramming us.

''Sailing master!''

As Ugo D'Orsini and his men watched, one of the low sail-and-oar-propelled felucca-rigged frigatas bore down on them from the windward, all sails drawing and every long oar flashing, the two methods of power combined giving her a respectable speed. Although the other two frigatas continue to fire off shots from their bow-chasers just as fast as the pieces could be reloaded, the lead vessel had ceased to fire, and knots of men could be seen gathering at midships and stern, bright steel of weapons and armor flashing in the light of the newly risen sun.

Aboard the *Spaventoso*, the starboard bank of twenty huge oars pulled mightily, while those twenty on the port side backed water every bit as strongly, and the high, long, ponderous galleass slowly moved about in place, in an effort to present her prow to the attacker in time. When he felt the frigata to be within range, Sir Giorgio ordered fire from those cannon that would bear properly, but every humming ball seemed to miss, although some splashed heartbreakingly close to the target.

"*Gunmen and moschettieri,*" roared Captain Predone, in a voice that Sir Ugo was certain could be heard as far away as Napoli, at least, "half an ounce of gold to the man who knocks the steersman yonder on his keel end!"

At this, the starboard rails became crowded with wheellock and matchlock-armed soldierery and not a few officers as well, for the offered reward was a princely sum indeed. After meticulously checking their priming, some tightening the springs of wheellocks, others blowing on and tapping ash from slowmatches before clamping them into the arms, the firing began. The steersman must have had a charmed life, for after the first dozen or so balls fired at him, he still stood and held the tiller rock-steady. However, the knots of fighting men assembled in waist and stern had not been so lucky, some of them. Some six or seven were down, either lying still or thrashing upon the decks, and all of those still on their feet were quitting the raised steering deck as fast as they could jump into the waist.

In a fury of frustration and fear for his vessel and men, Captain Predone himself stalked over to a base-piece, checked the priming of the long bronze inch-and-a-half-bored swivel gun, then snapped the question to the nearby gunner, "Solid or small shot?"

Fingering his forelock respectfully, the barefoot man said, "Solid, leaden ball, and it please the noble captain."

A grunt was Predone's only answer. Taking up a length of slow match, he blew it to a bright glow, then took up the cursive tail of the piece, leaned over, and squinted, sighting it, and abruptly jammed the lit end of the match into the powder-filled touchhole.

The frigata was by now come terrifyingly close, so Ugo did not need a long-glass to see the beefy steersman thrown completely over the stern rail as the pound-or-so ball of hard-flung lead struck him. He could even see five or six men leap up from the overcrowded waist onto the steering deck, hands outstretched to grab at the swaying tiller.

The sailing master of the galleass had seen what must come if none could reach the unguided tiller in time and had ordered the immediate shipping of both banks of oars. The shipping was barely accomplished in time to prevent damage or injury on the row decks of the *Spaventoso*.

Even as one or two of the Moors finally reached the tiller of their frigata, its solid brazen ram struck the metal-sheathed prow of the galleass, rode over its larger but shorter ram, and, still hard driven by acquired momentum, scraped its starboard side up the full length of the starboard side of the Genoan warship. All of that bank of the frigata's oars were snapped and splintered like so much kindling, and the hideous screams from her row decks were clearly heard on every deck of the *Spaventoso*.

And on board the galleass, every swivel that could be brought to bear, every arquebus, musket, dag, and pistol, was fired into the knots of Moors standing or kneeling or lying upon the deck of the frigata as fast as they could be pointed, discharged, and reloaded. Those few of the Moors who made to clamber up the sides of the galleass were all hacked or stabbed back down with sword or dagger or dirk or pike.

As wind in the untended sails bore the Moorish ship slowly away, Captain Sir Giorgio Predone grunted, upon Sir Ugo D'Orsini's word of compliment on his shooting, "A bit of luck, but we'll need more than a bit are we all to get out of this pickle alive. There're two more of the Ifriqan buggers . . . and to judge by this last lot, they know what they're about."

CHAPTER
THE FOURTH

A big, burly man with a three-forked chin beard, but no mustache, shoulder-length grey-streaked hair, and even greyer dense brows above grey-green eyes sat on a folding arm-stool at a low, heavy table in a stone-walled room lit by a dozen thick beeswax candles set in brass reflector holders.

All four walls, the floor, and the vaulted ceiling were of stone, unbroken by any apparent openings for door or window or even arrow slits. While everyone knew that such a room existed, few suspected just where it might lie, fewer had been within it, and only a bare handful knew any of the techniques required to gape supposedly solid and immovable stone walls and gain entry to it.

It was the strongroom, the royal treasury, of the ancient kingdom of the southern Ui Neills. The land was also called the Kingdom of Meath, and its king was also the *Ard-Righ* or High King of *Eireann* or Ireland. Round about the room reposed chests of all sizes and shapes, all secured to iron floor rings by lengths of thick-linked chain. Most of the iron-bound coffers were held shut by massive locks. One lid stood thrown back, however, and the big man sat studying a velvet-lined tray lifted from out that chest.

As often when alone, Brian O'Maine, *Ard-Righ* of *Eireann*, *Righ* of Mide (or Meath), and *Ri* or chief of the

Southern Ui Neills, talked aloud to himself as if to another person.

"The Seven Magical Jewels of *Eireann*, we choose to call them. When actually there are eight and including the one of Great *Eireann*, nine, could only some fisherman dredge up the long-lost Sardius of Ulaid from the murky depths of Lough Neagh. And I have two of them here."

His fingers, thick-calloused from gripping hilt of sword and haft of axe and from handling the reins of powerful destriers, lifted a piece from its fitted hollow in the rich cloth. In a wide, thick, heavy piece of that ancient alloy called electrum (silver and gold, giving a less yellow metal) were set three stones—a clear-yellow diamond of some inch across, a moonstone of about equal size but of a different shape, and a dark-green carbuncle.

"The Ancient and Most Holy Jewel of Ui Neill." He named its name. "Where in all this world did that pack of unhung thieves and despoilers that were my ancestors manage to steal such big, beautiful stones I wonder? They certainly were stolen, that or prized, for no man would ever part with them willingly, not for any price. Whenever I look upon it, I can understand just why our dear cousins to the north have never forgiven us Southern Ui Neills for insisting that it remain here, in the south, nearly six hundred years after the last Viking died or was baptized.

"Rest you well and ever safely, my joy." Reverently, he laid the piece back in its place, then lifted out the piece beside it. This a disk of reddish gold with a large, polished oval of fine heliotrope set in its center, the big gem being surrounded by a circle of twelve green garnets.

"The Blood of Airgialla, they call you, and we all know the myths of your origin, but I wonder what the truths are and if anyone ever again will know them. I doubt not that spilled blood, quarts or full gallons of the stuff, had much to do with your past, though. At least, you were delivered up to me in peace by a friend and ally—so bloodless a change of hands must seem strange to you. Well, I return you to your velvet couch, my pretty."

Around the two golden baubles with their glittering

stones, five other hollows of differing shapes and sizes gaped empty of occupants, their emptiness seeming to mock the aspirations of this puny, short-lived mortal man called Brian.

With one finger on his left hand tugging absently at the golden torque that encircled his thick, muscle-corded neck, he used a finger of his right to press into each of the vacant hollows in turn, while he mused on the absent pieces.

"The Shield of Laigin should come to me easily, for the *bouchal* who now rules there acknowledges that he owes me a debt for taking to a large measure his part against Rome. I think that when I'm ready to ask, he'll bring it to me with no trouble.

"The Star of Munster." His finger moved on to the next hollow. "That Italian conndottiere-type, di Bolgia, seems honest enough on the surface and even just below it, but all Italians are a sly, tricky breed. At least he's astute enough to recognize *Ri* and *Righ* Tàmhas FitzGerald for the incipiently dangerous slop-brain that he is. Now if I can ferret out just what it is that di Bolgia wants of me—and I know damned good and well that he wants something—I think that the Star of Munster will soon be in its place, here.

"Not that I like the idea of putting another FitzGerald onto the throne of Munster, for the blood is tainted, the entire line is eaten out with rot, like the most of the Norman ilk. But if there must be another of them, and I suppose that there must be, for di Bolgia has weighed accurately the sentiment in Munster and to place or try to place a new dynasty as kings of Munster would surely precipitate an uprising, and not just an uprising of the nobility, the FitzGerald kindred, but a general uprising of all the people . . . and that would be calamitous, at this juncture, giving as it would just the kind and size of an opening that Rome needs to start her mailed foot into the political affairs of *Eireann*. . . .

"No, I'll let them crown this Sean FitzRobert when they feel the time is ripe, and I'll give him a few years to show his stripes. Then, if he seems your normal land-hungry

FitzGerald, I'll just march down there and crush him and see if I can unearth one FitzGerald who is not a savage thief or a simpleton, which is about as likely as finding rubies in an old, rotten dungheap. But maybe, if I can find a brave, wise, cooperative man from among the descendants of the pre-Norman kings, the Ua Briains, the people and what I leave alive of the nobility will accept him as *Righ* of Munster.''

The *Ard-Righ*'s finger strayed to the next hollow pressed into the velvet lining. It was more than twice as deep as any of the other hollows and near as big as a man's clenched fist. "The Dragon of Connacht," Brian said. "That's one that I've never seen, since there's never been any long period of peace with Connacht during either my reign or my lifetime, but men and manuscripts say that it is a huge hunk of solid amber, clear but reddish, as if fresh blood had been mixed with it, and with a small dragon, one as long as a man's forefinger, encased within it.

"The thing surely came from the Baltic, that's where all amber comes from, but the various legends and manuscripts disagree on its age, how long its been in Connacht. Were it almost anywhere else, I'd surmise that it was brought in by Vikings, but there were never that many long-term Viking settlements in most of Connacht. So, like so many of the others of the Jewels, I suppose that the true genesis of the Dragon of Connacht is just another lost in the dim mists of the long ago, never to again be known as fact by any man.

"The Striped Bull of Ui Neill, now, the Jewel of the Northern Ui Neills, is supposed to be of Viking origin, and there are indeed some runes carved into it and a Norse sunstone set between the horns. Yet each time I've seen it, I've wondered where the Vikings who carved in those runes got that little statuette of banded agate. I'm dead sure that no Viking ever carved the thing, for who ever saw a bull with horns shaped like that one? Even the head and body are decidedly different from any living cattle I've ever seen, either in the flesh or drawn on parchment, nor has any one of the hordes of foreigners who've come to court ever reported ever seeing the like of such cattle as the sketch I had made of my cousins' Jewel.

"As far as getting possession of the Striped Bull is concerned, I think that all that is needed is to overawe my cousins with a strong force . . . Can I ever find the time to march north during Fighting Season? Perhaps this great captain that Cousin Arthur is going to send me can take his condotta up there?"

His fingertip tapped beside a long, narrow hollow in the velvet. "The Nail and the Blood, Holy Jewel of Breifne. Just an old, pitted, wrought-iron spikelet, cleverly encased in a crystal tube, the whole then set in a gold brooch and surrounded by small pigeon-blood rubies. All the people of Breifne and most of the churchmen to whom I've spoken declare that the nail is one of those that secured Christ to His Cross.

"It's possible, I suppose, for it does date back to just about the time that the men of the First Crusade to recapture Jerusalem would have been coming back, and I'd like to believe in the truth of at least one myth, but then I always recall what old Abbot Cormac used to say about supposedly holy relics."

"Look you, young king-to-be." The old man shoved into the center of the parchment-littered table a shred of one of his thumbnails he just had gnawed off. "What would you say if I told you that this was an authentic piece of a toenail of the Holy St. Lazarus?"

Brian, then in his early teens and completely at ease with his longtime mentor and teacher, had laughed and replied, "I'd say to find a fool to cozen, Father. What else would I say?"

"Ah," went on the elderly monk, "but what, say, if you were a ruler and in need for some reason of a holy relic to give lodgment within your holdings? What then would be your reply, eh? Let us say that the continued safety, security, and well-being of all your folk and kin depended upon your acquiring a holy relic—would you then agree that a piece of an old abbot's thumbnail might truly be part of one of St. Lazarus's toenails? Of course you would, for a ruler who will not do all in his power to see to the continued prosperity and peace of the people God has placed under his suzerainty is no true ruler, but a tyrant.

"Brian, in my travels as both youth and man, I have seen or heard of enough True and Most Holy Nails to be rendered into enough other nails to shoe every horse in *Eireann*, and the forge fire could be kept hot for the entire time it took by feeding it with bits and pieces of dusty wood avowed to be parts of the True Cross of Christ.

"But, Brian, listen you well and remember: While you or I may scoff and laugh at the naivety of those who truly believe such clear frauds, recall that those who originally perpetrated the conversions of a bit of iron from a blacksmith's scrap heap or a section of wood from a wrecked ship into holy relics very likely had most commendable motives for so doing, and that those souls who believe in the relics long after the fact are often uplifted, made into better people, by their firm beliefs, their sincere faith.

"When you are *Ri* and *Righ* and, perhaps, *Ard-Righ*, as well, my boy, be publicly open-minded and ever-doubting, for that is your nature and you must always be true to yourself in all things, but at the same time, be careful lest you undermine the faith in possibly spurious things that many a poor wight needs to simply survive in this world.

"When you face a liar, look not first at the lie itself, but try hard to learn more of the liar and reason out just why he tells such a falsehood before you render judgment upon him."

Ard-Righ Brian, sitting now in his bright-lit strongroom in his castle-palace at Lagore, sighed, missing his old, long-dead teacher and friend. Then, with another, deeper sigh, he let his finger go on to the next hollow, the seventh one, the last.

"Well, everyone knows where the so-called Jewel of Ulaid came from. It was looted in a raid on Mercia led by *Righ* Aed Allan, nine centuries ago, after the original Jewel of Ulaid was hurled into Lough Neagh by the defeated *Righ* Cathussach, just before Aed Allan caught up to him, killed him, and took his throne. Of course, where the Sassenachs came by such a diamond is probably a long and most entertaining saga . . . did any one of the *filid* but know its verses to sing.

"Getting it into this tray promises to be a very sticky, messy business, for it is said by those who know that *Righ* Conan, by-blow of a bastard Ui Neill, who has begun to style himself and his low, dishonored house Mac Dallain, has had the stone reset in a golden ring that he never removes at any time or for any purpose from his left thumb, having bruited it widely about that on the day he does remove the ring, he will cease at that moment to be *righ* and his life will be forfeit. So I know better than to ask *him* for the loan of *his* Jewel."

Brian leaned the full weight of his big-boned, muscle-rippling body upon the arms of the stool and stared down at the tray with its two Jewels and five yawning cavities. At long last, he spoke again. "I'd have to have a larger tray fashioned for me, of course, but for such a prize, I'd do that much and far, far more, and right willingly, too. It's been often described to me and I even own sketches and one full-color oil painting of it, but what pale thrills the painting, in all its true beauty, must be compared to seeing, holding, the real thing.

"The Jewel of Great *Eireann*. There, across the ocean, I understand that it's called by the name of St. Brendan's Plate, but in Connacht, they call it the Emerald of the West. That disk is a foot or more in diameter, and those who've seen it say that it's near as thick as is my smallest finger. But it's not pure gold, it's something they call white gold, though it contains no silver, it's sworn, rather some strange other metal peculiar to those lands that though colored like silver is much harder and more difficult to melt for alloying or for casting. That rare oddity alone would be enough of a marvel, but those stones, now. . . .

"Just within the rim of the plate is set a close-packed circle of small emeralds alternated with small yellowish pearls. A finger-width of space toward the center is another circle of the yellow pearls and sapphires, then, inside that circle, another one of opals and shiny jet-black stones. The next circle is of more slightly larger opals alternated with an opaque, whitish stone streaked irregularly with a bright green. The innermost circle is entirely composed of pearls—round, black ones and tear-shaped, bright orange ones. Inside that last circle is the Emerald itself, clear, dark-green, and large as a hen's egg.

"That fabulous plate is meant to be worn upon the breast, and each golden link in the chains is covered by a small red-gold disk, and in the center of each disk is set a tiny replica of the Great Emerald, each one identically shaped, each just as clear, each of exactly the same color.

"I wonder if, by a holy miracle of God, I'll ever actually see that plate, hold it in my two hands? Only God or one of His holy instruments could bring such to pass, I fear, and I am a sinful man."

His Grace Sir Bass Foster, Duke of Norfolk, Earl of Rutland, Markgraf von Velegrad, Baron of Strathtyne, et cetera, was just then thanking God that he had been blessed with a capable, intelligent, and, above all willing and seemingly tireless staff. After being exposed to the endless lists of minutia involved with transporting him, his staff, his squires and servants and theirs, his squadron of *galloglaiches,* their mounts, his, his staff's, and all of the squires' and servants', plus all the weapons, armor, firearms, clothing, equipment, food and drink, tents, bedding, necessary wheeled transport, and mules to draw them, he was very relieved that he was not in it all alone.

He recalled the early days of the war against the Crusaders, when he was a mere captain of cavalry and all of his possessions could be borne about in a single footlocker. Now, his field necessaries alone—and stripped to what his servants swore on the Rood was the barest of essentials, at that—required four waggons or large wains, plus six or eight pack animals, nor could he blame his servants for misjudging needful items or quantities thereof, for the most of the men all were former servants of noblemen killed in the wars, had been on many a protracted campaign with King Arthur's army, and presumably gave only good counsel.

Following a protracted, in-detail conference between his staff, his shipmasters, and his military leaders, with Sir Paul Bigod's secretary sitting in and Colonel Sir Richard Cromwell representing the king, it had been decided that the squadron and the trains, the spare mounts and draft animals, Bass, and at least half of his staff would march cross-country from Norwich to Liverpool, there to be met by the duke's personal fleet, plus as many horse barges as their staff deemed necessary. They would enship at and embark from Liverpool, sailing directly to Liffeymouth, where the beasts would be swum ashore, then to the Port of Dublin, where the troops and goods would be disembarked.

In a private meeting after the conclusion of the conference, Sir Richard had remarked, "Your Grace would, I know, enjoy a shorter and more comfortable trip around to Liverpool did he sail there aboard one of his fine big ships, I know well. But there is the matter of his squadron to consider, to be on the march through a peaceful countryside. Your grace has proven abilities to control those *galloglaiches*—indeed, to see the way that those murderous miscreants worship Your Grace is almost to be witness to idolatry—therefore, I am certain that His Highness would be quick to concur that the master must ride with his hounds, lest there be some regrettable occurrences involving Englishmen and their goods during the course of the march west from Norwich Castle."

"Which is a polite, roundabout way of saying, my friend," thought Bass, while Sir Richard sipped at his wine, "that my sovereign lord Arthur III Tudor, King of England and Wales, highly values the combat abilities of these *galloglaiches* I seem to have inherited, but doesn't trust them any farther than he could throw my destrier. Oh, hell, Arthur and Cromwell are both right, though, stone-cold sober, the most of the squadron are more dangerous to noncombatants or men of other friendly units than any other group I've seen or heard of on either world

—cold-blooded murder, rape, arson, robbery of every type and nature, lighthearted torture and maimings, sacrilege, these all would be everyday diversions for them, were they given their heads; and drunk, they're worse, if possible; drunk, they start attacking each other.

"But not for me, for some reason, be they drunk or sober—I seem to be completely safe from them, even if I've apprehended them in misdeeds and am in the very process of disciplining them, I've never had so much as one of them raise a hand to me, my gentleman, or their Irish officers. So I guess if anyone can prevent them from doing to the English countryside what Sherman did to Georgia, it's got to be me."

Then, a bare three weeks prior to his planned day of departure for the march westward, with Sir Colum, his squires, one of Cromwell's captains, and some members of Bass's staff already out reconnoitering the projected line-of-march, Carey Carr stopped off at Norwich Castle on his journey to Greenwich with word that the Archbishop, Harold of York, would like to speak with him at some time prior to his leaving for Ireland.

Lacking either the time or the energy for the hard, often long trip by road or the harder, though shorter, overland hellride, Bass, with Sir Ali—just returned from a pilgrimage to the Shrine of St. Thomas à Becket—Don Diego—also just back from a trip of a personal nature, having to do, he solemnly averred, with the good of his soul—and a handful of bodyguards and servants, boarded one of the smaller ships of his peronsal fleet, sailed up to Hull, there borrowed horses from the resident royal garrison, and rode from there to York. That ride, on the long, narrow, rutted and holed bogs that passed for roads, took longer than had the ship passage up from Norfolk. The only thing that Bass was really looking forward to in Ireland was that folk all said that the Irish roads were mostly far superior to those of England or Wales.

Late on the day of his arrival, in the spacious room that the old archbishop used for what he called in public his alchemical studies, the two men—one, of the twentieth century, one of the twenty-first century—spoke in a language that only one other person in the palace could have understood, the basic English of the United States of America of the last quarter of the twentieth century, for there were spies about and Archbishop Harold well knew it for fact.

One more time, he had carefully explained and demonstrated to Bass the workings and care of two examples of twenty-first-century technology—heat-stunners, weapons that, while they could incapacitate humans in the blinking of an eye, would never kill them if utilized properly.

Bass handled the two devices—the smaller looking a bit like one of the ball-point pens of his world and time, though about twice as thick, and the larger being about a third again thicker than the other, with a slight curvature of the butt end.

Old Harold had used the larger to quickly bring a bit of iron in a stone mortar to red heat, several times interposing his withered old hand between the instrument and the iron. "You see, Bass, when set on 'Heat,' these devices will only harm flesh if it is within close proximity to or actually in contact with metal, so you must direct the heat beam at some metal object.

"The 'Stun' setting I cannot easily demonstrate, unless you want me to show you what it feels like . . . and I somehow don't think that you would like it. Victims come out of it with a headache of inhuman proportions. Metal will not stop the stun beam, but there is no need to aim for metal, either. Directing the beam to the head will put your man down in a bare eyeblink of time, but should you not be able to direct it at the head, any available part of the body will do; it will just take a few seconds longer to do the job.

"The one real drawback to these smaller examples of the heat-stunner is that they possess only a very narrow beam and a short range of effective use, perhaps ten feet in the case of the smaller, twice that or a little more for the larger.

"The power charges, now." He thumbed back a sliding cover on the side of the larger device, exposing a cavity wherein nestled, end to end, two little cylinders of a brownish hue with shiny surfaces, each of them slightly less than an inch in length from one rounded tip to the other. "They are blue-black and shiny when fully charged, but as they slowly lose their charge, they become lighter in color and less shiny of surface. The forward one will, when weakened, draw from the rear one until it is emptied of charge, so if you note that the forward one is of a darker color than the rear one, don't be alarmed—it's only when the forward one begins to lighten that you should be ready to replace them with freshly charged ones.

"*Never, ever* throw these cylinders away or lose them, for only a few hours' exposure to bright sunlight will fully recharge them. You can't break them, either deliberately or by mischance, and the only way to discharge them is to use them in the devices. The small unit holds one, and, as you can see, the larger unit holds two.

"How you carry these weapons is up to you, whatever proves easiest and most comfortable for your quick use, but I have always kept my small one, the one that I brought into this world and time nearly two hundred years ago, strapped to my left forearm." He drew up the voluminous sleeve of his fur-trimmed robe to show the arrangement.

Bass nodded. "That looks as good as any other way to me, so long as I'm not in armor, of course. As for the bigger one, I'll have Nugai whip together a holster to go inside one of my bootlegs, I think. This little pouch of charges is flat enough—I can just have him stitch it inside a boot or in some other safe cranny. What are these other things you have over there? Do you intend them for me, Hal?"

The old man shoved the largest of the indicated items into the center of the tabletop. "This, Bass, is the unbreakable water bottle you took from the body of Colonel Dr. Jane Stone.* I boiled horsehide in wax and shaped it

*Read Robert Adams, *The Seven Magical Jewels of Ireland.*

around the bottle so that now it bears a close enough resemblance to not matter to a contemporary canteen that no one should question you about it. It holds exactly a liter of liquid.

"This lantern belt box, made of more of my *cour boulli*, contains the impermeable tubes of the emergency tablets she brought to this world and time on her ill-fated projection. They taste much better than they smell, incidentally, and each contains intensely concentrated food, vitamins, minerals, a powerful stimulant, and a mild general-purpose antibiotic. Never ingest more than three in any twenty-four-hour period, and always drink at least a pint of fluid whenever you do ingest one. The smaller reddish tube contains a much more powerful general-purpose antibiotic, twelve of them; actually, they are the longevity boosters, such as I used to save the life of the King's grandfather several times over, so long ago. The other small tube, the one that looks the color of old ivory, like the larger tubes, now holds a dozen pain capsules from my time and world. They will be effective against unbelievably intense pain for twelve, twenty, as much as thirty hours at a stretch, yet without so clouding the senses, such as does opium and its various derivatives, that a man cannot function normally.

"If you will open that flat chest there at your side, you will see yet another of my handicrafts."

Within the indicated leathern chest were what seemed to Bass to be patterns for a breast-and-back cuirass, plate spauldrons, and a velvet skullcap fashioned over something thin and rigid. On lifting out the two largest pieces, Bass recognized the dull, silvery-grey metal as that of which the projection device that had for so very long squatted in the ground level of Whyffler Hall's tower keep had been surfaced. Both the breastplate and the backplate showed bright, shiny splashes that his soldier's eye immediately recognized for lead.

Holding the thin, light pieces in his hands, he raised his eyebrows questioningly at the archbishop and asked, "Who shot the balls and why, Hal?"

"One of my guardsmen, Bass, with an eight-bore caliver

and at a range of under forty feet, and before you ask, yes, the weapon was fully charged. The balls struck the plates squarely and knocked each of them spinning for the full length of my inner garden and clanged them against the stone wall, but as you can clearly see, they were neither holed nor damaged in any way. I made two sets—I'm now wearing one, have been all day, and in relative comfort, as compared to a shirt of mail, such as I wore from the first attempt to assassinate me until I fashioned these.

"The sets are easy to put on or take off, alone, with no assistance. They are quite light in weight, as you can tell yourself, yet tough enough to stop anything short of a ball from a small cannon. That cap contains another piece of the same metal. I sized them from some of your clothing out of chests in Krystal's effects at my country palace, so they should fit, but try them on before you sail back to Norfolk. I can easily make any necessary adjustments. That done, you will be as well prepared for this new campaign the King has ordered as I can make you.

"Now, those matters aside, my old friend. I think that you should ride out tomorrow and pay your respects to your lady-wife. Wait, wait!" He raised a hand. "I know, she's become almost impossible, and I, like you, am not any longer certain that her mind is still properly balanced. She is not the Krystal I first met, years ago, she is not the Krystal to whom I married you, she has changed drastically from even the Krystal of last year.

"The Krystal who was projected here was friendly to almost everyone, great or small, egalitarian to an extreme, kind, generous, and of a forgiving nature. On the other hand, Dame Krystal, Duchess of Norfolk, is seldom seen to smile, now she either snarls or sneers; she has not a good word for anyone and is become extremely conscious of her rank in the social hierarchy. She throws insults at anyone and everyone and has driven all of her old friends from her, not wishing to have by her anyone who does not always and immediately agree with her in everything. She is both cruel and vindictive toward all those less powerful than she is become as your lady-wife.

"Are you aware that when one of your son's little playmates bloodied Joe's nose in a childish scuffle, Krystal tried to have one of your Irish knights behead him on the spot? When he quite properly refused to carry out the execution of the child, she threw a screaming tantrum that brought half the folk in the palace to that spot, then ordered the knight from out her sight, gathered her son and her ladies, and stayed in the wing she and they inhabit for the rest of the day, having the servants bring in food and drink.

"When Buddy Webster was informed of the incident, he forthwith moved the child and his entire family to my more distant estate, in the West Riding."

"Good!" said Bass vehemently, his face dark with rage. "Have you tried talking any sense back into her swollen head, Hal?"

The old man shook his head slowly. "Alas, my friend, I seldom even can squeeze out the time to get out to the country palace for so much as a single day. I've spoken to her but the once since you left here for Norwich. That was when she made to rail at me for not affording her the deference she thinks herself due. We had . . . ahhh, words.

"I did send Mr. Rupen Ademian, whom you met, out to talk with her; that was after she had Jenny Bostwick flogged. She refused even to receive him, noting that, emissary of mine or not, he was not a nobleman, not even a gentleman, and that her ladies all agreed with her that to receive him in audience would demean her."

"I was right all along, Hal," Bass growled. "The woman's flipped out, she's become nutty as a fucking fruitcake! No, Hal, I'll not go out to see her, not now. I'd probably beat her to death or close to it. I've arranged for little Joe to enter fosterage, you know, and I want you to have him taken away after I've had time to get out of

England. Yes, I'm a coward, so there! Isn't there some convent, maybe of a nursing order, that you can have her locked away in until I can get this Irish business done and get back?''

CHAPTER
THE FIFTH

Even as Bass sat talking with Harold of York, two other men met and talked in an out-of-the-way, benighted place in the countryside beyond the walls of York. Except for a clear difference in age, both the elder and the younger were so alike in appearance as to seem two peas from the same pod. They had met before in similar locations, and this latest meeting concerned some of the same topics earlier discussed. The mounts upon which they had ridden to this spot grazed placidly a few rods distant.

Speaking in a tongue that would have been imcomprehensible to even Bass or Harold, the younger remarked, "That is not much of a horse, Elder One. That beast you rode before was far better."

The man addressed shrugged. "This horse and those of the others of the party of Foster Bass were borrowed from the garrison at Hull. Yes, this one is rough-gaited, but still does it serve the purpose.

"Now, anent other matters, Younger One: Since last we met, I have journeyed long and far, both in distance and in time, both upon the nearer continent and the farther. No, I have yet to find just to where and to when the twentieth-century musicians were projected or exactly how the mistake could have occurred.

"But I journeyed also to Our Place, in the east, and

conferred with experts on the projectors themselves, as well as with those whose task it is to monitor units assigned to field personnel. We now concur in the belief that the ill-guided journeying was possibly not your fault, for the devices revealed that your unit was subjected to a substantial amount of abuse at critical moments of the activation; such degrees of abuse might very well, I am told, have caused slight slippages in the settings, and even minute deviations can, as we both know well, create extreme variations.

"Therefore, you should expect the imminent arrival of a 'merchant from the east.' You will know him, of course, and he will attune a replacement projector to you, as well as issue you replacements for all the items lost with your original projector. He will also explain and demonstrate some improvements recently developed in the projectors. With these improvements, you need no longer physically conceal any of your equipment, for now you may summon your storage casket at will.

"As for the matter of the now-lost projectees, copies of the records from the monitoring devices will be journeyed back to our world and time with the next shipment of metals and chemicals. With the more sophisticated equipment and interpreters there available, it is to be presumed that the exact error will be quickly found and corrected. Perhaps it has already been corrected and this is why my own hurried searches have been fruitless.

"At one point, in this last series of searches, I was momentarily certain that I had located the missing party of projectees, but then I realized that there was one too many of the projector auras in the group my device had detected."

"Who could that group have been, Elder One?" the Younger One asked with deference. "More accidental displacements wrought by one of those primitive projectors such as brought him once known as Kenmore Harold to this place?"

"No," replied the Elder One. "These auras were not the greenish auras of those unsophisticated contraptions, rather were they as pale as any of ours, invisible to the unaided vision. Until I journeyed to Our Place, indeed, I had thought that they might represent some special mission of ours, but no such mission exists, I found in the east. Now I and the directors are of the opinion that those invisible-auraed ones must have been of Them.''

The Younger One exhibited shock. ''*Them,* Elder One? Why must They haunt us in whatever time or world we visit? Do we not hide our true selves and activities from the indigenes diligently, never take enough of any one mineral to make our visits obvious, eradicate all traces of our visits when we are done at the sites and also do all within our powers to undo damages wrought by those fools who came from earlier times, such as that from which this current problem resulted?''

''How can we intelligently question Their motives, Younger One?'' was the reply. ''They are as far and even farther beyond us in all ways as are we beyond the indigenes of this world and time. We may only be certain of one thing concerning Them, and that is that They do indeed have reasons for being wherever or whenever They appear to us or on our sensors. All that we can do is follow meticulously the dictates They promulgated, for resistance would be unthinkable. We are as but lowly worms to Them, and They could crush us, even our world, effortlessly, were we in the slightest disobedient to Their directives.

''But such matters aside, for now. Upon the return of the party of Foster Bass to Norfolk, we all are bound for the next big island west, the one the indigenes call Ireland. When and as I can, I will make use of my own newer-model projector to contact you, projecting message holders to the receiver within your equipment casket, so you should be certain to check the receptacle daily, at least, for I will be projecting them in normal time. Should matters alter drastically in any way, here, you must message me immediately, setting the message holder for alarm. I only say this last because I somehow do not think that we have experienced all that we eventually will of the primitive projectors and the savage humans who operate them.''

*   *   *

"London is fallen, Your Grace." These were the words
Bass was given when, the day after his return from York,
Captain Sir Egbert d'Arcy one of Richard Cromwell's
officers, was granted audience.

"Angela actually surrendered the city, Sir Egbert?"
asked Bass wonderingly. "Surely she knows that she can
expect no parole or even quarter from His Majesty, not
after all she has seen done to him and his?"

"No, your Grace, the city was surrendered by a deputa-
tion of the soldiers and the citizens. The Regent and her
bastard both are dead. It is bruited about that she rendered
the bastard senseless with a draught and had a Ghanian
mercenary, her sometime lover, run the lad through with
his sword, then do the same for her, after sharing with her
a goblet of wine, which meant that he too was shortly
dead, as the wine was laced with a quick-acting poison.
His cries and gasps and thrashings about it was that caused
the outer guards to force the doors and find them all three
either dead or in the final throes."

"Thus cheated of his long-anticipated vengeance," said
Bass, "I would imagine that the King has the London
gutters running blood, by now. Once I heard His Majesty
swear that he meant to erect either a gibbet or a block at
every place two streets intersected throughout the length
and width of the city, when once it fell."

The young officer shrugged. "Oh, there have been some
executions, Your Grace—hangings, mostly, though with a
few beheadings, guttings, maimings, burnings, public rack-
ings, and similar torments. The Papal Legate and a few
others were broken on a wheel and the Archbishop of
Canterbury, who had crowned the bastard, was sewn into a
leathern sack with three black cats, then the sack was
flogged and, when he ceased to scream, thrown into the
Thames—but there has been little bloodshed, really. There
are not that many people left alive within London City,
Your Grace, what with the starvation and its attendant
illnesses, lack of fuel last winter, and a terrible outbreak of
siege fever, which last is even yet claiming victims.

"However," the officer said, smiling, "I was entrusted a bit of decoration for Your Grace's castle-gate arch. May my troopers bring it in?"

Despite a strong sense of foreboding, Bass acquiesced, and a brace of brawny, jackbooted troopers trundled in a small cask, sprung the topmost hoop, opened it, and lifted out—pale-white, slack-jawed and staring-eyed, dripping brine in ropy streams—by its hair the severed head of a man.

Smiling even more broadly, Sir Egbert introduced the "newcomer." "Your Grace, please give me leave to present his late grace the foul traitor Sir Jonathan More, onetime Duke of Norfolk. His Majesty knew that Your Grace would feel unjustly slighted unless the main gate of Norwich Castle bore the head of this infamous rogue in its proper setting . . . upon a spike."

Speaking through teeth tight-clenched, striving with every ounce of willpower to control his body's need to instantly spew up the full contents of his churning stomach, Bass Foster said that which he knew he must. "Sir Egbert, my thanks for delivery of this . . . token of his majesty's good offices. Please have it turned over to my castellan; he will know what disposition to make of it.

"Do you and your troopers bide the night with us, there will be food and drink for you all and bait for your mounts. Now, please go, for I soon must be on the march with my squadron and there is yet overmuch to be done before our departure."

Immediately the chamber was left to him alone, Bass stumbled in haste to one of the casement windows that overlooked a tiny garden court, thrust out his head and shoulders, and retched until nothing more would come and he could only gag and shudder.

Assured by his Portuguese friend, mentor, and onetime prisoner *Barón* Melchoro that such gestures were expected and necessary, Bass gifted Sir Egbert, along with his dawn stirrup cup, a purse of silver to divide amongst his troopers and for himself a golden ring—a bit of the loot of Gijón port—in which was set a malachite.

Then the officer and his troopers and their train of mules with their grisly cargoes were off to their next appointed stop: the town of Norwich where the mayor would shortly be in receipt of the upper right quarter of the body of the late and unlamented Sir Jonathan More for "decoration" of the town gates, a warning to all who saw of the certain and horrible fate of traitors to the Crown of England and Wales.

While he stood stock-still for the fitting of a new pourpoint into which the ultralightweight breast-and-back gifted him by Hal would shortly be sewn, Bass wondered if his mindset would ever truly adapt itself to this savage world and its barbaric, bloody mores.

"In my world," he mused, "there are . . . were far more people than live in this one. Hal estimates that there are less than a half billion people in all of this world, at this time, and something under a hundred thousand in this kingdom and Scotland combined, while there were between three and four *billion* in mine and nearly *twelve* billion in his.

"One would think that with so few people alive, human life would have at least the value that it had in most parts of my world. Hah! No such thing. The lives of most men, women, and children, here, are considered of less value than that of a horse or a trained hawk or hunting dog. No one seems to give a thought to the fact that in a bad winter, humbler people starve to death that said horses and hawks be properly fed.

"Some of the things I've witnessed since we were borne here would literally curl the hair. And some of the stories I've heard . . . like the poor bastard of a slate-roofer who was winged with a crossbow bolt and fell off a roof to his death because he had allowed his shadow to fall across the path of some West Country baron, back during the reign of Richard IV.

"And the killings and outright murders would be bad enough, God knows, but the people of this world, ninety-nine percent of all that I've met, anyway, don't seem to get half the kick out of seeing a poor wight put to death unless it's done slowly, agonizingly, or at least preceded by such tortures that would've made the Marquis de Sade of my world cringe and gag.

"The country people and those of the smaller, unwalled towns are all scared shitless of armies and soldiers of either side, and for damned good and sufficient reasons, not the least of which is that if companies on campaign are issued any rations at all, they're almost invariably of the worst quality that the commanders feel they can get away with, and if the soldiers expect to get anything better they must either buy it at vastly inflated prices or take it by force. And that latter is just what they usually do, taking time and opportunity for a little casual rape, here and there, and of course lifting any money or small valuables while they're about the main business that brought them to that particular place.

"The Kingdom of England and Wales is reputed to be an enlightened and humane land, ruled by just, merciful monarchs and nobles, and yet even here the value of human life, the price of human suffering, is incredibly low. Hal attests—and who should better know than a man who has lived in this kingdom for going on two hundred years?—that before the Crusader invasions and the late Angela Tudor's bloody mischief, things were slowly becoming less savage and sadistic in England. But even so, he can list nearly a hundred so-called crimes for which the almost invariable penalty is death, quite often a drawn-out, messy death at that.

"God knows, being who I am, what I am, and from where and when I am, my household and establishment is run—insofar as I am able to personally supervise it, which isn't much anymore, I fear—along decent, humanistic lines, yet every day or night at Norwich I find that I have to block my ears, pretend that I'm not hearing the screams of someone being hurt; for, as squeamish as I am still, my staff and guards and senior servants are men of their age to the nines, their minds and actions set an governed in a hard, callous, mediaeval mold.

"If a trooper breaks his captain's rules, he is flogged,

while his sergeant will usually just knuckle-massage him into bloody unconsciousness. A kitchen scullion who displeases a cook is beaten, but informally so is a stablehand who runs afoul of a groom, or a common servant—male or female—whose work or lack of same offends a superior, for even the slightest or most petty of reasons. I have to be damned careful in complaining about anything, lest my complaint be the cause for a poor bastard of an underservant to suffer wealed, bruised, bleeding flesh or broken bones, simply on account of His Grace being displeased in some more than likely trivial way.

"Worse, my own attempts to maintain humane behavior are misinterpreted to the farthest extreme. Because I cannot stomach driving a pikepoint or a blade into a helpless wounded man, I am considered widely to be a cold, hard man, taking private enjoyment in the thought of my enemies dying slowly of blood loss, shock, sepsis, or gangrene; and my signal failure on a few occasions to order a man taken to that particular room and put to what is euphemistically called 'the severe question' has been judged to my dislike of permitting torture when I've not the time to watch it.

"This worldwide barbarism must be infective, though, to some extent, because my wife, who was a left-liberal of the northeastern U.S. variety, egalitarian to a fault, warm and loving of all mankind, has succumbed to the brutality of this world, is becoming every bit as hot-temperedly cruel as any woman born here could be. Thus far it hasn't affected me to any great lengths, and I'm just as glad that it hasn't, for all that I might adapt a little more quickly and easily to the here and now if it had or did."

Having been forced to endure some hours of personal and very painful experience as the subject of it, Timoteo di Bolgia, like Bass Foster, did not like torture . . . unless circumstances dictated its use to achieve information or important ends, as in this present case.

Immediately His Grace di Rezzi and party had cleared the river bars and put out to sea, di Bolgia had set about the thorough rooting out of all the legate's spies and agents within his household, his mistress's, and that of King Tàmhas. When he had a goodly selection of them, he summoned the King's master executioner and they went to work, slowly untangling the Church's web of informants, without the stubborn old man himself to impede them.

Although Master Mohamad al-Ahmahr maintained the most scrupulously clean facility of the sort that Timoteo had ever before seen, not even he could rid the room of the odors of its true character—spilled blood, dung, urine, sweat, vomit, hot metal, and burned meat. Therefore, and also because of his other, time-consuming duties and tasks, Timoteo spent as little time as possible in the room, especially during the early stages of an interrogation, entering only when the subject had begun to say interesting things.

Having been so summoned by one of Master Mohamad's assistants, *il Duce* had taken only enough time to divest himself of his helmet and the heavier, more binding portions of his armor before hurrying to the room, a member of his staff providing him with a spice-scented pomander along the way. Leaving a brace of his guards outside, he entered and seated himself in the chair which stood close to the rack and its occupant, a Frisian serving woman hight Ingebord.

Whenever he had noticed the middle-aged, faded-blond cleaning woman while still she had served in his household, Timoteo had often noted that although her wrinkled face and turkey neck were about as attractive as the physiognomy of an aged bloodhound, her body looked to be, under the shapeless clothing, rather toothsome yet.

"No more!" he thought. "If any doxy shed her clothes to reveal a body like that one is now become to me, the first thing I'd do is puke, the second thing I'd do is run. Hell, I feel like puking now." He sniffed strongly at his spicy pomander and clenched his teeth, forcefully swallowing the sour bile that kept flooding his mouth.

A man of long and thoroughgoing experience in all aspects of modern torture, a true master of his profession, Master Mohamad had done no damage to the woman's face or throat; indeed, he had even kept in place a leather device during much of his work that had prevented her from biting her tongue, either deliberately or through mischance.

But below the neck, the body and limbs were become a horror of whip-wealed flesh, wide, deep burns, sprung joints, ruined digits, and certain signs revealing even more sickening abuse. For the nonce, Master Mohamad had placed a rough wooden support of boards and sawhorses under her body and partially slacked the ropes of the rack. As Timoteo entered, the executioner was trickling water into her mouth.

Looking up, the red-haired and -bearded Arab smiled warmly at his current employer. "My Lord, this subject has at last seen the great and most sinful error of her ways and is, thinks this unworthy one, now prepared to truthfully answer any questions that My Lord would care to put to her."

Once seated, his body more or less under control, Timoteo leaned forward and stated, then asked, "Ingebord, we already know that you were set to spy upon me. Three other spies have named you, independently one of the other, so your denials of your guilt were useless from the start. What I want you to tell me now is to whom you reported aught that you had learned in my service."

He "conversed" with the shattered female sufferer for some half hour. During that time, she only needed "prompting" by Master Mohamad twice, her resultant shrieks nearly deafening Timoteo in the enclosed space. Her answers to his questions filled in many gaping spaces in the puzzle, however, and he was well pleased as he arose to return to his more mundane duties.

At the door, he told the executioner, "Dose her well with opium, Master, and correct what you can of her injuries. Summon a physician if you feel it necessary, even a chirurgeon—though it has been my experience that men of your calling often know more of the human body, its functions and dysfunctions, than do any practitioners of *artis medicus*, even the best of them. At any rate, keep her alive and in as little pain as possible until I can determine her truthfulness, this day. If she lied, I'll still want the truth out of her.''

"And if she was utterly truthful, My Lord . . .?" inquired the Arab.

Timoteo shrugged. "I leave that up to you, Master. I suppose that, as she now is, the merciful thing to do would be to kill her.''

In a tiny, stonewalled room at the very tiptop of one of the defensive towers of the city walls, Timoteo met with his brother, Roberto, and *Le Chevalier* Marc. With their respective squires guarding the landing immediately below and with a section of the di Bolgia bodyguards on each of the next lower landings, the chamberlet was about as secure a place to talk as they were likely to find in all of King Tàmhas's capital city or anywhere else within the now-shrunken borders of the Kingdom of Munster.

"That old bastard is a shrewd one," commented the elder di Bolgia. "Wheels within wheels within still other wheels. You know, though I should've been suspicious when first I saw that Ingebord, for a woman doesn't keep a figure that good through a lifetime of drudgery and the rough fare of servants.''

"Then who or what is she?" asked the younger di Bolgia. "And why was she playing the part of a servant in our household?''

"Ingebord is the bastard daughter of a Dutch bishop, long deceased, and up until as late as fifteen years ago she was Giosué di Rezzi's senior mistress and housekeeper.''

"Uh-oh," said Roberto. "How badly did the torturer do by her?''

Timoteo shrugged. "So badly that it will be less cruel to kill her than to let her try to live on in such a state, my brother. I told Master Mohamad to keep her alive only until I'm certain that she told me the truth. But that part doesn't worry me; she'll be worm food by the time di Rezzi returns, if he ever does, and we'll just say she died of siege fever or something similar; such things happen, and she was, after all, nobody's spring chicken.

"What does bother me is something else she told me, gentlemen. It would seem that Ingebord spied not only for di Rezzi but on him, as well."

"For whom, pray tell? This, from *Le Chevalier*. "King Tàmhas?"

Il Duce di Bolgia made a rude noise. "*Righ* Tàmhas couldn't locate his arse with both hands and a pack of hounds, and we all know that for hard fact. His so-called spies were the first ones we caught, many of the inept bunglers before we'd been here a fortnight.

"No, the woman doesn't know just for whom she was spying on her onetime lover, di Rezzi, of this, I am certain. Not even when Master Mohamad did certain things to jog her memory, as it were, did she tell me more of her employer. She could only say that a man posing as a chapman came two or three times each year, made his presence known to her, met her in some out-of-the-way place, and had her impart to him anything of interest—especially as regarded singular visitors, miraculous occurrences, or rumors of wonders—that had taken place since last he had visited. She is certain that this stranger also had some informants in *Righ* Tàmhas's establishment and that he visited other *Irlandese* cities as well as this one, but she is just as certain that he was neither Irish nor even a European."

Le Chevalier pursed his lips and whistled softly. "How was she paid, did she say? In what coin?"

"In gold," answered Timoteo, "but not in coined gold. The way she described her earliest payments, it sounded to me as if they were just fair-sized nuggets of alluvial gold; more recently, she has been receiving little flat bars, each weighing exactly one ounce, but unmarked in any way, other than the random bumps and scratches you might expect of being carried loose in a bag for some time."

Le Chevalier shook his head. "Which tells us nothing, then. I know of a few places, mostly in Ifriqah and points well east, that sometimes use flattish bars rather than coins, but all of them I've ever seen have been clearly marked as to weight, purity, and place of origin. Faced with such a blank wall here, what we now need to do is to try to reason out what principality would need such information of di Rezzi or anyone else residing in this appalling little backwater pocket kingdom.''

"On the other hand, Marc," said Roberto di Bolgia, ''di Rezzi is a well-known supporter of the Italian–Northern European faction in Rome. Could this stranger, this non-European-seeming stranger, not have been an agent for the Moors or the Spaniards? Both factions have easy access to raw gold, and it would clearly be to their advantage to use unmarked golden flats, rather than, say, onzas or Moorish coins. Think you on that, eh?''

"Well, the only way we'll any of us know for certain is to catch this chapman or whatever he is," said Timoteo, adding, ''And we just might do that. According to Ingebord, he is about due for a visit, and as he most often came by ship up the river, this silly siege shouldn't hamper his incoming to Munster; merchants of one kind or another land on the river docks every day. I had a good description of the bugger of Ingebord, so I'll just keep my eyes peeled and my own agents alert for a man of that description. Once I have the man, I'll introduce him to Master Mohamad . . . and then we three will chat with him.''

Close-range cannon fire quickly sank the crippled Moorish galley, but the crew of the galleass could hardly rest on their hard-won laurels, for the other two galleys were both bearing down upon them, propelled by both the wind and their banks of flashing oar blades. Despite the big, long target thus presented to the threatening rams, Sir Giorgio ordered the galleass maneuvered about broadside to the enemy ships, that both the prow and stern batteries of large cannon might be brought to bear, as well as the smaller swivels mounted along the waist rails.

Not too many rounds had been fired off after the maneuver was completed when fickle fortune favored the gunners. The left-hand galley slowed, moved in a half-circle as only one bank of oars drew, then the crew could be seen frantically trying to jettison the heavy chaser guns mounted at prow and stern. With this one clearly in trouble, all the guns of the galleass that would bear were aimed at the one remaining Moorish craft. They did not score a visible hit, but, apparently no longer caring for the now-refigured odds, the vessel turned tail and withdrew as fast as oars and sails would take her.

Sir Giorgio Predone had his own ship, the galleass *Spaventoso*, rowed over closer to the obviously sinking galley that he had holed. With Sir Ugo D'Orsini and a contingent of the soldiery, he had the larger of his towed barges drawn up alongside, manned, and used to transport them to the doomed galley. The smaller barge was sent out to rescue any young, hale, unwounded survivors of this galley or the first that still might be in the water, for supplies of men to handle the long, incredibly heavy oars of the galleass were often hard to come by.

When finally the galleass sailed on toward the distant smudge on the horizon which was Sicily, she had garnered nearly three dozens of new galley slaves, two fine bronze chasers (one of twelve pounds and one of fifteen pounds), some seven swivel guns, an assortment of arquebuses, muskets, pistols, and edge or pole weapons, a few barrels of gunpowder, plus bits and pieces of armor, cordage, sailcloth, and ship's hardware. Sir Giorgio opined that it was not a bad profit for a few pounds of powder and shot expended and a little time lost.

After the formal meeting with Archbishop di Rezzi, whereat he had informed the old man that he shortly would be a cardinal and that, consequently, he would not be returning to *Irland*, Cardinal D'Este met privately with Sir Ugo D'Orsini in a solar that *il Duce* Timoteo di Bolgia would have recalled from his visit to D'Este's Palermo palace.

Immediately the servitor had poured wine, set out trays of sweetmeats, and departed on silent felt-soled slippers, D'Este said, "Well, my boy, how goes the so-called war in Munster?"

"You did not receive my letters, then, your Eminence?" replied Sir Ugo worriedly.

"Oh, yes, my boy, oh, yes, regularly, in fact. But I assumed that you did not put everything into written form. For instance, how did our condottiere and di Rezzi get along?"

Sir Ugo made a wry face. "Like a cat and a dog, both of them on the verge of starvation, Your Eminence. For some obscure reason, His Grace di Rezzi took an immediate dislike to Duke Timoteo and even made attempts, it was learned, tò undermine his influence with the king and his council."

D'Este smiled flittingly. "Not at all surprising, young Ugo, not when we consider that which has been learned since the demise of old Abdul. No, it seems that my good, trustworthy old friend and one-time mentor Giosué di Rezzi did some years back sell out to Abdul and the Moorish Faction in Rome. He became a willing spy within our camp, as it were, and *this* is the reason that Abdul and his people so vigorously resisted his being sent to fill the vacant archbishopric of Munster, back then, not—as we all then assumed—simply because he was one of us and not a Moor or a Spaniard."

"Then . . . then Your Eminence brought him back in order to kill him for his found-out treachery?" asked Sir Ugo, knowing even as he asked that such a solution was far too simple for the intricate ways of Rome.

D'Este raised his hands in an expression of what was obviously mock horror. "Sir Ugo, how could you, a Papal knight, think so of Holy Mother the Church or of humble priest and bishop like me? Fie, fie, young sir!"

Then he smiled. "No, son Ugo, we none of us need soil our hands or souls with di Rizzi blood. All that we need do is to send him on to Rome and I doubt not that the Moors and the Spaniards will do the task efficiently. You see, the Moors are aware that we uncovered di Rezzi's dirty little secret from amongst the secret correspondence of Abdul which we . . . acquired, just prior to his demise. If di Rezzi now returns to Rome and it is bruited about—as it certainly will be—that we are supporting him for one of the number of recently vacated appointments of cardinal, then they will have no other thought than that he has again turned his coat. You see, my boy, no one ever has complete faith in a bought spy, regardless the coin in which he is or was paid, regardless how long and seemingly faithful has been his service to the purchaser. No, when once he arrives in Rome, di Rezzi is dead.''

''And what then of Munster, Your Eminence?'' inquired Sir Ugo.

D'Este sipped and savored the wine in his goblet before he spoke. ''Ah, yes, Munster. Sir knight, we have great plans for Munster. It is just possible that those plans will result in the filling of two now-vacant sees—that of Munster and that of Rome.

''Look you, Ugo, can our faction be clearly responsible for bringing not only *Irland*, but England and Wales as well back under the sway of the Roman Papacy, why then no one—Moor or Spaniard or any of the rest of that ilk—would dare to stand against us, lest they lose those northerly islands all over again and possibly for good on the second occasion.''

''But Your Eminence, how can . . .'' began the young knight.

The cardinal waved a hand. ''My boy, I am certain that you, like most laymen, are of the belief that higher ranks of clergy must always be named and confirmed in their positions by Rome, but this is not a hard and fast doctrine. In past times, in times of great crisis, kings and other secular rulers have been allowed, nay, encouraged, to make appointments to fill vacant sees. The grandfather of the present Harold, Archbishop of York, was an example; King Henry VII Tudor did name him during a terrible outbreak of that pest that is commonly called priests' plague.''

Both men hurriedly signed themselves at mention of the deadly scourge.

''Well, if you cannot call the murderous insanity now raging in and about Rome a crisis, then I can hardly think just what could be so called. When you return to Munster, you will be bearing documents signed and sealed by the five most powerful prelates yet extant. These will take you first to the court of the High King of Irland, Brian VIII, then to the Kingdom of England and Wales, where you will seek and obtain audience with Harold of York. To him, to Harold, you will be presenting a proposition, two of them, actually, although if he should accept the first, you will immediately destroy the second and utterly forget that ever it existed. I know, I know, you do not understand now . . . but you will ere you set sail back to Munster, never fear.''

THE SIXTH

The march across the width of England at the head of his squadron of *galloglaiches* could have easily been much worse, Bass reflected as he stood with his squires, bannerman, bodyguards, and a few of his gentlemen observing the loading of troop horses onto the barges sent to Liverpool by agents of Sir Paul Bigod. Of course, his brainstorm decision to scatter the worst troublemakers around onto the ships of his private fleet, to serve under the rather strict discipline exacted by his no-nonsense Commander of Marines Fahrooq, had been of great help in maintaining relative order on the march. After the merciless young Turk had had six or seven of them severely flogged and two recidivists hanged on the main yardarm of *Revenge*, the others seemed to have gotten the message and behaved themselves for the remainder of the voyage.

In the hurried, harried days just before the squadron set out for the long march to Liverpool, Walid Pasha and Fahrooq had sought an audience with Bass, and he had finally been able to make the time to see them. When they appeared, both men were once more dressed in rich Middle Eastern garb, and Walid Pasha, at least, was less worried-looking than Bass ever before had seen him, save during sea battles.

"Sebastián Bey," Fahrooq had said, "I have received

correspondence from certain highly placed parties in Anqara. A part of the message is to the effect that whenever you have no further need of the ship, it and all of us will be most handsomely ransomed; however, so long as you do need the ship and us who handle her, we are yours by order of Omar III, the Omnipotent, et cetera. What he has heard of you has greatly impressed him, and he sends to you effusive greetings and gifts. Walid?''

Walid Pasha had then stepped forward and proffered a small chest, all carven and gilded. Upon opening it, Bass found a splendid, deeply cursive dagger of highly polished damascene steel, the hilt, guard, and case of which weapon were gilded and virtually encrusted with seed pearls and small precious stones, the pommel being an inch-thick sphere of rosy-hued quartz. Also within the dagger's fitted chest was a small silver-stitched silken bag, and within the bag was a heavy red-gold ring composed of several thick wires of gold tortured into an intricate design.

Walid had visibly started when he saw the ring and then had exchanged a meaningful glance with Fahrooq.

Stepping forward, Fahrooq diffidently had asked, "Your Grace, we had been ordered not to breach the casket, so we knew not exactly what it contained. Please, may I examine that ring for one moment?''

Wordlessly, Bass had handed the bauble over to the young Turkish officer. After a brief examination, Fahrooq had handed it back and said, "Your Grace *den* Norfolk, your grace must be made aware of the great, the rarely extended honor of the gift of the ring. No matter where your grace may find himself, all that he need do is to seek out the resident ambassador of the Christian Kingdom and Sultanate of Osmanli Turks, display the ring, and he and his will immediately fall under the full protection of the might of Omar III. Walid Pasha bears such a ring, as too do I, but only a bare handful of non-Turks ever have been so honored. The gift of the ring apparently is intended to bear earnest to the third portion of the message to your grace.

"Should ever your grace decide to quit England, for

whatever reasons, he will find a most cordial welcome and well-paid employment in Anqara. All that he need do is to contact any ambassador of Omar III and a ship will be dispatched to bring him in speed and comfort.''

Later, Sir Ali had slowly drawn and carefully examined the blade of the showy dagger, used its edge to slice a hair-thin shred off one of his fingernails, then said, ''Your Grace, it is true, first-water damascus, though the style marks it as having most likely been forged in Isfahan. It is a sash-dagger, meant to be thrust beneath a belt and sash— that is why the tip of the case hooks as it does, that case and all will not be dislodged when the blade must be drawn. The small grooves near to the point are there to hold resinous venom, if such is desired.''

''It is indeed a lovely item, a princely gift to a man never before met or even seen,'' agreed *Barón* Melchoro, adding sadly, ''It is too bad that Your Grace cannot keep it.''

''Now, dammit, Melchoro, it was given freely to me, no strings attached, so why can't I keep it?'' Bass had demanded testily, then immediately regretted the childish-sounding outburst, reflecting that this Portuguese noble-man had been of inestimable help to him in teaching him just how a man of his new rank should behave and bear himself in various situations.

But the baron answered readily, sounding neither intimi-dated nor peeved. ''Your Grace, my friend Bass, you rendered an oath of fealty to Arthur III Tudor, you hold your various English lands in feoff from him. Therefore, any foreign ruler who gifts you a valuable gift is actually gifting your ruler, your overlord, you see? If this came to you through the Turkish ambassador, you may be certain that others now know of it, so to not at least offer it to Arthur might well cause him to believe you either miserly to a fault or not fully loyal to him, and, knowing you as well as I do, I know that you want neither thought of you by anyone, especially your own, dear liege lord, the King.''

All of which had meant that Bass had had to send his herald, Sir Ali, with a suitably strong and impressive party to bear the gilded casket and its contents from the anchorage of his fleet off Great Yarmouth down to Thamesmouth and thence up the river to London, the newly rewon capital city.

Very, very near to the eve of departure for the west and Ireland, Sir Ali and his party returned, but by land, riding in company with *Reichsherzog* Wolgang and all of the Kalmyk troopers still remaining of his *Schwadron Totenkopf* after so many years and campaigns, some six or so score of them. A few of them still rode their scrubby, weedy, big-headed little steepe horses, but more of them now bestrode moor ponies.

Alone with Bass, the *Reichsherzog* had said simply, "No fighting in Englandt iss, not anymore. The witch-bitch Angela escaped me und Arthur, did, but the great pleasure we had of watching portions of the week-long tortures of the actual murderers of my niece und her little children, before Arthur had the *Schweinen* burnt on slow fires mit gunpowder rammed into their bodies. That done, my oaths carried out, I soon must return to my own landts. But before I do, another campaign I vould see."

"But Wolfie," said Bass familiarly to this old, dear friend and his overlord for his carpathian lands at Velegrad, "I thought that the electors and Emperor Egon had forbidden you to take any personal part in the fighting here anymore."

"Chust so." The bulky, powerful German nobleman, grinned. "Chust so, but forbidden war I to fight in *Englandt* or *Wales*, only, noddings about Irelandt was written. I grow fat und lazy, und my *Jungen* , too."

"The King has agreed to this, Wolfie?" asked Bass dubiously.

The German's grinned broadened. "Of course, *mein alte Kamerad*, else to be here I vould not." He then drew out a letter on a sheet of vellum, all properly signed, sealed, and beribboned. "Und Arthur ordered already has more barges for the transporting of the *Pferden* of me and *mein Jungen* . If to read the letter you vill, you vill findt vords of Arthur that say ve are free to go to serve Brian

VIII, but only if to approof of our inclusion first you do. Do you not want me und my Kalmyks on your campaign?''

"Wolfie," said Bass truthfully, "your Kalmyks fight like demons out of the Pit, and any field commander would feel himself fortunate to have them under his banner. You are personally a very brave and ferocious fighting man, but more important to me is your broad and deep knowledge and experience at warfare. In fact, you should really be in charge of this operation, if you are set on coming along. I'd be more than happy to serve under you, commanding only my squadron of *galloglaiches*, my guards and my gentlemen. . . .?''

"Oh, no, Bass," the *Reichsherzog* declared vehemently, "the *Hauptmann grosser* you are, *the Leutnant* I vill be. If to help gif or advices to offer to *mein Hauptmann*, I vill und most gladly, but to command, you must.''

"But . . . but, why Wolfie? Admit it, you arc far more qualified than am I for the command," Bass remonstrated.

"For vun thing," the massive German ticked off on thick fingers, "such Cousin Arthur's vish iss. For the second, to observe you in a field command, your decisions und the reasons behind them, I vould to sec for mein own self. Third, for mein own pleasure, partly, a point I am herein stretching und to flagrantly disobey the express orders of my own liege lord, I dare not, a very bad example that vould set for my peers in the Empire. *Nicht wahr?*''

On the march, Wolfgang had quickly proved himself to be a true boon; having commanded larger and even more heterogeneous forces/on marches through friendly territory so many times in the past, he frequently could act to head off potentially troublesome situations before they even began.

As for the Kalmyks, Bass was quick and surprised to note that usually fearless *galloglaiches* essayed to start no trouble with them, indeed seemed rather leery of them, which fact went far to relieve his mind on the march.

As he sat his horse there upon the Liverpool docks and watched the loading of the troop horses, he thought,

"There's little sense in warfare to begin with, but this particular exercise, at its very inception here, is completely nonsensical. Here am I, a twentieth-century American, in seventeeth-century—well, after a fashion—England. Weird? You're damned tootin' it's weird! Not only that, but I'm getting ready to embark on a Turkish ship to lead a squadron of Western Isles Scots and Russian Steppes Kalmyks, officered by Irish noblemen, English and Welsh gentlemen, a Portuguese baron, an Arabian knight, a Spanish knight, and the uncle of the Holy Roman Emperor to the aid of the High King of Ireland at the behest of King Arthur III of England and Wales. Back in my own world and time, if I or anyone else had written so farfetched a story, it would've—if any editor looked at it at all—been classed as purest fantasy or science fiction.

"And when you throw into the plot a two-hundred-year-old man originally from the twenty-first century . . ."

But Walid Pasha had sailed the private fleet of the Duke of Norfolk in with an even stranger, weirder story, plus two extra small ships. The *Revenge* had sailed into the crowded harbor with a low, sleek, fast-looking lugger under tow. As his tale of her taking went, she had come out of a fog bank almost under the bows of *Revenge*, her crew as surprised as were Walid and his by the occurrence. But the lugger's sailing master had recovered quickly enough, crammed on more canvas, expertly trimmed what was already on, and sped away at a good clip, knowing better than to try to outfight a full-armed ship of the battle line. Of course, when the lugger fled, Walid opened fire upon her, but she was very close to making good her escape when a chance lucky shot of the Fairley-made breechloading rifled chaser at extreme range took off her rudder and severely damaged her stern. Walid Pasha had developed a fondness for the fast, handy little lugger and suggested to Bass that she be repaired, there in Liverpool, to become a dispatch vessel for the fleet, and Bass acquiesced.

The mystery came with the other prize, a catte, out of Bordeaux, landen with French wines, cognac, brandies, liqueurs, and other assorted European goods of varied qualities and quantities. There also had been, upon the surrender of the vessel, a passenger, a passenger who had named himself a roving chapman of Provence, bound—as had been the little merchant ship—for the capital of the Kingdom of Munster, in Ireland.

"With the catte turned over to a prize crew, Your Grace," Walid Pasha had said, "the French crew and the passenger were all locked up in the hold, for all were good strong men and just the kind that slave dealers prefer. The prize had been keeping up well with the fleet when the crewmen below seemed to go mad, shrieking and screaming dementedly and essaying to force open the hatches with bare hands.

"The prize master signaled *Revenge* and Fahrooq was rowed over with a well-armed detachment. When the hatches finally were sprung and the crew emerged to find themselves surrounded by armored men with ready pistols and long arms, the prize master observed that one man of the number originally battened below and not come up.

"Your Grace, the little ship was thoroughly searched, from stem to stern, and the Provencal chapman was not to be found, only his pack and some of his clothing. Yet there was no way that he could have gotten out of that hold."

"What did the Frenchman say, Walid?" asked Bass.

The captain of *Revenge* shook his turbaned head slowly. "To believe the tale they all tell—and they have been questioned seperately, all of them—would mean that a man must temporarily suspend his rationality completely. They aver that they had been immured in that pitch-black hold, listening as the ship was worked above them, for some hour, perhaps. Then, from nowhere and suddenly, a softly glowing casket, wrought of a metal the color of dulled pewter, was there, suspended in empty air beside the chapman. It was rectangular—about six or seven feet long, two or three feet wide, and some cubit or so deep, with a strange design upon its lid and no hinges that anyone could recall seeing.

"But when the chapman fingered that design in a certain

way, the lid arose and gaped wide, whereupon the chapman climbed into it, not taking his pack, the lid snapped shut . . . and all at once, the casket was no longer there, it, its strange glow of light, and the Provencal chapman all gone together to who knows where."

"This casket," asked Bass, "it was in the hold all along, not found by those who inventoried the prize's cargo?"

Walid Pasha shook his head. "No, Your Grace, the hold was searched thoroughly prior to putting the crew in it. There was no such casket anywhere in it. Nor had any member of the French crew ever before seen it, they say; it was not loaded aboard with the cargo in the Port of Bordeaux, they all swear. And although they carried this same chapman as passenger to Munster once before, they did not see anything like that casket that time, either.

"Your Grace, it all seems as if some *djinn* of the tales used to frighten unruly children had borne off the chapman. Nonetheless, gone he assuredly is. And all of those Frenchmen so terrified that they have since willingly served as seamen aboard others of the fleet rather than so much as set foot back upon the deck of that catte. For that reason, if for no other, I must believe that they assuredly saw something very like what they all say they saw, rational or not."

For all that both Walid and Fahrooq had fumbled through its contents, Bass insisted that the chapman's abandoned pack be brought to Sir Ali, *Barón* Melchoro, Don Diego, and Nugai emptied it and examined each and every item within it, then dismantled the pack itself in search of anything that might have been hidden.

They found mostly small luxury goods—needles and pins of brass, buttons wrought of many and diverse substances from amber to rare woods, perfume-gloves of doeskin, small scissors and smaller tweezers of both brass and steel, laces, points for fastening clothing, gaudy items of gilt-brass jewelry set with paste stones, small cases of flint, steel, and tinder wisps, folding-blade penknives, a quantity of silken thread in vivid colors, two small, narrow bolts of a very high-quality samite (one a rich blue, the other an equally rich saffron), a double handful of buckles of various sizes and materials, a bagful of dried hare's feet with the claws removed, containers of a black substance that Sir Ali identified as fair-quality kohl, a cosmetic for darkening the eyes, about two dozen bone combs and a half-dozen of low-grade ivory, plus ones and twos or threes of a vast quantity of small fripperies, mostly feminine-looking.

However, sewn cunningly into the thickly layered bottom of the pack they found two pounds of flat rectangles of solid gold, each about of an ounce in weight.

"Now who ever heard of a humble chapman owning so much find gold?" remarked *Barón* Melchoro. "And is it not a bit odd that he'd be taking such a fortune along on a trip to a backwater place like the so-called Kingdom of Munster?"

But there was no answer to be given him, not then. The gold went, of course, to Bass, as it had been his ship that prized it. The others took any of the remaining items that tickled their fancies, and the rest was dumped, willy-nilly, into a sack and delivered back to Walid Pasha to be disposed of as he wished.

The examination of the papers of the other prize, the fast lugger, disclosed that she was the property of a group Sicilian merchants. Her last port of call had been Dublin, but she had borne no cargo of any description upon her capture, had rather been in ballast. The sailing master and his mates had been quite silent upon this highly suspect lack of a return cargo for the merchant owners. But when well filled with some of the brandy from the hold of the other prize ship, certain humbler members of the Sicilian lugger's crew had waxed more voluble, averring that the ship had indeed borne no cargo in the last three trips, either, only passengers, noble passengers, mostly.

Despite the Sicilian ownership, they said, they usually sailed under either Granadan, Catalonian, or Portuguese ensigns, and their home port of late had been Las Palmas, on the island of Majorca. The voyage preceding this ill-fated one had been concerned with sailing from Majorca to

Munster, taking aboard an archbishop, his secretary, guards, and servants, and a Papal knight and his squires, then turning right about and sailing back to Majorca, where their passengers had been put aboard a Genoan warship. On this fatal trip, they had, in Majorca, taken back aboard that self-same Papal knight and his squires (save that he had had one more than when last he had been aboard the lugger) and sailed out to land him on the Liffey River docks in Dublin.

They had been beating back southward for the Pillars of Hercules when the fog bank and the shrewdly aimed cannonball had undone them. Yes, they would all be very happy to serve as seamen aboard the ships of His Grace of Norfolk, for anything was preferable to being sold as slaves in a foreign land, with no hope of ever again seeing their homes and kin; this way they might be able to save their shares of prizes taken, eventually ransom themselves of His Grace, and work their passages back to the Mediterranean.

Upon landing, Sir Ugo D'Orsini discovered that the *Ard-Righ* was not to be found in either Dublin or the environs of Tara, but rather was just then dwelling with his court in a fortified palace at Lagore, to the south. Glad then that His Eminence D'Este had been most generous, he purchased decent riding horses and pack beasts for him and for his three squires and two servants, hiring on a couple more Irish servants who seemed to know the lay of the land and one of whom also owned a decent command of the archic Norman French that seemed to be the second language of parts of *Irland*. Alloyed with generous amounts of Church and Common Latin, as it was, Sir Ugo and all the other Italians in Munster had found the ancient dialect far easier to understand and speak than modern French, far and away more so than the guttural Gaelic or Irish.

Arrived at Lagore, Sir Ugo and his party were received with the ancient and customary welcome of foreign travelers by the Irish High Kings, given stabling for their beasts, and afforded lodging commensurate with their birth and rank. The knight was deeply shocked at the ease with which a private audience was arranged with High King Brian, his bit of golden palm grease, even, being courteously refused. The Roman did not consider such a way of running a royal court normal.

The *Ard-Righ* had, of course, been described to him by Timoteo di Bolgia in some detail, but Sir Ugo's personal impressions were even more impressive.

Brian VIII was well called the Burly, for he was a great bear of a man, for all that he moved with the grace of a panther. His beard was of the chin only, being cut in the modish Spanish style with one longer point flanked by two shorter ones. The soft-looking mass of wavy hair that fell to just past the antique golden torque that encircled his neck and throat was clearly all his own, and the eyes set back under the bushy brows shone with intelligence.

Where not darkened and dried out by the sun and weather of campaigning and hunting and hawking, his exceptionally hairy body and limbs were of a rosy milk color, with widely scattered freckles. There were widening streaks of grey in his hair, although his beard was still of a rich, dark auburn hue. His thick, corded neck fitted onto thicker shoulders, and his overall appearance was of one mass of muscle, sinew, and big bones. Sir Ugo thought that with but very few alterations, the body of the *Ard-Righ* could have passed for that of Timoteo di Bolgia, save that the hips of the monarch were nearly as wide as were his shoulders. The thighs were the flat thighs of a man who had spent overmuch time in a saddle, and the Roman thought that he personally would think several times before he decided to ride against this man with lance or any other weapon, and he silently wondered just how many men this ruler had killed with his own hands and weapons in combat.

"We welcome you to the court, Sir Knight," said Brian in a deep, powerful, yet ear-pleasing voice. The massive man sat in a canopied chair which must have been fashioned for him expressly, for it gave not a creak or a groan as he shifted his not inconsiderable weight.

Compared to the garish, ill-matched attire usually worn

by *Righ* Tàmhas FitzGerald, that of Brian was most conservative, almost somber. Over a sleeved shirt and tight trousers of a dark umber, the monarch wore a jerkin and calf-height boots of saffron-dyed doeskin. About his thick waist, a narrow belt of tooled leather, with a buckle of plain red-gold, gave support to a small purse that matched the belt, a triple scabbard of antler-hilted eating utensils, and a reasonably ornate dress dagger.

"You are, or at least were, one of the *Dux* di Bolgia's lieutenants, are you not, Sir Ugo?" said the monarch, in bland tones. At Ugo's affirmative answer, he asked, "Then how is it that you sail into Dublin-port on a lugger from Majorca? That lugger is said to have the cut of a smuggler or pirate and to own a whole chestful of assorted ensigns and merchant-house flags, far more than any honest mariner would have need to carry along."

"Your Majesty," replied Sir Ugo cautiously, "my travel arrangements were made by . . . others, not by me or mine. Yes, I noted that the ensigns were different at different times, Majesty, but I attributed this to the most unsettled times just now. Indeed, on my voyage to Sicily, the Genoan galleass on which Archbishop di Rezzi and I were traveling was attacked by three Moorish feluccas and was compelled by their ferocity to sink two of them."

Brian leaned forward, clearly interested. "You took part in this engagement, then, Sir Ugo? No, don't bother to answer; of course you did—you clearly are a man of mettle, an old-fashioned gentleman.

"Tell me, are you by chance a relation of the great and renowned philosopher Placido Pietro D'Orsini?"

Ugo nodded his head once. "Yes, your Majesty, Placido Pietro D'Orsini was my great-great-uncle. You have perhaps read of his works, Majesty?"

"My library holds all four of them, Sir Ugo; two were left to me as the behest of an old and most dear friend, one whose admiration of your eminent relative was unending, and the other two I acquired over the years. Their costs were staggering, but such works still are cheap at any price. *Fra* Placido Pietro was a brilliant man and would have made for us all far better a Pope than some recent ones of whom I can think."

"I sincerely thank Your Majesty," said Ugo, with obvious feeling. "We of the family had always believed just so, but it is indeed good to hear such sentiments from so renowned a monarch as Your Majesty. Nor can I but agree with Your Majesty that the last two or three Popes have been disasters in all imaginable ways."

A smile flitted across Brian's face, not just the lips, but the eyes as well. "You deliver your flattery as smoothly as any courtier, Sir Ugo; my congratulations on your expertise. But I still know that this particular renowned monarch is most likely regarded by the few Italians who have even ever heard of him as either a furs-clad, near-pagan barbarian or as an overly pretentious country bumpkin of a ruler of a pocket-sized kingdom of other country bumpkins. And, you know, quite possibly they are of more of a rightness than they think.

"But for all our wars and clan or personal feuds, here in my *Eireann* still are our people better off than those of you poor souls who live and die under the immoral misrule of this last batch of Popes and their criminal cronies. Within the last thirty-odd years, Rome—both ecclesiastic and civil—is become a true kakocracy, ruled interminably by those least worthy and least capable of ruling.

"But enough of idle discussion, for now. You spoke to my chamberlain of a sealed document you were bearing to me from someone of exalted rank in Sicily. Where is this document, Sir Ugo?"

Brian examined the outer seals meticulously, at one point using a magnifying lens from out his belt-purse. Satisfied at last that they not only were authentic but had not been tampered with, he broke them with his thumbnails rather than the more usual letter knife, unfolded the sheets of fine vellum, and read. Twice during that reading he started as if pricked by a point; once he grunted noncommitally; on another occasion he exclaimed, "Hah! Is it then so?"

Finished, the *Ard-Righ* gave a short jerk to the bell pull

of braided velvet at his side and, to the brace of guardsmen who popped through the doors, said, "Have a table brought, and an armchair for our guest. Tell the steward I'll be having a ewer of that pale French wine and two goblets. The *bouchal* here and Brian have things to talk on, and talking is dry work."

When once more they were alone in the room, the doors shut, the gilded goblets filled with the straw-colored French wine, Brian tapped a fingernail on the refolded letter before him.

"Have you read this, Sir Ugo? No, never mind, those seals were original and entire, by my axe, I'd swear it. And you are a man of honor, I believe. But this Cardinal D'Este, did he not perhaps discuss these matters with you?"

Again, Sir Ugo nodded once. "Yes, Your Majesty, His Eminence did discuss with me certain aspects of the letter he then intended to write for me to deliver."

"His Eminence really means this, then?" demanded Brian. "He is willing to help me to unite all of Ireland under my rule? But Sir Ugo, this is not like Rome, or Constantinople either, for that matter. Rome's traditional way has been to prevent or at least try to prevent the formation or expansion of any large, powerful kingdoms, preferring that all kingdoms remain small, weak, always in or on the verge of a state of war with neighbors and thus always in need of priest's powder, thus further enriching the Church. And also, it has come into my mind on more than one occasion, small, weak states are always far more vulnerable to pressures exerted by Rome than are or would be larger and more powerful states. So why this abrupt and radical change?"

Ugo spoke more slowly than was his usual wont, choosing his words and phrases carefully, wishing that he and the high king might converse in his native and more precise and descriptive tongue, rather than in a four-century-old dialect of French.

"Majesty, prior to the demise of His Holiness Pope Abdul, Rome and her environs were become a patchwork of armed camps. With him now deceased, the city is become a very battlefield, while warbands and hired condottas march over and fight each other on her rich fiefs, when not storming or laying siege to the walled towns or castles of the lay nobility.

"It is mostly a matter of the Moorish and Spanish factions against the two factions that represent the hopes and aspirations of Western and Northern Europe, although, of course, a number of private scores are being settled as well. Early on in this bloodbath, the Moors conducted themselves like an invading army, so now they have no friends or allies in all of Italy and have instead brought in condottas from Ifriqah, Spain, and even from Macedonia and Croatia, barbarians no whit less savage than any horde of Kalmyks or Tatars. Such warfare as now rages the length and the breadth of Italy has not been seen since the end of the Roman Empire, twelve centuries ago.

"But still is there hope, Majesty. The Kingdom of Napoli, the Republic of Venezia, the city-states of Genoa, Ravenna, Lucca, and some others, these all have fought the Moors and Spaniards and their foreign hirelings to a standstill, hurt the invaders so badly that they and their allies or client states are being strictly avoided. By mutual agreement by all factions, actual battle has moved out of the city of Rome, although assassinations still are rife there. Why, the holy Giosué di Rezzi, formerly Archbishop of Munster, was so slain by the Moors just before he was about to be elevated to the College of Cardinals.

"But as I say, Majesty, there still is hope. Can a compromise of some nature be reached, or can the foreigners be driven out of Italy or extirpated, then will emerge, God willing, a new and far better Rome, like a phoenix arising from out its ashes. Having seen, nay, rather experienced, just what atrocious enormities these Moors and their Spanish abettors be capable of, there can be little doubt but that the other European factions and the subfactions will decide that only in unity is there either strength or safety and join with the Italian Faction to pull the teeth of both the Moors and the Spanish.

"In the event of a compromise, the most likely replacement for Abdul will be Cardinal Siqil, a Sicilian Moor, but for all of that, a man who shares many of the beliefs of the Italian Faction and deeply distrusts all Spaniards and not a few of the Ifriqans. In the event, however, of a clear military victory or an alliance of Europeans, the three most likely candidates will be Cardinals Sicola and D'Este, both of the Italian Faction, or Cardinal Ermannus, Archbishop of Bavaria. As for this last, Cardinal D'Este has corresponded with him at some length and states that His Eminence of Bavaria holds beliefs that very closely parallel those of the Italian Faction.

"Majesty, no matter which of those four attain to the mantle of St. Peter, then will all of the world see a great and clean and cleansing wind sweep through Rome, sweeping away the greed and malice, the pride and the sloth, that have characterized the leaders of our faith for far too long.

"His Eminence D'Este says that the natural growth of states has been unnaturally stifled for far too long a time, that the time is upon Rome to remove the sacking covering the beds, lest civilization and faith both be smothered and die."

For a very long moment after he had fallen silent, King Brian just sat and regarded the young Roman knight. Then he nodded and said, "This D'Este sounds to be what Rome, what the Church, and what the faithful have needed for many and many's the long year. He also has demonstrated a rare ability to choose men. Sir Ugo D'Orsini, you will go very far, I trow, very far indeed. You are both eloquent and winning, even when speaking a language not your own."

For a moment, Ugo did not realize that the *Ard-Righ* was speaking to him in an almost pure, almost unaccented Roman Italian.

The High King went on, saying, "I will dictate a letter to His Eminence D'Este. It will indicate my willingness to indeed choose and see installed a good, holy, capable churchman to replace the most unfortunate Archbishop di

Rezzi. I also will note that I most eagerly accept his offer of the loan of your services in this matter, but I then will add that immediately this other mission for him he cites be completed, I will be wanting back you and your services for as long as you care to remain in *Eireann*. Your breed are exceeding rare, Sir Ugo, and it's a fool I'd be to pass up a chance to add one to my household and court. And never you fear about rewards and stipends, I am known far and wide for being generous near to a fault with those who serve me and Mide well and faithfully.

"It's down to Munster I'll be sending you soon, to arrange a very private meeting with di Bolgia for me. But before you go, I'll be wanting you to meet the great captain that Cousin Arthur is sending over to aid me, him and his condotta.

"Between your abilities and his, it's I'm hoping that this time next year will see a single great Kingdom of *Eireann*, and what a lovely, heavenly sight that will be."

THE SEVENTH

Bass Foster sat across a table from the High King, Brian VIII. On the tabletop was spread a large, very colorful map of Ireland, meticulously rendered on thich parchment by skilled hands. Using a slim, highly polished dagger as a pointer, the monarch was filling in his latest great captain on recent developments among the ever warring clans and kingdoms of the island.

"Two years ago, Sir Bass, there were eleven kingdoms in *Eireann*; now there are eight, as in the ancient beginning. Of these eight, three are definitely committed to me and have delivered up their Jewels, the symbols of their sovereignty, to me." He grinned and added, "One of the three is me, of course, in my persona of *Righ* of Mide and *Ri* of the southern branch of the Ui Neills. The other two are Airgialla and Laigin, which means that the only eastern kingdom still uncooperative is Ulaid." His dagger point moved up to tap the northeastern corner of the island.

Bass thought to himself, "Damn, even this altered world has trouble with Ulster. I guess some things never change."

"The present King of Ulaid is a usurper, a bastard and outlaw in the land of his birth, who took Ulaid by force of arms and is holding it in that same way. He is a ruthless man, and both his army and his fleet are strong and alert." King Brian went on, "I have tried to avoid a session at arms with him, since he is after all an Ui Neill after an illegitimate fashion, but now that I am allied with Airgialla—against which he has mounted raid after provocative raid—I may be compelled to march against him, send vessels to bombard and burn his ports and ships, and suchlike. Perhaps you and your condotta and fleet are capable of doing the job alone, or along with some of my seige train and some *bonaghts*, since your condotta includes no foot.''

The dagger tip moved due west. ''Now, this recently reunited kingdom is the original homeland of all the Ui Neills, or so the old songs say, though it could be the exact opposite, the other way about, and who today would know? These distant cousins of mine have been as yet loath to part with their Jewel, but I am certain that a display of force, a strong warband crossing their border, will quickly change their minds without any need for bloodshed.''

The dagger point drifted to the south of the map, stopping a bit north of the border of Mide, just southwest of a couple of largish extenuated lakes in which the artist had long-necked creatures that resembled plesiosaurs frolicking and chasing after silvery-scaled fishes.

''This, Sir Bass, is the Kingdom of Breifne, presently ruled by one Fergal. For all that he should have been an abbot or a bishop instead of a king, he *will* fight rather than surrender his Jewel to me, even on loan. You see, Sir Bass, he knows just what I am about in this quest for the Jewels, and he would love to see all *Eireann* taken over and ruled by and from Rome, deluding himself to believe that his lifelong piety—piety to a degree that borders upon lunacy!—would guarantee him the mantle of *Ard-Righ*. Although his is the very smallest and least populous of all the present eight kingdoms, his people all are firmly behind him, and that is why I'm saving Breifne for the last conquest; perhaps after they have seen the folly of resistance to me and also seen how generous I can be to those who offer me and my armies little or no resistance, they will think differently.

''Immediately you and your troops feel ready to undertake it, I'll be expecting you to march on Ulaid, to beard King Ruarc in his lair. Understand, I'll not be telling you how to campaign, just offering advice to one who doesn't know the various peoples of *Eireann* so well as do I. If you would rather sail your ships of the battle line up there and soften them up before you invade, feel free to do so, but in any case you can expect little or no help from my armies, not this year, for they are all busy in the south and the west . . . though the southern ones may soon be free, but then they'll be marching into Connachta to join the others."

"Then, Your Majesty," inquired Bass, "where would the *bona* . . . the foot you offered me to supplement my horsemen come from?"

Brian showed his strong, yellowish teeth. "Why, from the King of Airgialla, of course, Sir Bass. After all, he is now an ally, and it is his borders you'll be protecting now."

"Your Majesty," Bass asked, "please correct me if I have misunderstood, but I get the impression that Your Majesty wishes to achieve certain ends and cares not precisely how those ends are achieved just so long as they are achieved . . . and the sooner, the better."

The High King nodded forcefully. "Your understanding is perfect, Sir Bass. I want the remaining Jewels. How I get them is not in the least important, but get them, I must . . . and I *will*. Why do you ask?"

Brian's meeting place with Timoteo di Bolgia was in one of the two forts guarding the entrance to the fine anchorage at the mouth of the River Slaney, in southeast Laigin. Both had sailed to the rendezvous, High King Brian aboard a speedy little lugger but recently arrived from Liverpool to join the fleet of the Duke of Norfolk as a dispatch vessel—the sometime Papal lugger repaired and now fitted out with a dozen swivel guns and three of the smaller rifled breechloading tubes of Sir Peter Fairley's manufacture, two of them at stern and one at the bow on a pedestal mount which allowed for extreme flexibility of use. The extra weight had, of course, somewhat reduced the speed of which the vessel had originally been capable, but still she could sail rings around any other of the ships of the private fleet. His Grace had named her *Cassius*, noting that she still could flit like a butterfly, but that now she too could sting like a bee, fiery and long-ranging and most accurate stings out of the mouths of her one eight-pounder and two six-pounder rifles with their explosive shells.

Alone together, the king and the condottiere, both old campaigners and accustomed to privation, sat on the rough wooden stools with which the stonewalled chamber was furnished and sipped at their respective flasks of restorative.

Brian spoke first. "How much has Sir Ugo told you of events in Rome and elsewhere, *Dux* di Bolgia?"

Timoteo sighed and shook his head. "More than enough, Your Majesty. Alas, my poor native land and her miserable people. I have never really liked Moors, you know, even the Sicilian or Brindisi Moors. Not that I have anything against other Ifriqans, you understand—the blacker ones often make for top-grade soldiers, like the Ghanian heavy infantry or the Ifriqan cavalry that came to Munster with me and my condotta.

"To think of the Moors despoiling Italy is bad enough, but for the blackhearted swine to bring in such as Macedonians and Croatians! Next they'll likely run in pagan, barbarian hordes from the lands of Tartary. God help us all, even up here in *Irland*, if such as they get their way and retain the control of the Roman Papacy. I have written and dispatched to His Eminence Cardinal D'Este a letter asking if my condotta and I might not be of more use to him and his faction in Italy or Sicily than we are squatting there in Munster, but of course there has been no time for it to reach him or for his reply to reach me." He sighed and looked down at his big, hard hands, the backs of them so thickly grown with black hair that it was sometimes difficult to see the white cicatrices left by old wounds.

"I truly sympathize, *Dux* di Bolgia," rumbled the voice

of the High King, "for it is never pleasant to think of one's lands being laid waste by uncaring strangers when one is far away. But you need not be in Italy to help to forward the aims of the Italian Faction, you know? His Eminence writes me that can his faction regain *Eireann* and England for Rome, then there is little doubt that the man they support will be elected by the College of Cardinals, rather than another accursed Moor or a Spaniard, and I have replied to him that if he and his will aid me in firmly uniting all *Eireann* under its High King, I will not see it taken out from beneath Rome's sway, despite the love I bear my cousin Arthur III Tudor, and my own beliefs that a Rome in England might be preferable to a Rome in faraway Italy."

Timoteo nodded. "Your Majesty wants a new King in Munster. How soon?"

"Very soon," replied Brian. "As soon as is possible after you get back to Munster, that soon. Take Sir Ugo back with you, and as soon as Tàmhas is dead and this *Righ* Sean FitzRobert decently coronated, send our young knight up to me in Lagore with the sad news, the glad news . . . and the Star of Munster. At that point, I will lift the siege, send all my troops north, into Connachta, and you and yours will be then free to sail back to Italy, should you then so desire."

Timoteo nodded once again. "Simple enough, Your Majesty. You have no need for a crack condotta in *Irland*, then? It is said that you and your house have certain bitter enemies in the north . . . ?"

It was Brian's turn to nod. "And so I do, *Dux* di Bolgia, you are very well informed. But now I also have, thanks to my dear cousin, Arthur of England and Wales, one of his great captains on loan with his condotta of *galloglaiches* and Kalmyks. The man is Lord Commander of the Horse in England, has achieved many a stunning victory for Arthur, and even has his own private fleet of warships—three ships of the battle line and six smaller ones, including that fast lugger moored below. Between this innovative captain, his fierce condotta, and his strong fleet, I think that soon the Jewels of the north will be resting in my strongroom at Lagore.''

Walid Pasha courteously refused the suggestion and himself suggested that His Irish High Majesty and Sebastián Bey think up a less suicidal plan, for he was not about to essay to take *Revenge* and *Thunderer* into a place like Belfast Lough, for which he had no reliable charts and did not even know the tides, with God alone knowing just how the flanking forts might be armed or just how many warships might be moored within.

Bass could see the master mariner's point and supposed that he was just going to have to write off the use of the fleet against Ulaid, for the little kingdom's other deep harbor was even more of a deathtrap for a seaborne attacker than was the Lough of Belfast.

All right, what then? Nibble around the coasts, sacking islands and bombarding coastal villages and sinking fishing boats, such as Brian had first suggested? Or simply ride up into Airgialla, collect the supporting infantry and siege train, then march across the Ulaid border and lay waste the countryside until King Ruarc felt stung enough to bring out his army and fight? Bass was not afraid of pitting himself and his condotta against the forces of Ulaid. Like most Irish kingly armies, they were no such thing, really, being simply a warband of the king's cronies, relatives, and some of his subjects with a sprinkling, possibly, of foreign mercenaries.

The *Ard-Righ* had told him that Ulaid possessed no field artillery as such, only a few full cannon on siege carriages drawn by twenty span of oxen, with massive tubes twenty to twenty-four feet long. So they would not be expected to appear in any battles, for they would be of little good in a fast-moving engagement and not even King Ruarc could be expected to be so reckless as to risk the loss of such hellishly expensive pieces.

''You see, Sir Bass,'' High King Brian had said, ''to a large extent, the kingdoms of this *Eireann* still remain very conservative and of the old fashion. To every ruler here except me, war is the sole pursuit of gentlemen—that's why we have so many wars, and for any reason or none at all. Before I became *Ard-Righ*, wars were unheard-of except in the time between planting and harvest; I it was who began to really modernize my army on the European model, put it in the field in April and keep it there for six months, if the early snows weren't too deep. Of course, there were screeching howls when I did this, some from my own people, but mostly from my enemies, for this meant that they, too, were obliged to change their hoary ways, maintain their fighters for more months in the field, else they would stand to lose any gains to me and mine.

"I did this for a purpose, Sir Bass, for even then, in my youth, in the earliest years of my reign as *Ard-Righ*, I recognized that *Eireann* would never realize her potential, never become and remain a power of any sort in this world of ours, were her kingdoms not stablized in some way, not ever perennially at war one with the other or racked by rebellions and clan fightings. I realized that one of the ways to change the war-mad minds of the chiefs and the kings and the gentry was to show them that real war was not in any way or manner a game to be played for two or three months each year for so paltry rewards as a few acres of burned-out croplands, a few head of scrawny cattle and a new scar or three of which to boast around the fires of autumn, winter, and early-spring nights.

"Such peculiar mind-sets as my brother chiefs and kings own have ever been the weakness of the entire race of the Gael. Iulius Kaesar and his few Romans could never have conquered the land of Gallia had it not been torn by Gaels just like these of *Eireann*, whose hates and feuds for and with one another ran far deeper than fear and hatred of foreign invaders. Because of these deep rifts, divisions of the Gaels, all Gallia dropped like a ripe plum into the Roman hand.

"*Eireann*, ununited, is a plum no less ripe, only awaiting the proper hand to claim her, entire. I mean to succeed in uniting these Gaels of *Eireann*, where the great Werkingetorix failed in uniting his against the then-puny power

of Rome. But Gaels have always been a superstitious lot;
Christianity still in these enlightened days is but a thin
patina over a weighty mass of strong, deeply rooted mores
and beliefs, some of them as old as the hills and the
waters. And so, although I could fight and win suzerainty
over these other kingdoms, the great masses of the common people never would consider me other than a mere
foreign conquerer unless I held the sacred Jewel of their
land and folk. And if I took the other kingdoms by conquest, I might not get with the lands and the peoples
whose Jewels, which would then mean that there would be
rebellion after rebellion for me to fight year after year so
long as I lived or essayed to hold the other kingdoms as
mine.

"Such things have happened before, you see, in the
blood-splattered history of the kingdoms of *Eireann*. The
Jewel held by Ruarc is not the original, ages-old Jewel of
Ulaid. That one was cast into the depths of Lough Neagh
by a defeated king just before he was caught and slain by
an invader. The invader's divers could never find the
original, so he replaced it with a great gem lifted from
Mercia during a raid, but still are there clans of Ulaid who
will not recognize it or those who hold it as the lawful
Jewel or ruler of Ulaid.

"The legend sung by the *filid* has it that that last, really
legitimate King of Ulaid will be returned in the body of a
foreign warrior and that when this chosen one arrives at
Lough Neagh, the ancient Jewel will leap out from where
it has so long rested in those deep, dark waters and cleave
to him, showing all who see that he is the warrior-king that
Ulaid has for so long awaited. Just one of our folk tales."
He smiled.

Then he went on with his explanations. "Your ancient
Gael warrior uses no missile weapons of any sort, only
axe, spear, knife, and sword, sometimes with a light target
of wickerwork, and no armor at all, quite often too with no
clothes at all. The descendants of those men do use armor
today, even bows and crossbows and hackbuts or pistols,
but still they harbor an antique belief in the backs of their

minds that engines that hurl impersonal missiles really long distances are a bit cowardly, and though they'll all mount them on fortifications and ships quickly enough, they deliberately avoid obtaining artillery small and light enough to be handy on a battlefield. This does not apply to my army, of course, as you've seen, and King Flaithri of Connachta has begun to so arm his field forces as well, though he presently has no numbers of them and is clearly not completely sure how he should best employ them.

"What he has done is what I had wanted, in a way, in the beginning, but I much fear now that because of his steps to modernize the Connachta army, I may have to thoroughly conquer him and them and his kingdom. Of course, when he reaches the point of believing his cause lost, he'll simply enship to *Magna Eireann* with his Jewel and leave Connachta to me to hold as best I can lacking the Jewel. There are only two options, neither of which I would care to essay."

Throughout most of the voyage back to Munster from Slaneymouth, *il Duce* sat huddled in the bow, wrapped in a boat cloak and clearly deep in thought. When at last he roused himself, they were only some half hour from the city. Taking Sir Ugo aside, he said, "His grace di Norfolk, this noble English condottiere, puts a different angle to my gun tube, Ugo, as too does the carnage ongoing in Italy. You know, for I often have spoken privately of it in times past, that it had been my intent to serve out my contract to His Eminence, and to then seek employment for my condotta with the *Ard-Righ*, this Brian.

"But now the order is changed, changed utterly. Ties of blood that I never before knew I had in my fabric call me to Italy, to do all of which my men and I are capable to drive these foul Moors and Spaniards and their barbarian cohorts from Italian soil. Too, it now would seem that the *Ard-Righ* presently owns no need for me and mine.

"Brian told me, back there, that he is ready for us to make use of FitzRobert, that immediately the new order is jelled here, you are to journey back to him at Lagore with word and the Jewel.

"But I want you to do more than that, Ugo. I will send you back to Lagore right enough, bearing with you all that Brian requires; however, I will be sending Roberto with you. I want the two of you to wangle a way to accompany this *condottiere inglese* on the northern campaign and thoroughly observe, which should present you no difficulty, for the *Ard-Righ* seems quite impressed by you and most friendly toward you personally.

"My own affairs aside, for the nonce, you're a younger son, aren't you, Ugo?"

Sir Ugo nodded, with a wry half-smile. "Yes, Your Grace, one of several—my family is quite a large one— and with little to no chance of inheriting anything, barring some calamity. This is why my early acceptance by the Military Order of Rome was considered to be such a stroke of good fortune, and when I then was chosen, picked out of a number of young knights, to be a member of the staff and household of His Eminence D'Este, it was felt that my living was assured for life."

Di Bolgia nodded his head briskly. "And so it might have been, still could be, for that matter. But Ugo, consider, please, victory or defeat are sides of the same coin and each has an equal chance of turning up. Should D'Este or Sicola or even Ermannus be elected, then, yes, your fortune is made, your preferment guaranteed . . . for so long as he lives and his faction remains paramount in Rome.

"However, Ugo, having now been openly and thoroughly identified with the household of D'Este and, through that association, with the Italian Faction, if he and they lose this unholy war and Moor or a Spaniard is elected, then your life would not be worth a pinch of chicken shit within Italy, anywhere in Italy.

"Therefore, I would sincerely advise you to cultivate the *Ard-Righ*. No, wait, Ugo, don't say anything until I'm done. I'm not counseling that you turn your coat on D'Este— you wouldn't do such even if I did so counsel you, you're not that stripe of man, you're loyal and very honorable. No, all that I am saying is to consider that your true fortune and personal interest just might not lie in Italy, but here, in these more northerly climes, and since you do not now and most likely never will hold Italian lands, then why should you return if you find your prospects better elsewhere? With but a little effort on your part, I think that you can feel secure in the support of a most powerful patron; this Brian is a driven man, and I think that, ere long, he will be truly *Ard-Righ*—King of all *Irland* in all ways.

"Now, back to my own interests, Ugo. While Roberto studies the troops and the military side of the northern campaign, I want you to learn every bit that you can about the person and character of this *Duce di* Norfolk, as well as those of his principal lieutenants. While so doing, bear this thought of mine in mind: According to Brian, all of *di* Norfolk's land force are cavalry—mostly, heavy-armed horse, with a few Kalmyks as light horse. Now, all of my own condotta are foot; only a troop or so worth of heavy-armed axemen and officers are usually mounted. I am of the opinion that despite his denials, the *Ard-Righ* will see his grand design come more quickly to fruition does he have two, rather than just the one, present army, and I cannot conceive of a better army for him than my condotta combined with a really first-rate condotta of effective cavalry.

"I think that this was what His Eminence D'Este had in mind, but he chose ill in the matter of these Ifriqans. They're good enough soldiers, but they just cannot seem to adjust, adapt to this climate; at any given time, a quarter to a full half of the poor buggers are suffering of a bloody flux of the lungs, it would seem. This is bad enough in a permanent garrison on the most southerly coast, here, but can you imagine just how few of them would be effective were they to be marched up into the harsher climes of the north. It would be quite impossible. So, no, am I to combine and provide Brian with what he really needs, it must be with horsemen already acclimated to *Irland*, and so I need to know all that I can of this *di* Norfolk as soon as is possible, Ugo.''

Hurriedly glancing about to be certain that no one was close by, Sir Ugo asked in a hushed voice, ''How does Your Grace plan the . . . ahhh . . . demise?''

Di Bolgia shrugged his massively thewed shoulders. ''Probably, just let the individual die happy, a death in battle, what he would do doubt describe as an 'honorable death.' That way, I need do nothing myself save allow the reins to slip a bit in my fingers. The troops of him I spoke with back there will do the rest.''

''It sounds a reasonable plan, Your Grace, but how are you going to keep FitzRobert from riding out with him? Despite his good points, the man seems to be overly full of a suicidal degree of clan loyalty.''

The answer was another shrug. ''With cudgel across the pate, if it comes to the sticking point, Ugo, or mayhap a bit of poppy paste. I've worked too long and too hard to render that shaggy savage into the likeness of a civilized gentleman to see him just go down to dust with the rest of the addle-pated FitzGeralds.''

''With di Rezzi now become his late grace,'' said Sir Ugo, ''there exists little to prevent quicker and more expeditious method of ridding Munster of him, Your Grace . . . so long as a certain degree of circumspection is exercised, of course.''

Timoteo grinned. ''You truly own hidden depths, Ugo, my lad. Of what were you thinking—poison, garrote, sharp steel? Or mayhap a means less easily detectable, eh? But, no, I think that this plan of mine will be best. Besides, I've already told the man I spoke with back there in Laigin that that was how it would be done.''

But in the first meeting of the Royal Council, Timoteo called on the next day after his return from his surreptitious parley with the *Ard-Righ*, *Righ* Tàmhas proceeded to drop a bombshell.

Resting one elbow upon the tabletop and pulling at a lock of his greasy, matted hair with bejeweled and grubby fingers, Tàmhas FitzGerald said, ''No, I've reconsidered,

gentlemen. The righteous wrath of a *Ri* and *Righ* should
not be, will not be, wasted upon such scum as that dog
vomit *Ard-Righ* Brian chose to leave behind to hold his set
of ditches. They are all certainly cowards, else they would
have long since called me and us all to come out and fight
them breast to breast as men should, not just squatted out
of sight for much of the time, now and then shooting off a
gonne or engine—cowards' weapons, both of them.

"Yes, Sir Timoteo," he said solemnly to the condottiere, who on hearing his words had first paled, then
become almost livid of face, his big hands clenched until
the craggy knuckles shone white as snow against the weathered, hairy skin, "this *Ard-Righ*'s contumely is indeed
cause for anger, but it were better to husband both ire and
strength to wreak upon him and his better, braver troops
whenever they return to Munster. We have spoken."

That afternoon, the *Righ*—as he so often did—drank too
much with his meal to allow of his legs operating properly.
Four of the FitzGerald Guards, none too steady themselves, bore him almost to the top of the stone stairs before
he and they all tumbled back down them, breaking one
guard's leg and another's neck in the process. Servants,
cold-sobered men, took over at that point and bore the
still-singing *Righ* up to his bedchamber, undressed him,
and put him to bed, seemingly none the worse for wear.
But when some of his gentleman-cousins went in to awaken
him the next morning, it was to find him stiff and dead,
the body unmarked save for a lump standing up from his
pate and a trickle of dried blood that had issued from the
hairy depths of one ear.

"God be praised that that hard-nosed old bastard di
Rezzi is gone to God and not back here in Munster,"
Timoteo said vehemently to the emergency meeting of the
Royal Council. "Else he'd be railing at us all and accusing
us publicly of foulest regicide."

Le Chevalier let his gaze wander around the table with
its two empty chairs—Sean FitzRobert had not been asked
to this particular session—then asked blandly, "And is, or
are, one or more of us guilty of that crime, Your Grace?"

Il Duce di Bolgia snorted. "Of course not, Marc! Everyone here, you and half the residents of this palace complex, saw what happened yesterday. The royal ass got too tight a skin to walk and those damned cousins of his were in not much better shape, so the pack of them fell the length of a score and a half of steep granite stairs. One man was killed outright, on the spot, one is likely crippled for life, and the late royal sot was just hurt worse than he, in his drunken stupor, thought he was. The royal physician who pawed and probed the royal corpse states that the royal skull was cracked."

"Even so," *Le Chevalier* pressed on, "there are more things than a flight of stairs are capable of cracking a skull, even a royal one . . . perhaps, in this case especially, a royal one."

"Now just one damned minute, Sir Marc." Roberto di Bolgia came up half out of his chair, his face red and his right hand grasping the wire-wound hilt of a sheathed dagger at his belt.

Sir Ugo chose that moment to arise and say in a loud, firm voice, "*Gentlemen, if you please*! You're behaving less like polished and well-bred noblemen of France and Italy than you are like these savage, dirty, scabby, brawling FitzGeralds, did you know that?

"Your Grace, please to resume your seat and your composure.

"Roberto, sit down. If you try to put that blade into Marc, I'll be forced to put one of mine own into you.

"Marc, if you don't or can't believe that His Grace and Roberto and I had nothing to do with *Righ* Tàmhas's death, then take your ship of the line and sail back to France, to Sicily, or to hell, for all I care, but please cease your senseless questionings and baitings. Just what is it you're after this morning, anyway? Will you answer me that?"

When all were once more seated, *Le Chevalier* looked from beneath his brows at Sir Ugo, grumbling, "It . . . it's all just happened in too damned convenient a fashion here. I knew that the removal of *Roi* Tàmhas was neces-

sary, and I was willing to go along with letting him ride
out there and get his head blown off, for it was truly an
honorable death by any standards save your decadent Italian
ones. But to coldly murder a king is a something I cannot
. . . could not stomach, especially when said king is
obstensibly your employer, trusts you, depends upon you.
I'm sorry, I had until this morning considered myself to be
a man of the modern world, but now I know my true
nature: I am just an old-fashioned, honorable Norman
knight, who values truth and loyalty to his God-given
overlords above all earthly things.

"Had I that right, I would indeed board the *Impressionant*
and set sail for France, for Le Havre, and on this very day.
But I cannot, in honor, for I promised *my* king that I
would stay with his ship; that ship still is pledged to the
service of Rome and His Eminence D'Este, so remain here
I must. However, in light of words spoken this morning
here, and in light of what might or might not have been
done to speed *Roi* Tàmhas to Heaven, I must respectfully
withdraw from the Royal Council of the Kingdom of
Munster."

"Now, by Pontius Pilate's putrid pecker," roared
Timoteo, "we've told you we none of us killed that dimwitted, ever-sodden yokel of a king, Marc! What more do
you require of us? Solemn oaths?"

Shrewdly guessing that that was just what would impress the Norman and retain him on the council, Sir Ugo
drew the royal sword of state from where it rested before
the late king's empty canopied chair.

"All right, Marc, *Righ* Tàmhas always attested that the
pommel of this brand contained a fingerbone of St. Co-
lumbia." Clasping both hands about the oversized pommel, he said slowly, "I, Sir Ugo Mario Vittorio D'Orsini,
do solemnly swear upon this holy relic and upon my hope
of salvation that I in no way brought about or caused
others to bring about the demise of the late Tàmhas Fitz-
Gerald, *Ri* of that ilk and *Righ* of Munster."

*   *   *

The FitzGeralds all were forced to come to the city by way of the river, due to the blocking of all the landward approaches by the *Ard-Righ*'s siege lines, which gave each and everyone one of them a good look at the impressive ships, all bristling with cannons, moored out in the channel of the river. Within the city itself, they quickly were made aware that the only troops of any number were those of the Italian and Ifriqan mercenaries and that said mercenaries would favor the elevation of no one of the claimants to the throne save Sir Sean FitzRobert. Therefore, having care for their heads and wishing to get out of the city with them still in place, as well as admitting to each other both publicly and privately that Sean FitzRobert had about as good a claim to the throne and the chieftaincy as any of his peers, they announced after only a week of feasting, drinking, shouting, snarling, insulting, brawling, and bloodshed that their choice for *Ri* and *Righ* was Sean FitzRobert, who would be crowned as soon as Tàmhas FitzGerald had been buried properly.

Timoteo did not wait for the coronation. While almost everyone else was at the funeral service—sanctified, in the absence of a resident prelate, by a bishop brought in from Chaisil—and the burial, he and Roberto and Sir Ugo thoroughly intimidated, terrified, the royal treasurer and, with that functionary's trembling assistance, violated the strongroom, removed the Star of Munster, plus a little coined gold and a ring that took *il Duce*'s fancy, and set Sir Ugo and Roberto on the way to Lagore before Tàmhas's leaden casket was yet in its crypt. *Le Chevalier* had no part of this, indeed had no knowledge of its contemplation; he had been at the funeral mass and the encryption of the deceased *Righ* of Munster, along with *Ri* and *Righ*-elect Sean FitzRobert.

Of course, there was an almighty commotion when the royal treasurer was found in the strongroom with his throat cut and the Star of Munster missing from its chest, but Timoteo testily pointed out to Sean FitzRobert and a number of others that it was not and had never been the responsibilty of him and the other mercenaries to provide internal security for the palace or even the town; such duties were and always had been the exclusive provinces of the FitzGerald Guards and the Corcaigh Guards. He added that if the king-to-be and the other FitzGerald cousins did not like the quality of his work, he would be just as happy to load all of his troops aboard ship and sail back to Italy and let them deal with the besiegers themselves. At that point, all accusations of malfeasance, misfeasance, and nonfeasance were stilled.

THE EIGHTH

Her grace Dame Krystal, Duchess of Norfolk, *Markgrafin* von Velegrad, Countess of Rutland, the Baroness of Strathtyne, was summoned to the presence of His Grace Harold, Archbishop of York, then escorted to him by four of his halberdiers. The way was long, down the stairs from her suites in the north wing of the archepiscopal country palace, along the corridors to the main palace, then up more stairs to the archbishop's own suite. And at the guarded doors to that suite her ladies were courteously denied entrance, so that Her Grace was already in a fighting mood when the doors closed firmly behind her.

"What the fuck is this horseshit all about, anyway, Hal?" she snarled at the frail man seated across the room, near the bright rays of sunshine pouring through a window.

"We need to talk, Krystal," said the old man.

"Fine!" she snapped. "Let my ladies in and I'll talk your goddam ears off."

He shook his head. "No, Krystal, I have not long that I can remain out here, I must soon return to York. I want to talk to you without the constant titterings and hushed whisperings of that gaggle of noble-born geese you have collected about you.

"Krystal, there are those of us who are very worried about you. You have changed very drastically in a very short time . . . and not for the better, I must say.

"Krystal, before Bass left for the King's business in Ireland, he charged me with a certain responsibility, and the time is come for me to discharge it. On the basis of the things you have written in your letters to him, as well as on the basis of things he has heard from others concerning you, he feels that it would be much better for the sake of the boy and for you, too, were little Joe to begin his fosterage early."

She wrinkled her brow. "Fosterage? What the hell is that?"

"All gentleborn boys go through some years of living with another noble family than their own, sometimes a distant relative, other times not. Bass has secured a fosterage with an old and highly respected noble family; they already have three boys in fosterage and—" The archbishop broke off in shock at the appearance of the woman. She was become livid of face, tiny specks of froth had appeared at the corners of her mouth, and her eyes resembled more those of some wild beast than anything human.

"In a pig's asshole!" she shrieked, reverting suddenly back to twentieth-century English. "Not you or that fucking cocksucker I'm married to or anybody else is going to take my Joe away from me, do you hear me, you old motherfucker? I am the Duchess of Norfolk, and what I say goes, get that through your thick head! For two fucking cents, I'd call Sir Conn this minute and have him show you what . . ."

While the woman raged on, the archbishop, looking as if he bore the full weight of the world upon his frail shoulders, gave a pull to a bell rope. Rupen Ademian and three short but husky-looking women clothed in the habits of nuns entered from another room. It was a battle-royal, there in the little private parlor, and the nursing sisters and the furnishings all suffered for it, and at last Rupen put an end to it by cold-cocking the duchess and she was bound and easily borne away by the three women.

At a nod from the old man, Rupen opened the doors to the foyer of the suite and signaled the halberdiers to admit the seven agitated ladies of Krystal's household to the thoroughly wrecked parlor.

Seemingly oblivious of the chaos of splintered furnishings, stained carpet, and smashed bric-a-brac amongst which he sat, the old archbishop said mildly, but in a tone that brooked no argument or questioning, authority implicit in his every soft word, "Ladies, even as I speak here, there are those abovestairs who are packing the clothing and effects of the Duke of Norfolk's little son, in preparation for his imminent departure to a fosterage in Sussex. Without him to care for, Her Grace of Norfolk has entered a cloister for an indeterminate period of contemplation and a life of simplicity and prayer. All of her possessions are to be packed by you, and then servants will move them to a place of safe storage until she again is ready to enter the world of man. Sir Rupen Ademian here will be at your call should you need any assistance.

"With everything done here, I will make provision to return all of you and the other ladies to their homes or wherever else they may wish so go. Now leave me; Sir Rupen will join you presently."

Rupen still started when someone called him Sir Rupen. When old Earl Howell ap Owain and his cavalcade had ridden up from London to formally knight Pete Fairley, Carey Carr, and Bud Webster, only a hint of a word from His Grace of York had been necessary in order for the gruff old warrior to give the buffet to Rupen as well, no questions asked. Rupen's understandable objections had been answered by Hal.

"Shut up and go along with this, my friend. I'll tell you why after it's over. It's necessary—leave it at that, for now."

A few days later, he had said, "Look, Rupen, rank and birth are of much more importance to all classes of people in this world than they were in your world and time. I think that you, the man you are, could be quite useful to me in a great many respects and areas. But in order to serve most of my ends, you must be either a gentleman, a churchman, or a noble. Now, no one but the King can make you a noble, and I doubted that you cared much for holy orders, so the only thing for it was to make you a gentleman—a knight, as it turned out.

"That business of the earl was just too good an opportunity to let slip. Yes, I could've had some one of the local nobility knight you, but it wouldn't've had been the same as having Earl Howell do it. You see, that old man—old, hell, he's not as old as he looks, maybe two or three years your senior is all—he was King's Champion of both Arthur II and Richard IV Tudor, the present king's elder brother. He pled age and left court during the early days of the Regency, unable to stomach what was going on there, under Angela.

"Then when Arthur III Tudor raised his standard against the regent and Rome, Earl Howell raised and armed and mounted a squadron of heavy horse and led them to the King, putting them and himself at the lawfully coronated monarch's disposal. Interdiction and excommunication be damned, he said then, England and Wales were Arthur's rightful realm and he would be Arthur's man so long as a single drop of blood lodged in his body.

"Since that day, he has taken part in almost every battle or fight or skirmish in which Arthur's army has engaged. He it was who made the plans and commanded the famous ambuscade which virtually wiped out the regent's fierce and fearsome mounted raiders, Monteleone's Horse. Even better, he and his men that day slew Angela's lover himself, Captain Monteleone, in combat, then so thoroughly abused and maimed his still-warm corpse that it had the appearance of having died under torture. After they had reclothed it, they had it delivered to the Tower by a party of friars, along with a letter stating that when questioned, Monteleone had admitted to being the real sire of Angela's son that she still claimed was gotten upon her by her royal spouse, Richard IV."

"I'll bet that that created a merry old shitstorm," commented Rupen. "Or was she smart enough to just stonewall it all, Hal?"

"She tried to, of course," the old man replied, "between crying jags and screaming fits, but still that little bit of seventeenth-century propaganda cost her and her son quite a good deal of support, especially among the common people, the yeomanry, and the lesser gentry. Such folk continued to trickle in to fill out the army's shattered ranks, even though they all knew that by so doing they were leaving their lands and families unprotected, that they were losing all hope of salvation by fighting for an excommunicant, that the army of Arthur had little gunpowder and no way to obtain more save by capture, and that a Crusade had been preached against them and hordes of Crusaders were already beginning to gather on the borders and in nearby oversea ports, awaiting but the necessary transport to descend upon the troubled land like some pitiless swarm of armored locusts.

"Early in the fifth year of the civil war—for that is what it all amounted to, with noble and common families split, likewise the small standing army, the few ships owned outright by the Crown either burned or scuttled to prevent their falling into Arthur's hands, some royal garrisons holding out for either Arthur or Angela and a few of them fence-sitting, refusing to commit themselves until they were certain just who stood the best chance of winning the ruinous conflict—a raid-in-force, launched to capture a large store of gunpowder, of which King Arthur's force just then had almost none, developed into a full battle as both sides threw in additional units and ended in a pyrrhic victory for our arms in that while Angela's forces then available within the kingdom were routed, with all of their cannon and their entire baggage train captured, not only were the losses of men and horses bitterly heavy in Arthur's force, such gunpowder as was captured only barely replaced that which had been expended in obtaining it.

"You've of course seen the great camp, or what's now left of it, out there to the southwest of York? Yes, well, that is where King Arthur and his army were encamped, he and his staff—who understood better than the bulk of the army just how little chance they and their much-reduced

numbers had of winning against any of the four looming
hosts of foreign Crusaders with little or no gunpowder—in
the depths of despair.

"Then, of a day of blessed memory, a small party of
horsemen came riding down the borderlands, led by an
elderly but still vital knight of ancient lineage and famous
personal achievements, Sir Francis Whyffler—he now is
Duke of Northumberland, father-in-law of Emperor Egon
and Royal Ambassador to that monarch's court. In Sir
Francis's party were included Bass Foster, William Collier, and Bud Webster. They brought a brine-filled pickle
cask containing the head of Sir David Scott, an infamous
border riever, in earnest of their tale of having routed his
force of above two thousand Lowland Scots, but even
more important, they brought a pack train loaded with
gunpowder—a commodity just then and there more precious than gold dust.

"After some initial difficulties with some larcenous members of the royal staff, Sir Francis was at last able to meet
with Earl Howell, who, after hearing his tale and testing
the powder, conducted him directly to King Arthur.

"Now, as you no doubt know by now, Rupen, for the
last five hundred years, in this world and time, the Church
has held and savagely maintained a monopoly on the
manufacture and sale of gunpowder, trying to keep the
formulas for it secret and wreaking terrible vengeance
upon any person or group of persons rash enough to
formulate it on their own, without Church sanction. With
this monopoly in full force, the Church not only made
unbelievable amounts of profit from the sale of it, but also
was able to control and manipulate rulers and states to a
degree that the Mediaeval and Renaissance Church of our
world never even dreamed of, and they had thus been able
to keep most of the regions in their sphere of influence
from effectively uniting into nations of any real size or
strength, cynically preaching peace and brotherly love while
fomenting an endless round of small wars and selling the
wherewithal to conduct them.

"Those few brave or simply desperate souls who had in

the past made gunpowder from scratch had not, up until then, been able to turn out an 'unhallowed powder' as good as that of the Church, simply because the Church had developed a secret way of refining niter, and use of this in the mixture could, depending upon the proportions, of course, produce a more powerful powder than a more primitive niter.

"Now William Collier was, before he lost his reason, a multitalented and highly intelligent man, innovative, well read in many fields, and holding university degrees which included a doctorate or two in chemistry, in which field he also had done certain amounts of research for his government, involving propellants. Additionally, he was an avid amateur student of military history with an in-depth knowledge in a good many related subjects, and his sagacious counsel helped to revolutionize the then existent army, making it far more effective and easily controlled a fighting force, with units of set sizes and consistent titles of military rank.

"Two tandem cargo trucks, with their crews and cargos, had been projected at the same time as Bass, his house, and the other people. The cargo of one of those trucks consisted of some eighty tons of a powdered nitrate used in your world and time for fertilizer, and using this as a base chemical, William Collier and Pete Fairley had manufactured a variety of gunpowder far more powerful than the very best of the product of the Church's powder mills; experiments showed that less than half of this gunpowder was required to give results at least equal to a charge of hallowed gunpowder."

"Collier?" asked Rupen. "Isn't he the one who deserted Arthur and the army over some slight and went to Scotland, Hal? I seem to recall hearing something spoken of him when we all—you, me, Duke Bass, and some others—were up at Whyffler Hall. Didn't he eventually go mad, too, like the Lady Krystal? It's too bad, for as I now recall, the Duke said that his contributions were really trivial in giving Arthur and the army victories, that Collier had been the real hero of it all."

Harold of York shook his head. "Bass Foster is modest and self-effacing to a very fault, Rupen. You see, Collier was not a man of action, save with regard to experimental chemistry, but of ideas, theories. Even with regard to the powder mill at Whyffler Hall, it was Pete Fairley, Carey Carr, and Dave Atkins who did the actual work, lived through the always deadly danger of mixing the powder. As for the reorganization of the army, yes, Collier came up with the ideas, but it was Bass Foster and Bud Webster put them into practice, drilling hundreds of officers so that they might go back to their units and pass on the newfangled methods of drill to their men.

"Arthur took a quick liking to Collier, and the man was duly given a reward, being made Earl of Essex by the king. But he began to lose Arthur's and many another's regard and favor when he proved hismelf to be first a coward, then a bully. At length, in a pique, he went so far as to actually threaten to leave His Majesty, to take his learning and knowledge to the Church forces.

"Much to his surprise and shock, I would imagine, Arthur not only gave him leave to go, but even provided him with a neutral escort—commanded, incidentally, by the man who now is Holy Roman Emperor—to the court of the King of Scotland at Edinburgh. On the journey through the Lowlands of Scotland, however, the party was attacked by a savage clan of border ruffians. Most of them were killed, but some were taken for ransom. *Leutnant* Egon somehow escaped and fought his way out of Scotland, but by the time the Scottish Crown heard of it all and was able to force the lawless clan to release Collier, the man had lost his reason through torture and privation. For long, he was confined to the monastery of an order of nursing brothers somewhat southeast of Edinburgh, but I have been in receipt of recent news that he escaped twice last year; he was recaptured after slaying several peasants, but whilst he was being transported to the parent house of that order in far-western Scotland, he slew an abbot and again escaped and naught has since been seen or heard of him."

*   *   *

Around and about that ancient pile known to men as Whyffler Hall, the trenches and earthen ramparts of cannon emplacments that marked the onetime Royal Artillery defenses of the hall and the powder mill that then had been there established were slowly being filled in or leveled. In the park outside the bailey walls, new trees and shrubs had been planted to replace those cut down by the huge Scottish army that had twice surrounded and launched futile attacks at the well-defended hall during the ill-omened invasion of the Scottish crusaders.

Kings, princes, and every descending grade of nobility or gentility had enjoyed the hospitality of Whyffler Hall in times past, and a duke and the wife of an emperor had both been born there, but just now the sole gentleman resident on a permanent basis was Sir Geoffrey Musgrave, the bailiff of the hall and the surrounding Barony of Strathtyne, and even he was not always in residence, as the duties of his office often sent him clattering over hill and dale at the head of his troop of lancers. He and they also regularly patrolled the familiar though unmarked border between the barony and the Scottish lands beyond; for all that Sir Geoffrey and Laird Sir Michael Scott whose lands lay just to the north of the barony were bosom friends and drinking companions, too, on occasion, Sir Michael still was both a Scot and a Scott—full brother to the onetime, now fortunately deceased, Sir David Scott— and therefore Sir Geoffrey could not bring himself to fully trust his friend and near neighbor, much less his provenly deceitful and ever larcenous clansmen.

So it was no surprise to Sir Geoffrey, as he and his column rode back to Whyffler Hall after a swing through portions of the barony, to find Sir Michael Scott and a contingent of his own horsemen camped in the outer park among the young trees. At sight of him, Scott tightened his saddle girths, mounted, and rode to meet the bailiff at a fast amble.

In mock wrath, from a smiling face, he proclaimed, "Domned puir hospitality you extend y'r friends, Geoff

Musgrave! Yon gummen would nae e'en gape the gates enough tae bespeak me, just blew on their slow matches and shouted me tae withdraw intae the park until y' come back.''

In the same mock-serious tones, Musgrave said, nodding, ''A far warmer reception y'd of got had they not known y'r face and horse, Michael Scott. My garrison, they all hae their orders and they obey: Nae armed Scots are to be let w'in the bailey at any time whilst me and my launces be awa'.''

As the two aging knights rode along the road, knee to knee, Scott remarked, ''Mayhap 'tis time and muir for me tae speak to the lairds of Elliott and Kerr and eke Armstrang, for to march doon and level the unseemly pride of a sartain carpet-knicht of a bailiff, storm the ha', and distribute its wealth amangst the needy poor . . . north o' the border, of course?''

Musgrave snorted a laugh. ''Then best mark y'r wills ere y' a' do so, Sir Michael, my friend, and recall the end of y'r unlamented brother, not too lang since. Not a' the gonne-works King Arthur had put here has been took doon, nor a' the great gonnes ta'en awa frae Whyffler Ha'. I keep a very plentitude o' poudre aboot, too, an' muir nor enough bonny lads tae put paid to a parcel o' border ruffians o' the likes o' y' and y'rn. An' it still be room enough and tae spare in that meadow where we buried a' that were left o' the last rievers as rid doon here ahint Sir David Scott; the grass graes thick on that lea, and ever Scot under it by noo owns a cowflop cairn tae mark oot his place.''

Scott shook his head and chuckled merrily. ''An' y'd do it a', too, Sir Geoff, y'd blaw awa' y'r own friend's head wi' a caliver ba' an' think nae muir o' it. His Grace o' Norfolk has a guid mon in y', my friend. He, too, be a guid mon, so I pray a' o' his sairve him sae well. It's right mony the Scott wha' will hae food and fuel through a' the winter out'n the siller he paid for a' that clay, and I think me it would be mickle hard tae raise rievers out'n Scott lands, this year, did they ken that 'twas Whyffler Ha' or aught elst of this barony they was meant tae prey on.

"Be it a hard winter, it might be Kerrs or Armstrangs oot a-rieving, but y'll be seeing nae Scotts other than in peace. Nor eke a Elliot riever, either, y' ken, for Sir Andrew bears great love and respect for His Grace and the most o' his gillies gae in stark fear that it might be some o' His Grace's wild *galloglaiches* abiding at Whyffler Ha' yet."

Musgrave nodded. "What o' the Lindsays an' the Hays, d' y' think, Michael Scott?"

Sir Michael shrugged. "As to the Hays, I canna say one way or t'other, what wi' the auld laird dead an' the new still in Edinburgh, some hotheaded *toiseach* might tek it intae his mind tae ride doon on a rieving, but I'd think not, not sae harsh as the new king has been on rievers sich as Clan Johnston, of late times. An' the Laird o' Lindsay is one o' the chiefest supporters of King James, so y'll be seeing nane o' his ilk ride acrost the border save on the high road tae York or London."

At sight of Sir Geoffrey, the bailey-wall gates were gapped wide and the bridge over the ditch came rumbling down, and he, Sir Michael, and the Whyffler Hall Lancers clattered across it, followed shortly by Scott's remounted party of servants and retainers.

As most of the lancers and Scott troopers peeled off the cavalcade to make for the stables and see to their mounts, while the gentry, officers, and servants followed their betters up to the hall itself, one-armed Olly Shaftoe, the groundskeeper, could be seen to render Sir Geoffrey a military hand salute, where he stood watching the labors of his men. Solemnly, Sir Geoffrey returned the salute of the former cavalryman, one of the few survivors of the troop that Sir Francis Whyffler had taken to the king's service, the same troop that had been commanded also by Bass Foster when he still was only a gentleman-captain under command of Sir Francis.

Most of Shaftoe's busy workers paused from their toil long enough to raise an impromptu cheer for Sir Geoffrey;

only one old man, his thinning white hair showing clearly the jagged scars furrowing his scalp, his face all but hidden in a dense white beard, failed to make a sound, but he looked up and smiled to display a less than full complement of broken, rotting teeth and fingered the place where once there had been a forelock of hair.

Sir Geoffrey reined up beside the aged worker and spoke down from his saddle. "Hoo be y', Will? Be the work too hard for y'?"

His only answers were a wider smile to the first question and a shake of the head to the second.

Olly Shaftoe, when he came striding over, was asked, "Olly, cannae y' find Auld Will a pair o' breeks o' some kind? Auld bones ache muir nor y' youngsters' in oor cauld dews o' mornings."

"An' it please y', Sir Geoffrey, sir," replied Shaftoe, "Will hae been given two breeks, but he maun allus wear his kilt, a shairt and sometimes brogan-shoon. Cauld does nae seem tae plague him."

Musgrave nodded. "Weel, let him bide as he will, then. But be y' sartain sure that he owns an overthick mattress tick and a blanket o' nichts. An' a pot o' brown ale for him that nicht, Olly."

A gentle slap of the reins set his horse back in motion, and they proceeded on up toward the hall.

"Who be that auld Highlander, Geoff?" asked Sir Michael. "Cannae he speak?"

Musgrave shook his head. "He come tae the ha' a-begging, not tae lang after His Grace last left, whilst His Grace of York and Master Rupen, his servant, still abided here. He were naught save skin an' bones, then. An' nae, he cannae speak eke ane word."

"So, being the mon y' be, y' took him in." said Scott. "Who give him the name Will? Y'self?"

Again Musgrave shook his head. "Not so, Michael. He cannae speak, but he can write . . . well, his name, anyhow, 'twould seem. Tae do sich, for sartain sure he once were muir than a mere gillie. But how knew y' he be a

Highlander? The kilt, ainly? Yet Lowlanders wear it, too, some o' them.''

This time, Scott's head shook. ''Not the kilt, Geoff, but the sett. Auld an' wore doon an' faded oot as be that tartan, I cannae be sartain o' the sett, but I ken it be either Mac Ghille Eoin or Mac Neacail, both o' them clans o' the West Highlands an' the isles. Be Will the ainly name he writ?''

''Nae,'' answered Musgrave, ''he writ '*Uilleam Bheithir*,' he did, wi' charcoal on a flat stane. But I ne'er heared o' sich a family.''

''Nor hae I,'' said Scott, ''That word, in Scots, means 'monster' or 'wild beast.' Belike the puir auld soul be but a addled mon oot o' King Alexander's hosts, who either cannae find his way back tae his hame . . . or does nae want tae go back in his shame o' defeat an' degradation an' e'en unable tae say his name. God in His heaven wi' bless y'r charity to the auld wretch, Geoff Musgrave.''

At the front of the hall, grooms were waiting to take and lead away the horses. Within the foyer, other servants helped the two knights and the lancer officers to remove buffcoats, helmets, bits of armor, and weapons, offering soft, comfortable felt shoon to replace heavy jackboots, along with mugs of spiced ale to lay the dust of the ride.

The luck that William Collier had enjoyed on the night he had strangled the too gullible Abbot Fergus, slashed the throat of a sleeping gillie and despoiled him of all his clothing and effects, then managed to saddle the dead abbot's big riding mule and creep from out the sleeping camp of monks and Highland warriors undetected, had been the last he had been destined to know for some little time.

On only the second day of his new-won freedom, the hard-ridden mule had turned up lame, so he had had to take to his feet, leading the limping beast as fast as it could progress, still fearing that the inevitable pursuit might result in his recapture and a return to that foul, stinking bear cage and a continuation of seemingly endless miles of jolting, bone-bruising travel in that ox wain, this time with no simple-minded Scottish abbot to cozen with tales of spells and curses and witchcraft practiced by kings. And where would the end of that journey find him? Imprisoned in another tiny, stone-walled cell on a wind-swept island, to wallow in his own filth and howl away the freezing nights until death finally claimed what would by then be left of him. It might be easier to just let the Mac Ghille Eoin gillies take the blood price from all the blood he owned—at least that kind of death would be quick.

At length, he had rounded a bend in the road to come upon a crofter gnawing on black bread and hard cheese under a stunted tree, while an ass laden with wicker panniers of root vegetables and a brace of live chickens grazed the tiny patches of grass sprouting from between the twisted, knobby roots of the same tree.

Collier had bespoken the man, first in English, then, recalling just where he was and what he was supposed to be, in Scots Gaelic. But the crofter had been most unwilling to make the trade of his ass for the lame mule, and, after arguing a bit, Collier had been beset with one of his black rages, and when he once again was in his right mind, his stolen sword was in his hand and running fresh blood, while the crofter lay hacked and gory and very, very dead at the base of the tree.

Once he had dragged the crofter's body well away from the road and hidden it in a mass of prickly bushes, he returned to the site of his most recent murder, removed the panniers and chickens from the back of the placid, still grazing ass, and mounted the beast, taking his seat well back on the crupper, as he had seen men ride asses. Within seconds after he had mounted, he was on his back on the hard ground, his head spinning from rather violent contact with a lump of hardwood root. By the time his head had cleared enough for him to sit up, groaning, the ass was back to grazing, its long ears twitching. And a second attempt to mount and ride the small beast produced almost the same results, save that that time, Collier landed face-down and the pommel of his stolen dirk took him so hard in the solar plexus that he had to gasp for air and thought that he surely would smother before he was again able to breathe with great and painful effort.

Still keenly aware that he most likely was being pursued by the vengeance-seeking clansmen and probably the monks as well, he gave up on the uncooperative little ass. After finishing the bread and cheese of the slain crofter, he resumed his journey, leading the lame mule, though he did sling the brace of scrawny chickens—one foot of each of them forced between the bone and tendon of the other leg to make for easier carrying—to the pommel of the mule's saddle for his journey provisions.

But he was afraid to light a fire that night, lest pursuers see it and be guided to him by it. Not knowing what chickens eat and sure that the brace he had would need at least water were they to stay alive until he could kill and dress and eat them, he carefully pulled the whole legs from out the maimed ones and turned them loose, certain that so injured they could not get very far. Then he rolled himself in the scratchy, woolen tartan and slept the sleep of exhaustion on the cold, hard ground.

When a cold drizzle awakened him the next morning, neither of the chickens was to be found, and neither was the lame mule he had neglected to hobble. After a brief search, Collier had hurried on along the road to Glasgow, now carrying the mule saddle and gear in vain hopes that the beast might have strayed in the same direction he was traveling, but by midday he had thrown the heavy, awkward burden into a roadside ditch in disgust. Each time he heard travelers coming from either direction, he cautiously quitted the road and lay hidden, feeling like a wild and hunted animal, until they were safely out of sight and sound.

And soon he found that he had chosen the wrong road, for the trace began to wind down to the southward, becoming narrower and less well kept by the long mile until, at length, it petered out altogether at a collection of tumbledown huts and one-roomed cottages on the banks of a river. Although he entered them all, there was no recent evidence of human habitation, though beasts of various sizes and descriptions had established residence of a sort.

Some digging and slicing off in a a bit of an overgrown kitchen garden gave the ravenous man a double handful of turnips and beets, along with their tops, some herbs, and a couple of small, self-seeded onions, or what looked like onions to him. He first tried to eat the tubers raw, only to discover that so damaged and rotted were his teeth become through years of the abuse and malnutrition he had suffered that the hard vegetables were now beyond his abilities to masticate them, so he had to content himself with sucking on some of the greens while he laid a fire on the hearth of the best-preserved of the cottages, layered the tubers in riverside mud, and waited for them to bake to a sufficient degree of tenderness for his dentition to manage. For the first time in a long while, William Collier slept out that night with a full belly, as warm as the fire coals and the woolen tartan could make him . . . and completely free.

On the next morning, he began to tramp up, then down, the riverbank searching for a bridge or shallow ford . . . vainly. Just below the ruined hamlet was what looked to be the rotted remains of a pier or dock, and by straining his eyes, he thought to discern the stumps of pilings in the shallows on the other side. Then he began to search for a boat of some description . . . and he found one, but it was old and battered and waterlogged, and half its bottom had long ago been staved. Nonetheless, with great physical effort, he managed to drag the riverine disaster from the long-occupied bed of soft mud, only to see the wood flake away as it dried out.

He had lived in the deserted hamlet for a full week by then, and he knew that he would soon have to move on, ford or bridge or no ford or bridge, for he had dug up or cut almost all of the remaining food plants, and the small animals which had been almost tame when first he arrived were now become very skittish of the hairy, two-legged thing who slew with flung stones.

His swim across the river had been utter disaster. The

small raft of lumber stripped from some of the abandoned buildings and green animal skins had come apart in mid-stream, and with it had gone his targe, his sheathed sword and leathern baldric, and, worse, his warm tartan cloak-blanket. All that he had been able to snatch back from the racing current had been his dirk, his bonnet, and his hide brogans.

Exceedingly glad that he had elected to essay the swim wearing his shirt, kilt, and belt with its dependent sporran, he landed upon the opposite shore with them, the shoes and bonnet and only the dirk for either weapon or tool.

This far away from the scenes of his crimes, with the width of the swift-flowing river between him and them, Collier built a fire every night whether or not he had found anything to cook; it was either that or freeze to death with the loss of his tartan. This side of the river seemed, for some reason, to be deserted too. He had trudged on for days before he found any recent signs of man . . . and then he wished he had never found them.

CHAPTER
THE NINTH

Ard-Righ Brian the Burly shook his head as he gazed at the Star of Munster, cradled in his hand. To Sir Ugo and Sir Roberto di Bolgia, he said, "The *Dux* and you gentlemen were too rash, I fear. You siezed this bauble prematurely; you see, FitzRobert cannot be legitimately coronated without this Jewel . . . or very convincing facsimile of it."

All at once, he smiled. "However, this just might work out. The traditions hold that the owner in fact of this Jewel be the only true ruler of Muma or Munster, no matter who may wear the crown and sit upon the throne in Corcaigh. So what better way to impress all with the cold, hard fact that the Kingdom of Munster is become but another of my client states, eh?

"Therefore, what I'll do is this: A message will be sent notifying Sean FitzRobert that certain of my Knights of the Silver Moon met a small party of strangers riding in haste up out of Munster, o'ertook and slew them in a fight, then found the Star of Munster on one of the bodies, which Jewel they at once brought to me, of course. I'll assure him that the Star will be returned to him immediately he comes to me at Tara . . . as a suppliant, naturally."

"Your Majesty will actually return the Star to Sean FitzRobert?" asked Sir Ugo.

Brian's smile broadened and brightened. "Of course, Sir Ugo, I'll return *a* Star to him, one cunningly wrought with some speed for me by a certain master goldsmith at Tara. In return, this FitzRobert will be persuaded to, before ever he be crowned, give to me all lands over which he ever is fated to rule. Then I will give those same lands back to him as a feoff."

"Brilliant!" breathed Sir Roberto di Bolgia, his admiration of the *Ard-Right*'s ability to quickly turn unexpected happenings to his tactical advantage patent in his voice and on his face. "And then, should he someday become forsworn or try to wriggle out of his oaths, Your Majesty still will hold the authentic Star of Munster. I presume that the copy will be marked in some cryptic way?"

Brian laughed aloud. "Sir Roberto, you are a man after my own heart. Yes, there will be a barely noticeable mark hidden somewhere on the reproduction. Of course, if he remain a true liege man, no one ever will know of the substitution . . . until it suits my ends to disseminate the information."

Then, his smile fading almost away, he said, seriously, "You have a quick, shrewd, and unscrupulous mind, di Bolgia, much like that of your brother, much too like mine own. God be thanked that I need not anticipate you as an antagonist—you just might outwit me."

The time was to come when *Ard-Righ* Brian, Sir Roberto, and Sir Ugo were all to recall those words.

In Airgialla's capital, Ard Macha, Bass Foster was received almost like a king. The young *Righ*, Ronan, was as friendly and anxious to please as a puppy. Bass and his officers were granted audience, next paraded through the streets, then ushered into the main hall of the royal palace and grandly entertained at a feast that lasted for most of the remainder of that day.

All during the dining and drinking, relays of musicians strummed and tootled and thumped and droned. Between courses, there were bears wrestling and otherwise performing, tumblers, jugglers, knifethrowers, dancers of differing types, a sword-swallower, a fire-eater, two bards competing to come up with the funniest or most shocking doggerel verses extemporaneously in Gaelic, a sleight-of-hand performer, some dancing dogs, and several pairs of fighting cocks.

The *pièce de résistance*, whole roasted wild boar, was borne in to the accompaniment of two drummers and a war piper in royal livery. The full-throated pipes were deafening in the confines of the stone walls, and the drones brought the hairs prickling erect on the back of Bass's neck, bringing back to mind that terrible night of terror and blood and death when he and his squadron of English and Welsh heavy horse had held the waggon square against the attacks of the wild Highlander irregulars of King Alexander's Scottish Army at Denham.

Bass and Wolfgang, as the highest-ranking nobleman, flanked the *Righ* at the high table, King Ronan and Wolfgang paired for dining, Bass paired with the lissome, pale-blond *Bean-Righ*, Deirdre. The girl appeared to be about fourteen or fifteen, was very pregnant, and spoke a fair amount of English, having been reared at the *Ard-Righ*'s court, one of his quasi-legitimate (that is, illegitimate but recognized) daughters. Conversation with the merry girl imparted to Bass that not only was she a daughter of Brian VIII, but she was a second cousin of *Righ* Amladh IV of Laigin and a great-granddaughter of the famous Prince Emmett Ui Mail de Tara, he who first had made the prized Tara Steel.

At this, Bass could not help squirming a little, uncomfortably, for he still bore that very man's gold-hilted Tara-Steel sword and his dagger and his matched pair of wheellock pistols, all of them garnered from the Prince's corpse after a battle in England. At the time, he had not known the dead man's identity or rank; that knowledge had come much later from the mouth of Harold of York, who had been projected to this world and time almost two centuries ago along with Emmett O'Malley, from the twenty-first-century world that had developed the projector. The dead man's ring, which Bass had worried from off his cold, livid finger—that worn-down band that had borne the letters reading MASSACHUSETTS INSTITUTE OF TECHNOLOGY CLASS OF 1998—he had given to the Archbishop of York, once known, in another world and time, as Dr. Harold Kenmore.

That body had not even been granted the final dignity of a grave, but after being stripped by others of anything still usable, had been thrown into the cold sea along with all of the other corpses of the Irish Crusaders found upon that beach, food for nameles sea-beasts.

The feast itself reminded Bass to some extent of those well-remembered days and nights of feasting and drinking and good-fellowship with old Sir John Heron, Sir Francis Whyffler, Buddy Webster, and the rest at Heron Hall, before the invading Scots Crusaders had razed that place of good cheer and butchered its inhabitants.

The first course, put on the tables all at once, as were all the succeeding courses, consisted of tiny pasties full of codfish liver or beef marrow, a brewet of sliced pork in a spicy sauce, greasy fritters of more beef marrow, eels in a ginger-flavored aspic, bream fillets in a watery green sauce of herbs, a baron of tough and stringy beef for each pair of diners, boiled shoulders of pork and veal, and, to bring the course to an end, a seven-foot sturgeon, cooked whole and served with the skin replaced, surrounded by bowls of a sauce that Bass thought would have made a Mexican or Korean homesick, so hot was it.

But the sauces were all that arrived at low table or high table hot. All of the dishes served were cold on arrival, thick and tacky with globules of congealed fat afloat in the sauces. The wines—these only at the high table, the other tables furnished with ewers of beer and ales—were no cooler than was the room or cellar in which they had been stored; furthermore, as in England, Bass noted that no one seemed to have heard of serving of a certain color or sweetness of wine with a particular kind of meat or fish; the ewers were borne by cupmen who filled and refilled drinking vessels with whichever of the potables each nobleman or -woman demanded.

Far sooner than he was ready for more food, Bass saw the boar borne in with its accompaniment of pipe and drums. Behind it, servants brought poached trout and loach, a broth of bacon and onions, a tile of chicken and pork in a spicy sauce and garnished with whole almonds and cray-fish, pasties filled with goose liver or fish roe or the flaked flesh of bream or eels, and at last a monstrous caldron of blamanger—shredded chicken and whole barley grains sim-mered to a consistency of library paste in almond milk with salt and honey and anise and garnished with fried almonds.

There was another hiatus of drinking and entertainment which included an appearance by the court *filid*, Dungal Ui Delbna, a rather short, paunchy, jowly man who, accom-panying himself on a knee harp, sang a succession of rhyming verses in an archaic dialect of Gaelic. The verses went on and on and on, carried musically enough on the *filid*'s fine tenor voice, but so many of them were there that Bass was certain the song never was going to end. Worse, he could only understand a few of the words, for he had yet to really master the Gaelic in current use, much less a form of the language that most likely had not been a commonly spoken tongue for who knew just how many generations. From what little he could understand, he took the verses to be a compilation of the deeds and misdeeds of the royal house of Airgialla—wars and raidings, victories and defeats, murders and executions and famous judg-ments handed down by kings and chiefs.

Bass had witnessed almost unbelievable prodigies of memory in the England of this world, but the plump Irish *filid*, who paused at times to generously wet down his throat with full goblets of wine, assuredly took the cake in the memory category. Bass could not for the life of him imagine how anyone could remember or so smoothly com-pose and deliver extemporaneously close to an hour and a half of verses.

After the *filid*, the bears were brought back to dance lumberingly to the tune of the piper and his brace of drummers. Then came yet another food course.

This time, the opening pasties were filled with pease paste, chicken lights simmered in broth, pork brains, a very salty meat paste with chopped raisins and spices, and what at first looked to Bass like worms in slime, but which his royal dining companion identified as whole baby eels in a clear thickened eel broth.

The came venison—both joints and racks, larded and roasted—with the inevitable accompaniment of frumenty, fritters of forcemeat with chopped onions and garlic, lampreys in a sauce that made the previous hot sauces seem exceedingly mild by comparison, roasted whole breams stuffed with breadcrumbs and chopped mussels, whole capons stewed in broth with leeks and herbs and wine . . . and then came the sweets and fruits and nuts and honey-meads

For all that he had eaten far more lightly than the *Bean-Righ* or, indeed, any other personage at the high table, Bass felt stuffed—so very uncomfortably stuffed that he fleetingly regretted that the ancient Romans never had invaded Ireland and introduced the practice of the *vomitorium*—and, despite the hideous quantities of food he had forced himself to consume, he felt very tiddly and not a little drowsy. He now could easily understand how the *filid* and not a few of the more mature men and women of the court of Airgialla had gotten so fat, and he wondered how long the young king and his queen would retain their youthful slenderness on such overabundance of food and drink.

Although the sun was not yet fully below the horizon for more than a very few minutes, the serious drinking commenced immediately all of the ladies had departed. Bass drank as little as he could; in courtesy to his royal host, he had to drink some. When he saw a man of about his own age—he could not recall the terribly scarred and fattening man's name, but did remember that he was a half-uncle of the *Righ*—wave frantically at the waiting line of cupmen and be quickly presented with a container that looked a bit like an oversized chamberpot, into which he noisely regurgitated, Bass saw his salvation.

Once his own straining stomach was empty of its unaccustomed burden, he felt so much better that he actually could enjoy the next sips of strong Spanish wine, and an herbal cordial with an undertaste that hinted of spearmint was most refreshing. However, when Wolfgang, *Righ* Ronan, and certain others of his companions at the high table began to imbibe of mixtures of various wines and brandy, he decided it was high time that the Duke of Norfolk retired, and he made his goodnights, citing as excuses the long ride up from Lagore and certain old battle wounds that often plagued him of nights.

Escorted by a youngish knight of about the age of the *Righ*, in point of fact a quasi-legitimate half brother of the new-crowned monarch, who had been awarded the singular honor because he remained sober enough to walk and speak coherently, Bass and his party—four squires, two pages, and his two Kalmyks, Nugai and Yeuh, these last being combination bodyguards and bodyservants and both most accomplished at either task—were led up stairs and along corridors to a suite of rooms large enough to accommodate them all. While palace servants who had come along behind bearing the baggage set themselves to striking fire and lighting lamps and tapers, Nugai and Yueh, looking very grim and businesslike, padded around and about all the rooms, especially the largest, wherein their lord would abide the night.

Their jobs done, the servants would have departed, had a word from Bass not sent several racing off to fetch back water, both hot and cold and in such quantities that they began to silently wonder if the foreigner nobleman was not either drunker than he seemed or a little mad or both.

In their absence, two of the squires set themselves to unpacking, brushing, and otherwise caring for Bass's clothing and effects, while the other two began to undress him. Yueh took the pillow-sword from its sheath, checked the point and both edges for sharpness, then resheathed it and put it in the sword rack built into the bedstead, before going about the making of the bed with Bass's sheets and blankets and pillows.

By the time the palace servants had returned with buckets of cold well water and lazily steaming caldrons of hot, two of the squires had brought up their lord's copper bathtub along with the small chest containing the lengths of cloth he used for washcloths and towels and the casket of fine milled soap that Sir Peter Fairley had had manufactured for him in York; the stuff did not lather very satisfactorily, to Bass's way of thinking, but neither did it take off skin and often burn it as did much of the contemporary so-called soap, and the scent of the fresh crushed lavender with which it was infused reminded him of the aftershave he once had used years ago in another world and time. The very innovative Sir Pete was now working to formulate a decent shampoo, but had not yet gotten it to the production stage, he had averred when last he and Bass had talked.

"Bass, it ain't as if I ain't trying, see, but it's just so many hours in a day, too. And right often, too, I got plans to do suthin' of the next day and *bang*, I wakes up with a idea's been slipping away from me for weeks and I knows if I don't git on 'er pronto, she'll be gone under again.

"See, from the time I's just a kid, I read whole bunches of books and all 'bout old guns, muzzleloaders and cap-and-ball revolvers and cannons and I don't know whatall. Then, after I come back from the Nam and was trucking and had me some money to spend, I bought some reproductions—both percussion and flintlock, too, and even a minychure cannon, a Napoleon twelve-pounder that shot a fifty-caliber ball—and shot 'em alone and at matches with a muzzleloaders' club. That's why I knows so much about old guns and how they was made and all; but Bass, old buddy, knowing it, having it somewheres in your head, and being able to remember it when you wants to is two diffrunt things . . . and it don't all the time work out and come up when I want it and what I need to remember when I want it.

"Like them friction primers for cannons, see, I knows they had the bastards back around the time of the Civil War and I knows they was a whole lot simpler to make and use than what I done come up with here, but I can't up to right now remember just what the damn fuckers looked like exac'ly or exac'ly how they worked, so I just had to play around till I come up with somethin' that I know is too damn complicated and all, but at least it works mosta the time.

"So you and me and Buddy, we'll just have to wash our hair with the soap until I gets the time to work on mixing up the right stuff to make shampoo. I got me a idea, too, on making up a batch of paste to go underneath armpits, stuff like they use to make before sprays and sticks come along; if I can put powdered talc in it, it might cut down on sweat-staining shirts and all. Then too, ol' Carey Carr, he ain't worried 'bout no shampoo, 'cause he's losing his hair fast, but he does want some kind of shaving soap that'll lather up stiff and thick, and I'll work on that one, too, whenever I got the time or can make time."

When he had made use of the chamberpot, bathed, and been dried and draped in his silken nightshirt, Bass sat on the edge of the high bed, sipped at one of his cordials, and chatted with Yueh, wondering idly just to where the usually faithful Nugai had wandered off with the young knight who had guided them all up from the feasting hall. At length, when he had finished the sweet, spicy draught, he bade Yueh good night and slipped under the bed coverings, his damp hair bound up in a guilted silken drawstring cap. He composed himself and was teetering upon the very verge of sleep when he heard a soft noise just outside the door to this room, where Yueh and Nugai would sleep each night that they remained here.

After a few moments, Nugai opened the door and padded in, trailed by a smaller, slighter figure draped in a voluminous hooded cloak. Since first he had been given to Bass's service by *Reichsherzog* Wolfgang, years back, Nugai's English had vastly improved, although his accents of German and his own harsh guttural language still surfaced on occasion, especially in his construction of phrases and sentences.

His yellow-brown face split in a white-toothed smile, he said, "Pliss, Your Grace, custom iss here to giff guest bedwarmer. When to refuse I tried, the *Irischer* knight to misunderstand did and offered his own bed services for His Grace this night, so better I thought it to accept young woman. She called Ita. So long in coming we were because to wash I made her to do, as Nugai knows His Grace wants womans to be. Nugai also to examine her hair and body and find no fleas or lice on her, also no sores she hass and teeth not rotten. Cannot send her away, Your Grace, or *Righ* Ronan offended will be iss said.''

"Oh, all right, Nugai, put her over on the other side of the bed—it's wide enough to sleep me and four or five women in. But sleep I mean to do, and sleep only and that damned soon. Get you to sleep, too . . . unless you brought up more of them for you and Yueh,'' said Bass, a little exasperatedly.

Again, he was almost asleep when he felt hesitant, starting and stopping movement on the rope-springed bed. Then a soft, warm body was pressed against his back and a tiny hand crept over his hip to seek between his legs and find what it sought there. He willed himself not to respond, but his body knew its needs far better than did his conscious mind. His duties in King Arthur's service had kept him much apart from Krystal, his wife, and, of recent months, whenever they had been together and had tried sex, she had not seemed to take much if any enjoyment from it, so it had often been unfulfilling for him as well. And so, hating himself, but uncontrollably driven, he rolled onto his back and drew her slim, light body up onto his own.

Taking her head between his hands, he kissed her eyelids, then her silken-skinned throat, then at last her lips, soft as rose petals, teasing the sharp tip of her small tongue with his larger one. Leaving her head, his seeking hands found first her breasts, now pressed between them, then her creamy-soft buttocks, which he kneaded powerfully, as the kiss lengthened and deepened and both of her own hands kept up their maddening work between his trembling legs.

At last, she tore her lips and mouth away from his, then

slid down the length of his body, pulled up his nightshirt, and began to apply her tiny tongue and soft lips and little nibbling teeth to his penis and scrotum, all the while pulling at his chest and pubic hair, pinching his nipples and rolling them between her fingers.

Bass's agony was exquisite. He felt as if he had been suspended in boiling lava, and it took the still functional, still rational part of his mind long seconds to realize that the man he could hear groaning . . . in pain? . . . was he. And when, after short, endless, eon-long minutes of suffering unbearable pleasure wrought upon his flesh by this so-welcome torturer, he ejaculated, it seemed that, he feared that, he prayed that, it never would cease, that all his blood and life and being would escape in pain and joy through his spasming urethra.

But even after the last spasms had died away, the girl's mouth continued to enfold him, her tongue and lips now working gently, lingeringly, up and down and around, while her palms caressed his sweat-soaked, trembling body in circular motions. And slowly, ever so slowly, his utterly spent body began to recuperate and he felt a feathery tickle of desire returning to his damp loins.

The girl became aware of these developments, too, and commenced again her earlier activities, but Bass pulled away from her in a swift, abrupt movement. Rearranging her slender body and limbs, he knelt between her splayed legs, grasped her buttocks in his two hands, and lifted her up to where his tongue and lips could have easy access to the tangle of curly blond hairs and the red-pink labia that they failed to conceal.

Oblivious to the girl's moans—first soft, then louder and still louder—whimpers and, finally, piercing screams, he busied lips and tongue and now-nibbling, now-pinching teeth upon her hot, wet flesh. When at last he lowered her body to the bed again and drew his shoulders out from beneath her legs, she just lay there, eyes tight shut, gasping and breathing in great, ragged breaths, the entire length of her jerking with muscle spasms.

He allowed her the time to recover to a point at which

she was once more breathing almost normally and had all but ceased to jerk and gasp, then he once more lifted her flat buttocks, but this time to place a pillow beneath them. Her eyes came open—pools of tears misting over dark-blue irises—as she felt his weight upon her, and her mouth opened as if to speak, but by then he was slowly entering her body, damp and hot as live steam to his swollen flesh. Not until morning did he recall how she had whimpered and sobbed, gaspingly, that first time he entered her, tensing her body and sinking her blunt little nails into his shoulders.

Bass was awakened at dawn by Nugai, who had borne in a tray which held Bass's specially made teapot, softly steaming with the familiar herbal tea that the talented Kalmyk brewed so artfully that Bass found it not much dissimilar to the green teas of his own world and time and relished it and its sovereign restorative powers.

Grinning so widely that it seemed his broad face must surely split, the short, powerful man said, "Good girl, yess? His Grace much less tense seems today."

"Mind your own misbegotten business, you grinning yellow ape!" snapped Bass, then he relaxed, smiling himself, and said, "Sorry, Nugai, I didn't mean it, you know that. Yes, a good girl. You know, since the Lady Krystal and I . . . well, I'd forgotten until last night just how good and satisfying it all can be. There is simply no substitute for good sex shared with a willing and responsive partner."

Nugai nodded, still grinning, though not so widely as earlier. "Nugai will wake up girl and take her back belowstairs, yess?"

Bass shook his head. "No, Nugai will go into the other rooms and waken my squires and tell them to set up the bathtub in here again, then Nugai or one of them will go below and get servants up here with enough water for two baths. For food, his Grace will have bread, cold bacon, cheese, and some hard-boiled eggs, this gray dawn. Enough to feed His Grace, four squires, two pages, two Kalmyks . . . and one small female."

As the door softly closed behind the cat-footed Kalmyk,

Bass slipped from beneath the coverings and fumbled for the chamberpot . . . and that was when he took notice of the profusion of dried bloodstains adorning the front of his nightshirt.

"What the hell . . . ?" he thought. "Did the little minx really *bite* me? Or did I . . . ? Wait a minute, that first time that I . . . that we . . . and she . . . God in heaven, don't tell me she was a *virgin*?"

Affairs of his bladder forgotten, he raised his gown and found more dried blood—his public hair was matted with it—but not one break in the skin anywhere on him to account for it. That was when he gently peeled back the sheet and blankets from off the still-sleeping Ita. There were streaks and smears of blood on the backs of her thighs and on her lower buttocks, all of the lower parts of her body he could see, since she was sleeping curled up on her side. However, the sheet just beyond her and his third pillow looked as if someone had been slaughtering hogs on them.

Weak-kneed, he sank down onto the edge of the bed once more. "My sweet Jesus," he muttered to himself, "what kind of a ravening beast has living in this world made of the Bass Foster that used to be? How old is this poor child, sixteen? Maybe only fifteen? And last night I . . . but wait a minute, if she was a sheltered virgin, how the hell did she have her felatio down so pat, huh? How . . . ?"

Then there came a knock upon the door, and he hurriedly drew the covers back up over the stirring, naked, bloody girl and over his own bloodstained lap as well, before he bade the knocker enter.

Righ Ronan seemed a little puzzled by Bass's words, and had they two not been speaking English, Bass would have thought he had said the wrong thing in the Gaelic and Mediaeval French he was trying hard to learn quickly. He repeated himself.

And Ronan replied, "Your Grace of Norfolk, I have no *bonaghts*, this is the principal reason why my borders are ever so vulnerable to the inroads of that unhung bandit and oathbreaker who chooses to style himself King of Ulaid these days. The Airgialla army, such as it is, is all in Connachta, with that of my patron, the *Ard-Righ*. I would have thought you knew, since you serve him too.''

With a sinking feeling, Bass began to wonder just what the overjovial Brian VIII was up to with him and his squadron. Did the *Ard-Righ* really think that he was dumb enough to try to take on the whole Ulaid army—said to number a couple of thousand, foot and horse—with only an unsupported squadron of *galloglaiches*, a hundred and twenty Kalmyks, and six light field pieces? It would be suicide, pure and simple. Before he'd do it, he'd reboard his ships and head back to England, and if Arthur wouldn't have him for deserting Brian, he'd sail to the Empire and look up Emperor Egon and lay claim to his Mark of Velegrad and to bloody hell with Ulaid, Brian, Arthur, and their bloodthirsty games of statecraft.

Later, after he had left the *Righ*, he voiced some of these same bitter thoughts to Wolfgang, Sir Ali, and Barón Melchoro, where he had found them all lounging in the reception room of his suite, dipping cups of wine from out a keg they had found and appropriated somewhere in the palace or the town below.

"Be not rash, *mein gut Freund und Vasall*," said Wolfgang, shaking a big forefinger at Bass. "Brian a most devious man most assuredly iss, but gut troops he still values, and to fritter them avay he vould not. No, a gut mind he knows you haf, *Herzog* Bass, and to use it he thinks you vill, faced with such an impossibility, militarily."

Melchoro put in, "Bass, this Ulaid cannot be attacked from the sea without anticipation of far heavier losses of ships and men than we could endure, nor can we do more than hit-and-run raiding with our available land force, all mounted, as it is. Despite the impression left you by Brian's words, Airgialla has no available foot to support us. Therefore, we must devise some other means to achieve the ends desired by our employer. Yes?''

Bass thought to himself, "Von Clausewitz of my world

and time called war diplomacy by other means . . . or was it Bismarck? Anyway, if that's so, then isn't diplomacy war by other means? Maybe if we have no way of shooting this chicken-raiding fox, we can trap him or go into his den and smoke him out.''

To Sir Ali, he said, "Go find my squires, will you. Send one to fetch those two Italian knights up here, tell another to seek out Nugai, and yet another to try to find Sir Conn and Sir Colum. As for the fourth . . . Melchoro, do you know where Don Diego might be just now?''

The column crossed from Airgialla into Ulaid northeast of Armagh, near to the southern shore of Lough Neagh, taking the road that skirted the lough and following its way through croplands and wastes. Although gates of small castles and hilltop palisades slammed shut and hastily armed men appeared on wall walks, with the smoke spirals of slow matches plain to be seen, no one of the mounted men made any move toward these pitiful defenses, for this was not a raid they rode, but a diplomatic mission.

When the road crossed another which led away to the north, they followed the new one, still skirting the lough, which looked grey and cold under a soggy, lowering sky full of rainclouds.

Clad in court attire covered for protection from the elements and journey soil with jackboots and a hooded cloak, Bass forked a dark bay rounsey troop horse. Not sure just what might chance on this risky business he was undertaking, he had left his invaluable spotted destrier, Bruiser, in Armagh, in the dedicated care of two of his squires, his pages, and his servants. A fine high courser was being led behind him by one squire, while the other led the packhorse laden with his armor and most of his weapons. But his Tara-steel sword was at his side and the loaded and primed flintlock horse pistols rode in the pommel holsters, ready for whatever might chance.

Behind him and his gentlemen and officers trailed a column of his more easily controlled *galloglaiches* and Wolfgang's disciplined Kalmyks—a large enough force to discourage bandits and to make any prospective attacker think twice, but not sufficiently large a number to give the impression of an invasion of Ulaid. They all rode warily, erect in the saddle, swords loose in the sheaths, holsters unbuckled, axes or long wheellocks borne across the withers of steeds, spears unslung from shoulders and gripped in hands, ferrules in sockets. All these riders were veterans; their eyes were never still, darting gazes here and there, their ears listened intently for untoward sounds or sudden orders . . . in vain.

Bass was surprised. He was come to within actual sight of *Righ* Conan Ruarc Mac Dallain's new capital of Oentreib, at the northeast corner of Lough Neagh, before he saw a party a bit larger than his own riding upon the road down from the north. He halted the column then and called for Sir Ali, his herald, and Sir Colum, who spoke both Gaelic and French, as well as English, in case there might be need of a translator between the Arab herald and whoever was leading the Ulaid force now bearing down on them at a fast amble. They rode fully armed, that force, their helms in place though not yet closed, their advance preceded by a mighty clanging and clanking, squeaking and rattling of their equipment and horse gear that almost drowned out the clip-clopping of shod hooves on the road.

Feeling as much as hearing the ripple of movement behind him in his own column, Bass raised his empty hand warningly, for a shot accidentally discharged now or the sudden flash of a drawn blade might well precipitate a pitched battle, and that could be disastrous this deep into Ulaid with a relatively small force.

But he kept his gaze locked upon the leaders of the approaching horsemen. One pistol shot, or if those spears standing up above the ranks of riders should be lowered to the horizontal, and he would give the order that would put his own force into battle formation. They looked to be somewhat outnumbered and they might all be slain in an engagement, but knowing his troopers and gentlemen as well as he did, he knew damned well that they would take a fair proportion of their attackers with them.

The splendid Venetian long glass that Walid Pasha had temporarily loaned him in exchange for his binoculars showed that, although well and fully armed by mediaeval standards, the oncoming troops were not all bearing firearms of any description and that many of those who were looked to be supplied with antique matchlocks.

"And there is not much more difficult to use in battle on horseback than a two-foot long matchlock pistol," he thought to himself, recalling his early days with Sir Francis Whyffler's troop when a good number of the troopers were so armed and thus had been forced to depend upon strong right arms and edge weapons than upon the tricky, often useless (save as an unwieldy club), always unreliable handguns.

On the other hand, he and his force all bore either wheellocks or Pete Fairley's best flintlocks. The *galloglaiches* carried one brace of pistols in the pommel holsters and a second brace in their boot tops, and like as not yet another one or two thrust under their belts, or a wheellock long gun slung across their backs. The lighter-armed Kalmyk's long guns were flintlocks, like their brace of pistols, in addition to which, about a third of them still carried their old crossbows, for emergencies, they averred when questioned.

So, yes, he and his force could easily empty a fairish number of the saddles of the approaching column long before it came to the point of hack-and-slash.

Suddenly, he noted something not before seen at the head of the oncoming troops, and he again lifted the long glass to his eye.

CHAPTER
THE TENTH

Harold, Archbishop of York, sank back into his chair and regarded his still-unemptied plate, saying to his dining companion across the small table, "Rupen, something about those lamb patties tickles in me a far, far distant memory of how food tasted when I was just a little boy, in twentieth-century America."

"In what year were you born, Hal?" asked Rupen. "And where, if I may ask?"

The old man nodded. "Of course you may, my friend. I was born in 1968, in Tempe, Arizona. My mother and my father both were educators at the university there. I was the first of their three children."

"Then that answers your memory-tickle, Hal. A whole lot of folks then cooked outside, over charcoal grills, and that's just how I did these hamburgers. I rummaged through the palace kitchens until I found a grill that would more or less fit one of these larger braziers, but that wasn't the real problem. No, getting ground lamb at all was what drove me into a near-tizzy.

"You see, cooks here and now either have their assistants chop meat up fine with a knife or render it into a virtual paste with pestles in humongous mortars. Nobody here ever heard of a damned meat grinder—just another labor-saving device nobody here seems to need or want."

"So then how did you obtain one, Rupen?" inquired Hal. "Make it?"

Rupen grinned. "Not quite. One of Pete Fairley's smiths made one to my specs and drawings. You know, otherwise primitive as the most of them are over in the Royal Armory, a lot of them are damned bright, verging on brilliant, a few of them men who can't even read or write."

"Oh, come now, Rupen." Hal shook a finger chidingly at his host. "Of all people, you must know that mere education has little to do with the native intelligence of human beings, that in fact it may stunt natural abilities to some degree. No, many people here and now cannot read and write, have never had the opportunity to learn, but this very fact means that the memory of your average man or woman, here and now, is astounding—by the standards of those worlds from which you and I came. I have met and worked with common men owning a prodigious recall. Moreover, I understand that in societies even more primitive than is England—the Highland culture of Scotland or the Irish, for instance—those inheritors of the old, pagan druidic cult, called *filid* by the Irish and something akin to *fahda* by the Scots, are still capable of recalling and chanting at one sitting literally hundreds of rhymed verses of genealogical and historical accounts that go backward in time for a millennium or more."

"Speaking of the Irish, Hal, have you had word from His Grace of Norfolk? You did receive a letter from Ireland, I believe?" said Rupen.

A slight smile tugged at the corners of the archbishop's thin lips. "You are well informed, Rupen. But, in answer, yes, I did receive a letter from Ireland but no, it was not from Bass Foster, but rather from an old and dear friend, Gilbert de Courcey, Bishop of Dublin." His smile became a frown, and he added, "That letter included a few facts that I find most disturbing, too, Rupen.

"It would seem that the High King, Brian VIII, King Arthur's actual cousin—who at one time was so anxious to see Arthur and England triumph over the forces of Rome that he dispatched a full squadron, fully equipped and with mounts and baggage, of gallowglasses to help to fill out the ranks of the royal horse—may be having second thoughts on the matter of a New Rome in England. De Courcey owns proof that not only is Brian corresponding with a certain Cardinal D'Este and clandestinely meeting in out-of-the-way places with agents in Papal employ, but he has adopted two such agents—both Italian knights, most likely Papal carpet-knights—into his royal household and has dispatched them both to Bass Foster's entourage, most asssuredly to spy upon him for their masters, both lay and ecclesiastical.

"Perhaps a more telling point is that Brian has temporarily canceled the long-planned visit of Irish clergy to York to take part in the ongoing conferences to establish a Northern European Church which would be completely free of Roman domination or influence. He gives Gilbert— who was to have led that delegation—one excuse after the other, each thinner and less believable than the one preceding it.

"Gilbert de Courcey has come to believe that in order to retain him and all of Ireland for Rome, this Cardinal D'Este—who is a very powerful man in the Italian Faction of the College of Cardinals, only a little less so than the acknowledged leader of that faction, Cardinal Prospero Sicola—has laid before the High King some extremely tempting offers of one kind or another and that Brian is trying to see just how much more he can squeeze out of D'Este before he makes a decision to go or to stay."

Rupen grimaced. "And I would just bet he hasn't bothered to mention this possible change of heart and allegiance to his cousin King Arthur, either. Meanwhile, he's using some of his cousin's best troops to what ends, would you imagine, Hal?"

"Why, to do what he has been trying to do as long as he's been High King, of course, Rupen," declared Hal. "He burns to make himself true High King of all of Ireland, the only real monarch on that island, with the same kind and degree of power that Arthur enjoys in England and Wales, or that James enjoys in Scotland.

And, actually, what he desires, if ever he brings it to pass, might be the best thing that ever has chanced in that deeply riven, always unhappy land of endless wars, cruel warlords and rapacious armies constantly on the march.

"And, as I sit here thinking of it, that just may be the valuable something that Rome, in the persons of Sicola and D'Este, have offered the power-hungry High King of Ireland; in point of fact, Rupen, were I inclined to gamble, I would bet every ounce of gold I own that that is precisely what those conniving Italians have proffered to Brian VIII: support of the Church, henceforth, in his warring to unify Ireland under his sole dominion.

"You may not know this, Rupen, but the Church of this world has done everything in her power to retard or actually prevent the small, weak states of the Christian sphere from uniting or being united into larger, more powerful ones. True feudalism has been kept in full flower far longer here than in our world and time scale. Simply to retain power and make money from the sales of gunpowder and niter, the Church has been a truly divisive force in the affairs of men, splitting any natural allies, fomenting wars, and bending temporal rulers to her will with threats of excommunication, interdiction, and the refusal to sell gunpowder to those whose actions or attitudes were displeasing.

"The principal reason that Ireland is not today united is the action of the Church, Rupen. Brian or his father and predecessor would long since have conquered or otherwise won over the whole of that island had not Rome repeatedly hindered their aims through support of their opponents. And even at this late date, were Roman support and aid to be withdrawn, a very few years would see Brian precisely where he and his father before him always aspired to be."

"You'll send word of this to the king, of course?" asked Rupen.

Harold of York shook his head. "No, Rupen, nothing of this is as yet hard, provable fact. Why should I unnecessarily perturb His Majesty with mere happenings in Ireland and some of my suppositions as to what they might portend? Poor Arthur has more than enough problems to weigh down his mind and occupy his time already. Besides, there would be nothing that he could do about any of it."

"Well." Rupen Ademian set his jaw. "He could at least bring back His Grace of Norfolk, his men and his fleet. Why should he let them fight and suffer and die for his enemies . . . or for one who seems about to ally himself with Arthur's enemies?"

"Never you fear," said the Archbishop matter-of-factly. "When or if Arthur III Tudor has need of Bass Foster, he will be brought back to England . . . and that quickly. But he has no real need of him and his squadron and fleet just now, in this kingdom. They all—the men and the horses— must be fed, in war or in peace, so why not let another realm take of its substance to feed and provide for them, eh?

"And, Rupen, you have clearly misunderstood many aspects of this discussion. Brian is in no way Arthur's enemy. Indeed, he and the late Emperor of the Holy Roman Empire were the only two then-ruling monarchs to offer our excommunicant king sanctuary in their realms during the very darkest days, a few years ago, for all that had they taken him in, they could then have been themselves excommunicated and the lands they ruled been put under interdict. No, Brian is a good friend both to his cousin Arthur and to England, but he is too a very ambitious man, living with a fixation that he die as the real High King of all Ireland, and he is willing to do anything that he must to win to that lifetime goal.

"Nor is Rome any longer an enemy, Rupen. Abdul has been dead for more than six months now, and they are no closer to electing a man to succeed him than they were upon the very day he died. The whole length of Italy is become a battleground between the competing factions of the College of Cardinals and their lay supporters; the very city of Rome, indeed, was a veritable slaughterhouse before the factions came of one mind and declared that no more fighting would take place in or close around it. The

Moorish Faction and the Spanish Faction, which two have
for long been loosely allied, have brought vast numbers of
their more warlike countrymen into Italy and have even
gone so far as to use Papal funds to hire mercenaries from
the Balkans to further ravage and intimidate Italy and
Italians.

"Thus outnumbered, the Italian Faction and the European Faction, also long loosely allied, have brought or
caused to be brought into Italy troops and mercenaries
from Hungary, Burgundy, France, the Empire, Languedoc,
the Low Countries, and even Scandinavia. There has not
been fighting of this breadth and scope in most of Italy for
a century and a half, or more, Rupen.

"So, as matters now stand, as of my most lately received letters, Rome is become completely incapable of
handling her own affairs and businesses, much less med-
dling in those of other, secular realms. If the Moors or the
Spaniards win, of course, it will assuredly be back to dirty
business, as usual; but should the Italian or the European
faction be triumphant or singe the opposition so sorely that
an accommodation of some nature can be worked out, then
we may find that what I and the others have been here
planning may, after all, be unnecessary and best dismantled and abandoned, before it go farther."

Looking troubled, Rupen said, "Hal, how much do you
know of Bass Foster's life before he was projected to this
world? It's not just idle curiosity—I have a pressing reason
for asking you, but I'd like to know more about him before
I say anything more."

The old churchman shrugged his bony shoulders. "Not
too much, I'm afraid, Rupen, only what he has volun-
teered from time to time over the years I've known him.
He was a man of forty-three years of age when he came to
this world, which would make him close to fifty now. He
had been married back there, back then, two or three
times.

"His entire house was projected here, you know, with
him still in it, as well as several cats, some house mice,
and even some flying squirrels, which last became accli-

mated and are slowly spreading out from the environs of Whyffler Hall. I believe that he was born in Virginia and he was living somewhere on the banks of the Potomac River in either a suburban or a rural setting at the time of projection. He had at one time seen military service, I think, as an officer. When I once asked of him why he had had in his house the equipment and the supplies for reloading shotgun shells, he mentioned something about shooting skeet . . . whatever kind of bird or beast that may be.

"He speaks and behaves and carries himself like a cultured, educated man, and he once mentioned that his family's roots went far back in Virginia, to or near to the colonial period. But I doubt that he was really wealthy; his house, though comfortable enough by any standards, was not that of a person of real means."

"What did he do for a living back in that world, Hal, do you know that?" probed Rupen intently.

"He was a writer, Rupen, a writer of fiction, mostly. His personal library was extensive, very varied, some fiction, but mostly nonfiction reference books. He gave me some of those books when he noticed my interest in them; the rest I'm keeping here in my palace for him until he decides upon and establishes himself in a permanent seat. Some of the works of fiction in that collection give him as the author. Now, why do you put to me these questions, Rupen?"

"Hal, when you have me oversee the packing of the effects of His and Her Grace of Norfolk, out at your country palace, it was a damned good thing you did. Those so-called ladies were all of them the most light-fingered and larcenous types that I have run into in a lifetime of dealing with real sharpers and outright criminals. I finally was forced to bring in some of those nuns and have those hussies-in-waiting strip-searched, and even then, I'm sure that some of them got away with some goodies here and there. Had I not been on the scene, there might well have been damn-all to pack left, by the time they had all taken what they wanted of it.

"One of them, I don't know exactly which one, had

hung a pouch of gold and silver coins under her skirts, and the nuns found it and gave it to me. None of them are coins of this world, Hal; all are from my world, though most are older than my actual time, or Foster's either, for that matter. All of the silver and many of the gold coins are from late-nineteenth- or early-to-middle-twentieth-century America; the rest of the gold coins are what were then called 'bullion coins'—each of precisely an ounce or a half-ounce weight of a certain purity of gold, weight and purity both stated on the coins—and the ones in that bag came from the Union of South Africa, Canada, Mexico, and Switzerland . . . with a single exception."

He reached into his belt-purse, fumbled for a moment, then drew forth a small silken drawstring bag. From the bag he extracted a not-quite-round golden coin about two centimeters in diameter. He laid it upon the table between them.

Naturally, the Archbishop picked it up, and after straining to read the worn lettering on the obverse, he drew a silver-framed lens from out his own belt-pouch and adjusted its elevation up and down until he could pick out the lettering.

"Rupen, this is a Sicilian coin. It was minted at Palermo. It looks quite old."

"As I recall, it was about two hundred years old when it was bought and defaced by someone I knew, Hal. Turn it over and tell me what it says."

The Archbishop found that the reverse of the antique coin had been shaven or possibly ground down, and upon the thus-smoothed surface had been engraved letters and numbers in a flowing, flowery script.

He read aloud, " 'From C.A. to R. A., My Prince Charming, Honeymoon, June, Sicily, 1970.' But Rupen, why would anyone so ruin an old thing this way?"

Rupen looked as if he wanted to spit. "Because she was a spoiled, selfish bitch, Hal. I know, please believe me, and that is a gross understatement of the woman's character, too. She 'gave' it to me, but she was the one who had it pierced and wore it to flaunt about, after we got back from a thirty-two-day honeymoon that ended up costing me an average of seven hundred dollars a day . . . and that was only the bare beginning, too.

"Hal, my second wife, Carolyn, could go through more money in a day of shopping than I could've imagined possible before I married her, and with less of value to show for the money she'd spent, too. She would be on hand without fail, charge plates in hand, every time one of the big stores had a junk sale. We ended up having a cellar and an attic actually crammed with boxes of useless items she'd bought 'because they were reduced'—shrimp deveiners, egg slicers, cheese wires, three-minute hourglasses of cheap plastic, bales of plastic dishes and bowls and tumblers and cups and cutlery.

"That she bought clothing and jewelry and shoes and whatnot was far easier to understand than her endless collection of pure junk. And God knows she loaded up on clothes and shoes and jewelry, hats, belts, toiletries, a million and one assorted accessories, furs, you name it, and always only the best that my money would buy, too.

"Hal, I was making damned good money, but I couldn't seem to make it come in as fast as she could shovel it out. Not only was she a big spender, she was a big giver, as well; she thought nothing whatsoever of writing thousand-dollar checks to one of her 'causes,' a large number of which seemed to have to do with radical or at least left-liberal politics, these being the exact antithesis of the culture in which she had been reared.

"But she was always giving money to various members of her family, too, and not only money, either. I recall coming home from a busines trip to find the entire dining-room set gone—table, chairs, sideboard, matching custom-made corner china cabinets, serving cart, the works. Carolyn was not home, of course—there was a junk sale on somewhere downtown that day—but the cook told me that Carolyn had had some movers come in, load the furniture on their van, and deliver it to the home of one of her brothers.

"Hal, when that happened, we had only been married

about eight months and living in that house only about two of them, and that set of furniture was brand, spanking new and had set me back over five thousand dollars. I phoned the company and told Bagrat that I was back in town but I wouldn't be at the office until the next morning, then I settled down to wait for Carolyn.

"She didn't show up until well after eleven that night, reeking of whiskey and loaded down with shopping bags full of plastic and metal and glass junk . . . plus a bracelet that I'd never seen before.

"When I demanded to know why she'd given our furniture to her brother, who happened to be a thirty-odd-year-old doctor working for the Veterans Administration and could, conceivably, afford to buy his own damned furniture, she began to scream that I was a selfish bastard, that since I had not even been born in the U.S. I had no right to be making the kind of money that I was making, but that since I was making it anyway, she meant to see that it went to benefit the people who should rightfully have it. She pointed out that as she was my legal wife of record and that as the Commonwealth of Virginia had on its books a community property law, she had as much right to dispose of any property bought after marriage as I did. She went on to say that if I didn't like what she did or the way she did it, I could pack my bags and leave and she would charge me with desertion and divorce me, and that she had no doubt but that in such circumstances a court of law would give her everything she asked for, which would be everything I owned, plus a hefty amount of monthly alimony.

"She snagged a bottle of Scotch out of the kitchen and kept belting it down straight between screaming and cursing and threatening me with financial ruin and telling me candidly just why she really had been willing to marry an unpedigreed mutt like me to begin with. Finally, she threw the empty bottle at me, then passed out cold, and I undressed her and put her to bed.

"It was a few minutes later, when I was rambling through the huge purse she habitually carried, trying to find the receipt for the new bracelet so I could know how much I'd been soaked for, that I found a gift box, custom-wrapped. Feeling a little guilty for the fight we'd had, I opened it. Inside was a gold cigarette lighter and a case of what was patterned like snakeskin with gold fittings; the lighter had been engraved and the engraving read, 'to S.F. with all my love C.'

"Well, Hal, I dumped the purse at that point, found her checkbook, and figured just about what she'd written on our joint account since the last statement, and the next morning, while she was still snoring, sleeping off her drunk, I went out and rented a panel truck and a storage garage, then took everything that I really treasured out of that house and put it either in that garage or in a new, large safety deposit box. Then I withdrew from the joint account all but a few hundred dollars over the amount of checks she already had written. Then I went and found myself a damned good divorce attorney and asked a hell of a lot of questions, and armed with his advice, I started laying plans to get out of *l'affaire* Carolyn as painlessly and inexpensively as was possible, given the way that the divorce courts of Virginia seemed to be loaded in favor of the woman in almost any proceeding.

"Still acting on my new attorney's advice, I continued to live with Carolyn, for all that it became pure hell after she became aware that I had paid off all her charge accounts and then closed them and I was no longer depositing to the joint checking account, and I threatened to close it too if she overdrew it again. I gave her a thousand dollars each month, paid weekly in company checks, drawn on an Ademian Enterprises account in a Fredericksburg bank.

"I also found and hired on a private detective, none other than my old friend Mr. Seraphino Mineo, Sara the Snake, Herr Kobra, and God knows how many other *noms de guerre*. By then he was operating a security business, though how a man with his mob connections had been cleared for a private detective's license was and still is a mystery to me . . . maybe the CIA helped him as he'd helped them, years before, in Europe."

In a plain, painfully neat single-room office over a luggage-repair business on Main Street in Richmond, Sam Vanga (Rupen had nearly laughed himself sick at the in-joke; in Italian, *vanga* was a word for shovel or spade), referring to a spiral notebook from time to time, said, "Mr. Ademian, your wife is flat no good, but I guess you know that a'ready, or you wouldn't of hired me, huh? I'm just glad I can fin'ly do somethin' to help you, 'cause you sure as hell pulled my balls out of a deep crack back you remember when, and I ain't never forgot it, neither. But back to your wife. She ain't just got one stud, she's got at least three, maybe four. One of them's a nigger, too. The main one though, the one she's with the most, anyhow, is a writer what lives up in . . ." He riffled through the pages of the notebook briefly, then continued, ". . . up in Fairfax County, Virginia. It's real boondocks where his house is, right on the river. The road down to it won't take no real car; I had to rent a Land Rover to get in there. He's got a Jeep pickup and he comes and meets her in this little hick town called Dranesville.

"He ain't a bad-looking feller, forty years old, divorced, lives with two, three cats in a trilevel house, mostly keeps to hisself, but the folks in Dranesville I talked to who'd met him said he was a reg'lar feller who paid his bills and didn' seem to be a drunk or doper or nothin'. But he don't socialize much and some the folks was wondering if he wasn't queer, till he started picking up your wife there in town and taking her out to his place for sometimes as much as a week at a time, they say.

"But like I say, Mr. Ademian, he's just one of 'em, and prob'ly the best of the bunch at that; most her taste in studs is a pure taste for shit. All three the others lives right here in Richmond." Again, he riffled pages until he found the one he wanted.

"Arnie Mohr, he's a Jewboy. He ain't a doper, and that's about the only good thing I can say about the fucker. He's wunna the ringleaders of a Commie-front outfit called

Southern Students Strike Against War and Poverty and two, three other outfits just like it. You want that one hit, just say the word, I'd really like doing it to him . . . real slow and hard. He tells ever'body he's twenty-seven, but I got good, firm info he's thirty-five and he's been throwed out of colleges all over the place. Your wife, she ain't his only cooze and meal ticket, neither, see, he's got a whole string of women with more money then sense, plus a little fairy that lives with him, too.

"The other white boy she's banging here in town is a feller useta be her teacher at the city college. He teaches soshology or somethin' like that and he's married, but his wife's crippled, can't get out of the bed without help, and he and your wife bang right in the room next to her, but here again, she ain't the only broad he's screwing, some of 'em are still his students, too. I got some bona fide info on him, too, from some folks I useta do jobs for, years back." He winked broadly.

"This fucker's tied up with the Commies too, useta be one, maybe still is. He's forty-five, was in the army in World War II but didn' never go overseas. When they tried to call him back in for Korea, he suddenly turned up with a punctured eardrum. He's alla time tryin' to raise money for all kinds of hell-raising groups . . . but the word is that don't much of what he c'lects ever get where he said it was going to.

"Now the nigger, he's a doper—grass, hash, acid, coke, horse, morph, mushrooms, he does it all and some I prob'ly ain't never heard of besides, plus booze—and when he can get hisself a gig, he plays guitar and sings and they say he ain't half bad. They say he and your wife useta be a big thing, but she don't see him much anymore sincet you cut off the bread she was laying on him so's he could buy dope and all.

"Here're the pictures, Mr. Ademian, but just of her and the Jewboy and her and the college teacher; like I say, she ain't seein' Eugene Gentry, the nigger doper, much anymore, and that feller out in the boondocks, he keeps his drapes drawed up tight whenever she's in the sack with him, and even when he's alone there, too. But that's a good way to live, 'cause ain't no good burglar going to bust into no winder he can't see what's waitin' for him through, I can tell you that for a fact.

"Now, if you want them all hit, Mr. Ademian, I'll do it for you. The Jewboy and the teacher I'll do for free, 'cause I don't like fucking Commies, see, the damned Commies hurt a lotta my family when they took over Cuba, see. The other two, I'll take out for a rock-bottom price, but only for you, Mr. Ademian, I'll—"

Rupen had shaken his head. "Thank you sincerely, Sera . . . Sam, but I don't want any of them killed, I just want out of an unfortunate mistake of a marriage, as cleanly as possible, cheaply as possible, and quickly as possible. Your report and testimony and these pictures will, I'm sure, get me that which I'm seeking from the courts: justice."

"This willing murderer you hired," said the Archbishop, "never gave you the name of the other man your wife was committing adultery with, then, Rupen?"

"Yes, I'm certain that he did, that it was also in the written report that I received from him and took to my attorney along with the photographs, but I simply cannot recall what that name was. Maybe I need to take some lessons from your Irish or Scotch memory experts?" Rupen shook his head ruefully.

"Nonetheless, you now think that that nameless adulterer and home-wrecker who so wronged you was Bass Foster," said the old man bluntly.

"Well, Hal," said Rupen, "a lot of the things I do remember about that man do seem to dovetail in to things you know about His Grace of Norfolk, you know. Writer, living by a river in northern Virginia—what would you think in my place, especially, if you had found this"—he flicked a fingernail against the edge of the old gold coin—"in effects supposedly the possessions of that person?"

Harold of York sighed and shrugged. He really had no answer.

*   *   *

In far-off Italy, the warring raged and the land bled and men, women, and children died horribly. After an epic defense, besieged Perugia finally fell to the Moors and their mercenaries ran wild and uncontrollable through its streets—looting, raping, torturing, maiming, killing, burning, and otherwise destroying. When at length even the Moors had had enough, they tried to check the orgy of death and destruction and ended having to wage pitched battles to do so, losing more troops thusly than they had lost in the actual intaking.

Florence, besieged for the third time since Pope Abdul's death, held firm as she had on both previous occasions, taking severe and steady toll of the Spaniards and their Macedonian mercenaries in sally and in defense of their city walls.

The city of Rome, policed by completely impartial Pontians hired from Omar of Turkey, lay relatively peaceful, aside from a recent rash of assassinations which had taken clerical and lay lives from all of the four major factions and not a few of the minor ones as well. But there was no open fighting of any sort; the coldly merciless men of Pontos saw to that.

A force of Moors, Spaniards, and Greek mercenaries laid siege to Montevarchi, in Tuscany, only to find their entrenchments shortly surrounded by the entrenchments of a force of Italians, Hungarians, Goths, and Burgundians, who proceeded to besiege the erstwhile besiegers.

At sea, the warships of Genoa, Venice, Naples, and the smaller Italian maritime principalities did their best to keep the shipping lanes free from Moorish and Spanish privateers and other sea-robbers. These ships suffered cruelly for their efforts and right often were compelled to put into the closest well-equipped port or naval basin for repairs, which meant that strange sights frequently were seen—a Venetian frigata undergoing the fitting of a new mast in the yards of her traditional enemy, Genoa, a ship of the battle line of King John of Naples being repaired in Palermo.

Such things as this had never before happened in the memories of living men.

In his ornate and comfortable palace, safe from all mainland strife, Cardinal D'Este sat in the warm Sicilian sunlight and read with sadness of the deaths of old friends and wondered if ever the carnage would end . . . and if it then would end in his favor.

Unknown to him and the rest, he was fated to have his answer and an end to the Italian chaos far sooner than he could imagine. For even as he sat musing, an army of above thirty thousand fighting men was slowly moving through the passes of the Alps, headed south, toward Italy. There marched therein grim knights of the Teutonic and other orders, fur-clad Poles and Rus-Goths, squadrons of slant-eyed Kalmyks and Lithuanians, Prussians, Bohemians, Saxons, Bavarians, Brandenburgers, Tyrolers, Styrians, Carinthians, Savoyards, Switzers, men of Franche-Comte, Marburg, Munster, Cassel, Frankfort, Koln, Luxemburg, Stuttgart, Regensburg, Hamburg, and Bremen.

At the head of this mass of men rode a young man whom Bass Foster would have immediately known—Egon, Emperor of the Holy Roman Empire, leading his vassals and allies and mercenaries down to put an end to the Italian anarchy and to see a new Pope firmly installed before he led them all back through these same passes again.

Like most monarchs of Christendom and all other men of reason who believed in order and fairness, he had been sickened and very angered by what had followed the death of old Pope Abdul, not that he, personally, had been any too pleased with all that had transpired while still the devil-spawn Moorish bastard had lived and misruled the Church *from* Rome but *for* Ifriqah, the Spanish kingdoms, and his own selfish ends.

Unlike most of the aforementioned monarchs and other men, however, Emperor Egon was in a position to do something about the situation roiling through the Italian peninsula. He had only waited as long as he had because gathering such a host had taken time and effort and he had wanted to be certain that when he made his appearance in Italy it would be in such numbers that no one would even consider offering him battle, demur, or argument as he saw matters set right in Rome.

The electors had come as close as they ever before had come to refusal and open rebellion when he had presented them with his estimate of what this heterogeneous army would cost to raise, marshal, field, and maintain during the marches down to Italy and back. But he had managed not only to cool them all down but to get everything he had asked of them, in the end. He doubted that he could so easily have done so much with them a year back, but since his wife had recently given birth to a set of male twins, thus granting reasonable assurance to the succession of his house, he now wielded far more real power than in the past.

He meant to settle some old scores in Rome, set some flagrant injustices right—such as those wrought by Moorish malice upon his good friend King Arthur III Tudor and his unhappy, much-persecuted realm, and some serious vengeance must also be wreaked upon some of the Moorish bastards for the shameful treatment and eventual murder of his elder sister, Arthur's queen, by the Moorish minions in London. But he knew that he would have long enough in Italy to hunt them all out, try them in order to broadcast their misdeeds, and then arrange suitably impressive ways of publicly executing them; for entering Italy this late in the year, he knew that it would be next spring before the Alpine passes would be sufficiently free of snow to allow for the march back north.

THE ELEVENTH

His every nerve drawn tense as wire, Bass sat his mount, watching Sir Ali ibn Hussein, clad in his white herald's tabard, pacing his barb mare at a slow walk, and trailed by one of his squires, who bore the headless lance shaft from which depended the plain white square of linen cloth. From time to time, the Duke of Norfolk shifted the long glass to scan the head of the now-halted column of mounted men of Ulaid, over and among whom now coiled serpentine spirals of gray smoke from countless slow matches. Then, as Sir Ali drew closer to his objective, Bass concentrated entirely upon the possible foemen, for if a single shot was fired up the road there, if but one blade flashed free, he must immediately give his Kalmyks and *galloglaiches* the order to loose a volley from their long guns, then charge close enough to deliver a few deadly caracoles or pistol volleys loosed by one rank at a time. And finally, had the foemen not already either charged or broken and fled, it would be, must be, bladework.

But no one fired on or drew steel against the sacred person of the herald. Sir Ali sat his barb easily, his empty right hand gesticulating as he conversed with the riders gathered around him. Abruptly, the semicircle of mounted men opened enough for the Arabian knight to turn his mare about, and, now accompanied by three of the

Ulaidians, he returned toward the spot whereon Bass sat his own horse, with Wolfgang and Barón Melchoro flanking him a bit to his rear.

Carefully turning his head to allay any suspicion of sudden movement—for things still could quickly get very sticky if someone out there should even suspect possible treachery—Bass summoned Sir Conn to act as translator if such a need should arise in this coming parley.

As the party led by Sir Ali got closer, Bass was able to see the faces of the three who had come back with him and make some hurried estimates of them, of with just what sorts of men he would presently be conversing and dealing.

The two who trailed Sir Ali, with that knight's squire behind them, wore fair-quality three-quarter plate, with both halves of the visors open. Their scarred, weathered faces and that indescribable aura of the veteran marked them both as either professional soldiers or very close to such. As they drew still nearer, Bass could see that their plain armor was nicked and dented, scarred and showing competent field repair here and there, but not the slightest speck of rust. Their rounseys looked to be about as well bred as was Bass's.

The man who rode a big mule beside Sir Ali was altogether of a different mold—florid of face, his cluniacal tonsure marking him as some degree of cleric, but for all, he rode fitted out in an antique byrnie so recently sanded and oiled that the steel rings looked like silver beneath the patina of road dust; the barrel helm that hung on its chain at his side was probably of more venerable age than even the byrnie, but it too had been scoured shiny and oiled.

All three of the Ulaidians carried long horse pistols in pommel pipes. The two old soldiers' baldrics held broadswords with pierced steel baskets, while that of the florid, mule-mounted man was weighted down with a cross-hilted brand that would not have looked out of place on the First Crusade or at the Battle of Clontarf and thus blended well with his archaic armor.

Bass squirmed uneasily in his sweat-damp saddle. If these men—leaders? spokesmen?—were examples, he might not be confronting some kind of army or guard at all, but rather a rather large pack of banditti of the stripe who often haunted roads in out-of-the-way places, trying to coerce or intimidate "tolls" for uncontested passage out of those too strong to be robbed and killed outright; such collections of lawless scum had plagued the English and Welsh countrysides all during and just after the civil war and foreign incursions until he and the Royal Horse had had the time to hunt them all out and exterminate them like the dangerous vermin they were.

Arrived at last before his lord and leader, Sir Alai said, stiffly and formally, "Your Grace, these be the commanders of yonder force, which is all the cavalry that their army owns. It would seem that the *Righ* we seek and his still-loyal forces are at this moment besieged in the city up ahead there, Oentreib. These men lead the entire besieging force and rode out when they heard of our coming because they feared us to be mercenaries summoned from afar by the *Righ*, Conan, to take them from the rear and possibly break the siege.

"The man beside me is a priest, Father Mochtae ui Connor of Mag-Bile, who has raised the common people of the countryside to fight in support of these two mercenary captains and their troops against the *Righ* and his coterie.

"Captain Sir Lugaid ui Drona and his company were sent by this honorless fool of a *Righ* on a dismounted raid-in-force into Airgialla last month. They returned to Oentreib to discover that the all save penniless *Righ* had, in their absence, sold all their mounts and baggage beasts to a horse dealer out of the Ui Neill lands, across the River Ban, in order to raise enough money to pay the other two companies of mercenaries in his employ. Quite naturally, they at once took leave of *Righ* Conan and his city, seizing such horses and mules as they could along their way and shooting or cutting down any opposing their seizures or progress.

"One of the other two companies, that of the other captain with Your Grace's herald, Sir Ringean Mac Iomhair, joined them, no longer willing to serve a forsworn employer of the likes of *Righ* Conan Mac Dallain, by-blow of a renegade, outlawed Ui Neill.

"They pray that Your Grace may see fit to join them, for they sorely lack for horsemen of any description and the most of their trenches and homemade engines are manned by raw, untrained farmers and herdsmen and fishermen and suchlike."

With Wolfgang, Sir Colum, Fahrooq, and a few troopers making fast tracks back to Ard Macha—Sir Colum to bring back the rest of the squadron, the baggage train, the field guns, and any spare horses available, the *Reichsherzog* to use his unquestioned powers of persuasion and debate to try to get the young *Righ* Ronan to recognize and exploit this splendid opportunity, to scrape up every fighting man, horse or mule, transportable cannon or bombard, cask of powder, every other weapon or tool that might be used in warfare and proceed with all haste into Ulaid to aid in the final ruination of his own kingdom's long-standing enemy, *Righ* Conan.

Fahrooq, however, was to remain in Ard Macha only long enough to change horses, he and his escort, then to spur hard for Dublin, where lay the fleet brought by His Grace of Norfolk. Bass had been repeatedly assured by knowledgeable-sounding men that the River Ban, though too shallow the most of its length for ships of the battle line or large merchanters, would easily pass doggers, howkers, bugalets, belandres, pinks, luggers, and all manner of smaller craft. Indeed, the principal reason that Oentreib still stood against their arms and landward interdiction was that the city could be and had regularly been resupplied by small vessels sailing south on the Ban from the riverine port of Coleraine into Lough Neagh and offloading at the tiny port just below Oentreib, the roadway to which was protected by two lines of earthworks and palisades defended by light cannon and swivelguns.

Was the Ban deep enough for large warships as far as

Coleraine, then? Yes, full galleons could easily sail up from the sea and unload cargoes there, Your Grace.

Then, if all the countryside, noble and common, was up in arms against *Righ* Conan Mac Dallain, and if he was so impecunious, why did the merchants of Coleraine continue to supply him and Oentreib? They all are rabid supporters of *Righ* Conan, Your Grace, most are not of Ulaid at all, but out of Ui Neill lands, across the River Ban, and they would see all of our Ulaid as naught but a humble, exploited client state of the Ui Neills. Had we had enough men and guns, we would have interdicted Coleraine, as well as Oentreib

Dismounting some of his *galloglaiches*, Bass saw a party of river pilots, who all swore familiarity with the Ban, set out at the gallop for the headlands at the mouth of the river, but made certain that Captain Fahrooq knew them before he sent the other party southward.

When the merchants and residents of Coleraine on Ban rubbed the sleep from their eyes and rose up from their beds of a morning, two huge, long, high, multidecked men-of-war lay anchored in the channel of the Bann, along with a number of smaller armed ships. All flew an unfamiliar ensign, looking like the arms of some noble house rather than those of a principality. One of the larger ones also flew the war banner of—of all kingdoms—Turkey. Pulling on hurriedly only enough for decency's sake, men, women, and hordes of children and slaves flocked down to docksides to view at closer range these new, strange ships on their river.

Smoke rose thickly from both of the warships, rose in too much quantity for mere cookfires, thought some of the watchers uneasily. Then signal flags were run up the halyard, and immediately thereafter, gunport covers were raised and all the larboard guns run out on both of the huge liners. Steam poured out of most of the gaping muzzles, and the few men ashore who realized just what a horror this fact heralded—the reaction of red-hot solid iron cannonballs with water-soaked wads that prevented the shot from detonating the propellant charge prematurely—had barely the time to turn to run or take a breath to shout warning.

Belowdecks on the *Revenge* and the *Thunderer*, double gun crews went about the ultradangerous business of preparing, transporting, loading, and firing red-hot shot into the houses, warehouses, careening basin, docks, and shipping, letting the smaller deck guns and swivels do for the screaming, roiling crowd ashore with loads of langrage and grape. But the perilous labors of the crews of the main batteries were brief, for within the space of time that it took to discharge two or three full broadsides from each of the two ships, the entire port was blazing merrily and the shores were thick with bleeding, still or feebly twitching bodies and pieces of bodies.

Coleraine on Ban would not be sending any more ships up to offload at Oentreib, not for many a month to come.

The roars of the heavy guns, only some twenty-five crow-flight miles away, were clearly heard that morning by both the besiegers and the besieged; the latter cheered lustily, knowing full well what the distant sounds portended, while the consensus within the city was that yet another day of rain was in the offing.

Downriver, his first mission for Sebastián Bey thoroughly done—one might say done to a crisp—Walid Pasha led most of the fleet of His Grace out of the river and set sail, first bearing eastward, then southeastward. He and His Grace both had been very pleased to hear that Ulaid now no longer possessed warships of any consequence nor yet any really large pieces of coastal ordinance, all having been sold to the Ui Neills and various foreign parties to provide money for land forces to extend the borders of Ulaid at the expense of Airgialla.

The townsmen of Benchor, on the southern shore of Lough Loig, first ran, hid, and cowered in an excess of terror at the strange, awesome fleet of warships, but when Ulaid pilots had been rowed ashore and had told that these foreign ships were come to aid in the overthrow of the well

and widely hated *Righ* Conan, those same inhabitants all
went a little mad with joy.

The ships were piloted to safe anchorages, and, at his
needs being translated, Walid Pasha was shown a narrow
strip of beach below a low cliff, with a full six fathoms of
water only twenty-five yards out from the beach. Within a
few hours, demicannons and culverins were being rowed
to the beach, heaved ashore in heavy-duty cargo nets, then
winched to the clifftop by sailors who did not lack for a
host of willing, helpful hands and arms and backs from the
men of Benchor and others come in from the smaller
settlements and holdings round about Lough Loig. Others
of the inhabitants of the country had been sent far and
wide to bring back such draught oxen and sturdy wains as
could be found, for roads hereabouts were few and poor
and the shipboard gun trucks would be useless on them, so
the guns, the trucks, powder, shot, and all related equipment needs must be transported by wain or on the backs of
asses and men. But all here keenly aware that possession
and use of such big, powerful, far-ranging cannon must
speed the fall of Oentreib and so frighten *Righ* Conan that
the Ui Neill bastard would remove the ring in which he
had had mounted the sacred Ulaid Jewel and abdicate the
throne he had seized and held for so many bitter years,
with his hired, foreign warriors.

Squire John Stakeley, once a cavalryman, had been
discovered by Walid Pasha to be a born seaman, with a
feel for a ship that cannot ever be taught by even the most
accomplished instructors. The vastly experienced captain
of the Turkish warship had kept the man aboard the *Revenge*
until he had taught him the mechanics of ship handling and
the basics of navigation, then had had him posted as one of
the master's mates aboard *Lioness*, the ship of Sir John
Hailley; then, when Sir John and both of the other mates
had been slain during the mighty sea battle with the French
galleon-liner now called *Thunderer*, Squire John had taken
command, fought the ship better than well, and brought it,
despite rather drastic damages, back to port.

Being apprised of these sterling qualities and shining deeds by Walid Pasha, His Grace of Norfolk had knighted Squire John and had promised him a command whenever one should become vacant.

When the prized Papal lugger had been repaired and refitted to His Grace's and Walid Pasha's instructions in Liverpool and sailed over to Dublin by seamen left behind for the purpose, Walid—knowing how busy was Sebastián Bey with other things—had had Sir John Stakeley brought to him and had given the Englishman command of the now-armed lugger, with its rakish rigging and sleek lines.

Even with three Fairley-made breechloading rifled cannon mounted on heavy wrought-iron swivel bases, and the dozen swivel guns now mounted along the rails, the lugger still drew far less water depth than was required for any of the liners and many of the other less sizable warships. That was why she was the only one of his ships that Walid Pasha would allow to essay the higher reaches of the River Ban, local pilots or no local pilots, and he had also admonished his newest ship captain to take great care, immediately turning back should he even feel discomfort with the journey.

Two fishing boats had escaped the carnage and conflagration of Coleraine, and these Walid Pasha had had loaded with powder, shot, waddings, a few casks of langrage, and assorted other supplies, plus enough seamen to sail them and Fahrooq with a score and a half of his fighters. These vessels had closely trailed the once-Papal lugger, now rechristened *Cassius*.

Sir John had experienced no trouble at all, all the soundings of his leadsman having shown more than enough water depth for his little ship all the way south to where the river began as an outlet for Lough Neagh. The wind having suddenly failed him, he set his men to the long sweeps with which the lugger was provided and moved out onto the waters of the freshwater lake, its waters colored brownish with the stain of peat deposits near into the shores, but being a grayish-blue farther out toward deep water. Trailed by the fishing vessels which, with the lack

of a breeze, were being towed by oarsmen in the long-
boats, Sir John moved along to the eastward, keeping the
passing northern shore in sight off his larboard.

Following the advice of his native pilot, Sir John flew
no ensign or banner of any description as he came within
sight of the "Port" of Oentreib. It would have been
laughable under other circumstances: three rickety listing
wharves, supported if they could be called such by warp-
ing piles driven into the peat at the head of a little bay
closest to the walled town. There were no warehouses or
other port facilities of any description, only a cleared space
at the lough end of a more or less level dirt road and a
couple of wattle-and-daub huts, out of which came a few
men at sight of the lugger bearing in from the lough.

The men started to come out on the longest, levelest
wharf, then stopped in the cleared space when they saw
the ship, propelled by the efforts of men straining at the
sweeps, swing broadside to the shore and heard the rattling
as the fore and aft anchors were dropped to the lough bed
not far below.

Possibly more prescient, certainly more than experienced at saving their hides in sticky situations, the gaggle
of men scattered, running when they saw the gun crews
begin to swivel about the tubes of the fore chaser rifle and
one of the stern chasers. Their screams and cries of alarm
quickly brought the full attention of the men manning the
light cannon along the palisaded embankments guarding the
road from landward assault, and a few of these men began
to try to start manhandling the guns on their clumsy carriages about so as to bring them to bear upon the now
clearly hostile lugger out in the bay.

But it was too late for them, even at the outset. There
was a puff of white smoke from the bow chaser and a
screaming shell struck and exploded, dismounting one of
the six-pounders, the flying shards of iron casing killing or
maiming every member of that gun crew and several caliver
men besides.

Another shell, hard on the heels of the first, but from
the stern chaser, ploughed into the embankment before

exploding, harming no men, but tumbling down ten or twelve feet of palisade stakes. As the guns kept firing and the shells kept exploding, with men screaming and bleeding, being blown apart, and dying all around them, those who had been manning the road and port defenses apparently decided almost as one that to longer remain at their posts would be suicidal, at best. In a formless mob, they started up the road to the lough gate at a dead run, making a splendid target for shrapnel-loaded rifles and swivel guns loaded with langrage. A few of the mob actually made it into Oentreib . . . possibly they attributed such good fortune to the vaunted luck of the Irish.

But *Cassius* had not come through the action entirely unscatched, either. Two men had been killed and another seriously hurt when one of the rail-mounted port pieces had backfired, blowing apart its removable breech. Sir John himself, standing half the length of the lugger away, on the low afterdeck, had suffered a deep gash along his jawline from a piece of the gunmetal shrapnel. Holding a wad of his linen neckband pressed against the heavily bleeding wound, as clean-cut as if made with a sword, he carefully examined the port piece and, finding not the trace of even a hair crack, pronounced it safe for use, but advised all of the gunners to be exceedingly careful in checking each removable breech in turn and be certain that they were not double-loaded in use. Then he had Captain Fahrooq signaled to send over a boat to take off the wounded man and bring from the supply boats resupplies of shot and shell, plus three men to replace those he had lost.

The tall, brown-haired ship captain smiled broadly, despite the renewed and intensified pain that such movements brought to his gashed jaw. He smiled with the deep satisfaction of an assigned task well done. He also smiled with the pleasure that captaining the ship and commanding this action had brought him. It was all much less of a deadly danger than riding a skittish horse into a battle with the bullets humming all around you and uncountable yards of cold, sharp steel flashing ahead of you, with your bowels turning to water and your bladder nigh to bursting, your mouth as dry as ashes and your eyes bugging out at the sight of the man beside you still riding along, still erect in his saddle, and still grasping both reins and broadsword but without a head, a great ropy gouts of red blood spouting up out of his jagged stump of a neck and showering over everything behind him.

No, this naval business was much preferable to the service he had seen in King Arthur's Horse.

From atop a small ridge some hundred yards away from the nearest of the lines of palisades, all those who could crowd upon it watched, many of the humbler sorts awestruck, as the lugger's well-aimed and highly destructive cannonfire wrecked the guns and defenses that had for so long thwarted their aims and ambitions. But when the defenders left their positions and their now-useless six-pounders, dropped their calivers, and fled toward the city, only to be almost all cut down by the fire from the ship, the humbler besiegers—and not a few not so humble—screamed, shouted, cheered, and hugged each other in an excess of unbridled glee.

Bass, on the other hand, felt no joy at the sight, only a soul-deep sickness. Yes, it had been mostly his plan, but the carrying out of that plan had been a butchery, not a combat. None of the defenders had had even the ghost of a chance to strike back at the attackers. Yes, the butchery had been a necessary butchery, under the present circumstances, but a disgusting, sickening butchery nonetheless.

The palisades were all set afire after the cannon had been dragged away and all usable weapons, supplies, and equipment had been garnered. When the half-dozen leaders of the rebel besiegers seemed intent upon staging an immediate all-out assault upon the city, Bass demurred, pointing out that the walls of the place still stood undamaged and still mounted cannon and bombards enough to make such an assault by men unsupported by their own artillery very, very costly and quite possibly doomed to failure from its inception.

It was not until he told them of the big, hard-hitting, far-ranging cannon that he had ordered be brought in from the seacoast that he was able to convince the leaders to wait. Grumbling from the ranks he handled by the simple expedient of ordering the entrenchments lengthened, continued on through the once-palisaded area to entirely encompass the city with an endless ring of trenches and emplacements for the promised siege guns.

They all waited for two more days, and fidgeting and grumbling was once more beginning to fill the ranks in the trenches, but then proceeding from the southeast came a long column of wains, each drawn slowly by twelve to thirty span of lowing oxen, the shrill protests of ill-greased axles screaming out far ahead of them. Walid Pasha had arrived with the big guns, and Bass breathed a sigh of relief, for he had by that time about run out of convincing arguments to use in further forestalling a suicidal assault against Oentreib's walls and guns.

Another day was required to get the tubes out of the wains, set back on their trunks, and dragged or wrestled up to the places prepared for them, protected as well as possible with combinations of packed earthen embankments, palisades, logs, and thick bundles of faggots on three sides and doorframes to which were hinged thick plank doors to give protection during reloading operations.

A week to the day after the destruction of Oentreib's sad excuse for a port and its indefensible defenses, the first resounding boom of a thirty-two-pounder demicannon from off His Grace of Norfolk's ship *Revenge* sent an explosive shell over the walls of Oentreib into the streets of that unhappy city.

With Walid Pasha's batteries fully engaged and Sir John Stakley's rifles firing over the heads of the entrenched besiegers against the lough side of the city, within three days every gate had been blown down if not apart, much smoke and occasional flames could be seen above walls that were themselves beginning to show clear signs of damage and weakening of fabric with the repeated pummeling of iron cannon balls and cylindrical explosive shells. Counterbattery fire from atop the mediaeval-style walls had been mostly from huge but ancient bombards throwing stone balls, and those few guns that had seemed to cast too accurately for comfort had quickly been sighted and subjected to concentrated fire of every besieging gun that would bear, or could by rearrangement be brought to do so, until put out of action. Now, counterbattery fire from the walls had become desultory, the dwindling number of losses from gun crews mostly being the result of long-range sniping with big bore wall-mounted matchlock calivers, but there seemed a dearth of notable marksmen within the city, for hits were rare, though the inch-or-more-in-diameter balls were almost certain to be the death of anyone so unfortunate as to be caught in the path of one.

On the morning of the fourth day of the bombardment, at about the third hour after dawn, Walid Pasha received a message from Sebastián Bey and ordered a colored rocket fired up into the sky above the embattled city, whereupon all the guns ringed about the place ceased to fire.

After some of the debris had been cleared away, a mounted party of men debouched from out the damaged arch where once had stood the main gates of Oentreib and walked their horses slowly to the verge of the first line of entrenchments, the rider following the stout man at their head bearing a rectangle of white cloth bound to a reversed pike shaft.

There was no way to get the horses across the broad trench, but boards were brought up and thrown down over it to make a springy but passable footbridge so that the party might cross to the spot where the commanders of the besiegers waited in the space between the first and second lines of trenches, one of their number also bearing a plain, near-white banner.

Face to face with the *Righ*, Bass found him to look anything but regal, while his manner and bearing seemed more those of a swineherd than a ruler of men. Standing a bit behind Bass, Sir Conn translated the discourse that followed.

"Where in the fuck did you get that shitty ship and those fucking guns, Lugaid?" *Righ* Conan Ruarc Mac Dallain demanded angrily.

He was answered by Father Mochtae, however, who said in a mild tone, "Your Majesty might say that they were a gift from God, were Your Majesty not a heathen murdering bastard, unfit to sit on any throne, much less the high and ancient and holy throne of Ulaid."

Snarling, his face suffused with clear rage, the *Righ* grasped his swordhilt and started to step toward the priest, only to be frantically restrained from doing either by the men flanking him, for to break the truce here in this place would be quick suicide, death for all of them, not just the *Righ* . . . who more than one of them was silently thinking should be dead, and soon, for the good of the rest of them.

Halted, but not in the least cooled down by his lieutenants, *Righ* Conan Ruarc raised his left hand where all might clearly see the huge diamond mounted in a massy golden ring on the thumb of his big, hairy bridle hand. In a ringing voice, raised purposely to reach those in the trenches as well as those leaders now before him, he spoke.

"Hear me, men of Ulaid. You back-stabbing, ill-born rebel swine and your pig-turd great guns may drive me out of Oentreib, but in it or out of it, I still will be your rightful and lawful king so long as I bear or wear this, the Sacred Jewel of Ulaid. And because God has recognized me as lawful *Righ* of Ulaid, this ring will not, cannot leave my thumb. You see?"

He lifted up his right hand as well and gave what looked to Bass like a real effort to pull or twist the ring over the joint of his thumb, but the band would not pass the obstruction.

Behind him, Bass could hear an increasing spate of whisperings and mumbling among the humbler men who made up the most of the rebel force. A few yards down, he saw some of them beginning to clamber up from out of the trenches, dropping their makeshift weapons and milling about aimlessly. A few more minutes of this bastard's oratory and showmanship to the superstitious common men whose dispositions and mind-sets he seemed to understand so well and this almost-victorious rebellion just might fall apart at the seams.

"I wonder," he mused, "I wonder if he really tried to get that ring off?"

Without really conscious planning, Bass peeled down the cuff of his left gauntlet and drew out the small heat-stunner. After setting the stud for heat, he tried to point it from the hip, so as not to be noticed, then depressed the stud as Hal had shown him to do.

For what seemed like at least a quarter hour to Bass, nothing at all untoward happened; the *Right* continued to orate and more men came up out of the trenches to swell the throng already out and empty-handed and murmuring amongst themselves. Frantically, he tried varying the direction of the device by fractions of millimeters—up, down, left, right.

All at once, *Righ* Conan Ruarc Mac Dallain, in the very midst of yet another appeal to the God who had supposedly coronated him to rule Ulaid for the rest of his life or until He signified His Holy displeasure by causing the ring containing the Sacred Jewel of Ulaid to come from off his thumb—why, had they not seen, time and time again on feast-day gatherings in Oentreib and other places, how neither he nor other men and women, noble and humble and even priestly, had been able to remove from his thumb the ring that God Almighty had ordained to there remain?—a look of agony and terror came over his florid face. He moaned softly, then groaned loudly, then half screamed. His features became twisted and the muscles cording his thick neck could be seen all hard and tensed to the fullest, veins stood out and throbbed strongly at his forehead, his jaw joints bulged and worked as he clenched and ground his teeth.

Then, with a hoarse, bellowing scream, he jerked down his left hand and did some unseen something with the fingers of his right hand. When the bauble dropped from off his thumb, Bass and a few others could see that where it had for so long been emplaced, there now was what looked like a severe and terrible burn circling the thumb, which thumb he then instinctively began to suck at and lick.

Conan Ruarc Mac Dallain, clearly no longer King of Ulaid, did not suffer but bare minutes. Someone of the men clustered around him—none of Bass's party could see among the press clearly enough to ever say just who—drew and rapidly, cleanly thrust a dagger into the unarmored back of the former *Righ*. His eyes opened wide, his burn clear forgotten; he fell facedown upon the ground, and the hilt of the weapon could be seen standing up out of his back, just below the left shoulderblade.

Looking down at the death-gurgling body of Conan Ruarc Mac Dallain, Bass wondered aloud, "But now who is there to rule in Ulaid?"

When once he had completed his rather rushed holy rites, Father Mochtae looked up and said, "Oh, ye of little faith. Never you fear, Your Grace, God will provide us a new and a better *Righ* for Ulaid."

Not anticipating taking the hideously heavy and unwieldy guns and trucks back the way they had been brought with any real relish, Walid Pasha put men to making of suitable timbers and boards that had been used in the defenses and entrenchments rafts to be towed and guided by polemen down the Ban as far as the ruins of Coleraine, where they could then be gotten back aboard *Revenge* with far less trouble and strain.

When the rafts were ready, they were dragged out to water deep enough to float them and launched, then pulled close up to the side of the strongest-looking pier and there tied in place securely while the seamen speedily erected a strong beam and support and stapled and lashed to the beam a huge iron pulley.

Four of the long, wide rafts had been fully laden and were being poled out to *Cassius*, that the towlines might be rove, when Sirs Ali, Ugo, and Roberto di Bolgia rode up, dismounted, and wandered to the land end of the dock to observe the process being done by a mixed work gang of seamen, ship's officers, marine fighters, and Ulaidians. When tired, sweaty hands seemed to be slipping on a guiding line in the lowering of the bronze tube of a massive thirty-two-pounder demicannon, Sir Roberto hurriedly kicked off his jackboots and ran out onto the wet, mud-slimy, uneven boards to add his strength to the task. Halfway to the work crew, his feet slipped in a muddy puddle and, all the while snarling foul Italian curses and blasphemies, the big, hefty man plunged feet-foremost into the peat-murky water that lapped against the uneven line of pilings.

As he splashed into the water of Lough Neagh's northern shallows, Sirs Ali and Ugo, Walid Pasha, and the entire work crew paused in place to have a hearty laugh. But Sirs Ali and Ugo, who had come out onto the ill-built pier at a slower and more cautious pace, ceased to laugh and make broad jests at and to their unfortunate companion when he snarled and spoke.

"Damn your wormy lights, you sons of sows, help me out of here. Something's stabbed me in the sole of my foot, down in that muck. I can't reach the fornicating thing!"

Hearing the words, Walid Pasha brought a rope, and once Sir Roberto had got a good hold on it, they three and a couple of Ulaidians easily drew him up and out and onto the pier, dripping thick mud and water.

Squatting beside the soaked knight, Sir Ali grasped one of his muddy ankles and, after a moment, drew the long pin of a brooch from Sir Roberto's sole just under the arch of the left foot.

Whistling softly, he held the brooch on the palm of his hand, saying, "A lucky fisher you are, my fine Italian friend. If I am not blind, this thing that came out stuck to your foot is pure gold, heavy stuff, too, and set with what look much like small rubies, six of them. Now, what's gotten into these men, Walid?"

The two Ulaidians, upon seeing the brooch, even before

Sir Ali had pulled it free, had dropped to their knees and
were shouting a spate of Gaelic words to their fellows still
working. The only words any of the non-Irish could understand were "*Righ*" and "Ulaid."

CHAPTER
THE TWELFTH

In a windowless, doorless, stone-walled, -floored, and -ceilinged room well hidden within the recesses of the *Ard-Righ*'s royal palace at Lagore, Brian the Burly sat once again in his backless arm-stool at the table on which rested a velvet-lined tray taken from the only unlocked and opened chest of all the many lining the walls of the strongroom.

Where once, not too long ago, only two of the oddly shaped depressions sunk into the tray had been filled, now five were occupied, with but three still gaping empty, and so one would have expected Brian VIII, *Ard-Righ* of *Eireann*, to be pleased with himself and with recent events, but such was not the case, far from it, in fact.

Poking roughly at a diamond set in a ring of heavy gold that filled one of the depressions, Brian snarled like some wild beast, talking to the otherwise empty chamber as if to another person.

"I had thought—and that not too long since, either—that never would you grace this tray with your presence, you *Sassenach* pretender, yet here you are, for all the good your ownership does me or can do me or will do me. But who would ever, could ever have imagined that a Jewel—the long-centuries-lost original Jewel of Ulaid, having lain hidden in the mire and peat of Lough Neagh for near a full millennium—would've suddenly appeared, reappeared in this world of men, sunk into the foot of a damned Italian knight-for-hire, fulfilling to the very letter a prophecy made who knows how many hundreds of years ago? Hell, it makes one almost believe in the old religion that gave genesis to such arrant nonsense.

"Sir Roberto di Bolgia, *Righ* of Ulaid—the very words are enough and more to make a shit-eating dog puke. I hope the Italian swine gets the damned black-rot from the wound that that blasted Jewel put in his foot! Damn him and his damned impudence to the deepest, hottest, foulest pits of hell, anyway! The sly, backbiting by-blow bastard of a Satan-spawn Italian proceeds to send this now-valueless—well, for my purposes, valueless—piece of shit to me by way of Sir Ugo D'Orsini, along with a letter written as if to an *equal* in rank, saying that in a short while, when he has settled affairs in *his* kingdom, he will consider whether or not to continue the practice of exchanging hostages with me and the other kings and advise me in due time of his decision on the matter.

"The southern-bred pig! Why, not long since he was squatting in Corcaigh with the rest of the honorless mercenaries sent to Munster by the Jew-shrewd Cardinal D'Este to foil my then plans. Now, thanks entirely to a stroke of luck so incredible that a superstitious man might think he'd signed a pact with Satan—and maybe he did, I've long thought that Satan was certain to be an Italian, if not a Moor, pest take them all!—this foreign trespasser on the sacred soil of Holy *Eireann* is being hailed by every caste of the people of Ulaid as the authentic, God-sent king that will restore their lands to the power and the glory they think their distant ancestors enjoyed. Pah, the fools are all self-deluded; Ulaid was never one of the original Fifths, only a part of one."

Knotting up his right hand into a fist, he slammed its scarred knuckles into his hard thigh once, twice, thrice, each time harder than that preceding, the pain and action helping him to drain away his righteous indignation and rage.

Then, almost wistfully, he said, "This new, alien *Righ* might at the very least have sent me the real, the ancient Jewel of Ulaid, for surely his brother, *Dux* Timoteo di Bolgia, has told him of my needs, my high aspirations of completely uniting all of *Eireann*, of making my kingdom a force as strong in the world as the Empire or as Rome herself. It would've been returned to him . . . eventually. Well, at least he would've received back a facsimile so perfectly wrought by my goldsmiths that no one not knowing exactly what to look for and exactly where to look could've told the difference between the old and the new. And I would never have told a living soul of the substitution . . . unless the time came that I thought it best for Ulaid and *Eireann* that he be deposed and replaced."

His finger, that same finger that had stabbed so cruelly hard at the nearby diamond thumb ring, now moved to gently, lovingly caress a large golden brooch of ancient workmanship. It centered a lustrous sapphire, and four isosceles triangles, formed by lines of much smaller sapphires, lay at each point—north, south, east, and west—of the larger, roundish central stone.

"That's what I did for you, my sweet, my lovely," he crooned to the bauble of stones and cold metal. "That's why you still are here, safe with me, you know. Your replacement took a bit longer than I'd thought it would, when first I envisioned it; the goldwork was not difficult, it had long been roughed out and waiting only the finishing and careful comparison with yours, but the stones I had gathered were mostly of the wrong shade and I had the devil's own time speedily finding enough others of the proper shade. but it's all done now, and you're safe, you'll stay here, with me, in your velvet bed, unless there be more trouble with Munster, of course, and I need to prove the new king, this *Righ* Sean FitzRobert, was never truly coronated by the ancient rites and therefore cannot, has not ever truly been, *Righ* of Munster and *Ri* of FitzGerald. So, sleep you well, my pet."

Turning away from his pleasure, he frowned sourly at the three still-empty depressions in the rich, well-padded cloth. "*Hmmph*! I'll have to get my hands on a pattern of that rediscovered Jewel of Ulaid, then get a new tray made for the Seven Jewels and One. As for the old *Sassenach* diamond, it can just go into the chest of precious stones yonder—it's a fine enough specimen, but no longer a Sacred Jewel of *Eireann*, of course.

"As for the other three, well . . . my war in Connachta just seems to drag on and on and on. Christ damn that *Righ* Flaithri, anyway! The old fart has his bolthole, and he knows it and he knows I know it, worse luck, and I'm beginning to think that the only way to run him finally to earth, corner him and get what I want of him, is to somehow, someway close that bolthole in his ugly face. But how, pray tell?

"Maybe send the elder di Bolgia and his condotta, and that Ifriqan and his to *Magna Eireann*, perhaps? Without that place to flee to, I'm certain Flaithri'd come to quick terms with me. But no, not di Bolgia, not as yet. FitzRobert is too short a time *Righ*, and at any time, any day, one of those drooling, idiotic FitzGeralds could decide he or one of his nearer kin has better claim to Munster and either slay FitzRobert or raise a warband or both, and in such case I might be faced with just the same troubles I had with *Righ* Tàmhas the Unlamented, all over again, without a strong force on hand to quell any such FitzGerald-spawned foolishness at the onset.

"His Grace of Norfolk? Hmm, now there's a distinct possibility. He's even got his own ships, good ones, too, two of them better than anything I own, and were that French liner down in Corcaigh added to the private fleet, I dare to say that the resultant flotilla would be unbeatable by any fleet west of France or north of the Mountain of Jibal Tariq.

"Of course, His Grace's land force is unbalanced—only horsemen and a few, light cannon. I wonder . . . ? *Righ* Roberto . . . fagh! That good Gaelic title coupled with that foreign name sounds like an obscenity and leaves a taste of ordure on the tongue. Anyway, though, that man is certain sure to be in dire need of hard money after so many years of Conan Ruarc's misrule. Sir Ugo tells me that he has in Ulaid no less than three condottas, all now foot, since the late *Righ* sold all the horses of the cavalry in their absence. He seems on friendly enough terms with His Grace, so maybe His Grace, backed by my money, of course, could arrange to hire away from him enough foot to give some balance to that agglomeration of Scots *galloglaiches*, Kalmyks, Turks, Irish, Germans, English and Welsh, Provençals, and God alone knows just how many other breeds of man.

"But, thinking harder on the matter, I think I'd best wait and see what sort of a job His Grace does for me with my northern cousins. I don't know—he seemed a very catalyst of sorts in Ulaid. Yes, he got me what I had sent him north to get, but he got it in a way that has begat yet another problem for me—a newfangled problem that just may end in costing me more money, more blood, and, worse, more time than the original did and might've cost. Another such 'victory' for me by this great captain of Cousin Arthur's may well serve to ruin my plans for *Eireann* altogether, may mean that I'll not live long enough to collect all the Jewels, leave my tray of pretties part-empty forever.

"No, I'll just wait and see how His Grace of Norfolk goes about getting me the Striped Bull of Ui Neill, before I do aught else than get him some foot out of Ulaid, perhaps. Hmmm, yes, I'll do that . . . or at least try to, for that will not only help him and therefore me and my aims, but it will also weaken the available force of this new *Righ* of Ulaid, a laudable end, in itself.

On the return march to Airgialla and *Righ* Ronan's capital of Ard Macha, Bass had been expecting to meet the vanguard of the young *Righ*'s scratch-force army just beyond every bend of the road, but he led his squadron back into the Airgialla capital without so doing.

Even before he dismounted, Bass was informed by *Righ* Ronan's chief councillor that there was to be a great feast to celebrate his victory in Ulaid on the morrow, but Bass was just then in no mood for feasts or celebrations of any description. Signing his officers to come with him and his gentlemen, he stalked into the palace and through its corridors, salons, halls, and chambers, he and his armed gentlemen intimidating guards and terrifying courtiers at every turn with their grim, businesslike, no-nonsense manner.

They at length found *Righ* Ronan and *Bean-Righ* Deirdre lying side by side on a wide couch set in the garden behind the palace, sipping wine from a loving-cup of gilded silver and listening to the girl Ita sing a sad-sounding song in Gaelic while her so-slender fingers struck notes from a lap harp. Neither of the royal personages altered position or even bothered to look around when the sweaty, dusty men in their heavy jackboots tramped up behind them to a jingle and clank of weapons and equipment, so Bass deliberately paced around the couch to take his stand between them and the still-singing girl, whose small, heart-shaped face had brightened at the sight of him, despite the sad words she still sang and the doleful notes her hands extracted from the small harp.

Obviously more than a little tiddly, the youthful *Righ* smiled up at Bass and said languidly, "Ah, our good friend and most doughty champion His Grace of Norfolk has at last returned. Do you know that I have ordered a full feast, with suitable entertainments, for the day after whatever day you returned to Ard Machta?"

"Your Majesty," said Bass, bluntly and without bothering to try to mask the exasperated anger in his voice, "when first I came upon a very promising situation in Ulaid, I sent Sir Ugo D'Orsini to you with word of it and a request that you immediately bring all available force to Ulaid, along with such spare horses, guns, and supplies as you could quickly amass, the better to take advantage of that situation to your benefit and that of Airgialla. Your Majesty told Sir Ugo that you intended to do just that and in some haste. But Your Majesty clearly did not do that or anything else of note that I can discern. Why not?"

The *Righ* shrugged. "Oh, Your Grace of Norfolk, look at me; you do not see here in me some sweaty and muscle-brained and bloodthirsty savage of an Irish warrior-*righ*, nor yet a captain-general such as dear Cousin Brian, the *Ard-Righ*. I did not come because I could see no point in aping the warrior and possibly getting all of my fine guardsmen—the only men of arms left in Airgialla, since I loaned the army out to Cousin Brian—disfigured or maimed or even killed.

"You see, my dear Sir Bass, I had great and abiding faith in you, in your abilities to bring to a halt all inroads upon my borders by that rude, crude ruffian Conan Ruarc Mac Dallain ui Neill. I knew that you would be triumphant. You have been, and now that you are returned, we will have a grand feast."

"Yes, I won . . . in a way," agreed Bass, then adding, no less coldly and forcefully, "but I might just as well have lost. Because you did not come, chose to not come for poor reasons, I was forced to cart in shipboard guns to use for siege pieces against the walls of Oentreib, not even to mention bombarding and burning to the ground the River Ban Port of Coleraine, killing God alone knows how many men, women, and children. Even if you were loath to send your palace guards to fight, you might at least have taken a half-dozen of the fortress-size guns from your walls and laid them in wains and sent them and gunpowder and shot up to me. Your Majesty is, after all, supposed to be the *Ard-Righ*'s sworn ally, and I am one of his captains."

"Take guns from off the walls, Your Grace?" The *Righ* looked and sounded slightly shocked at such a suggestion. "Oh, heavens no. Why, those things are frightfully heavy and terribly clumsy; they weigh, each of them, thousands and thousands of pounds. My guards and my servants together would not be able to accomplish such a thing. I would be obliged to bring in hordes, just hordes, of dirty, smelly, sweaty common workmen from the outer city, bring them into my very palace. Why, such a thing is unthinkable!"

Bass shook his head. He was getting nowhere fast with this so-called *Righ* of Airgialla. He wondered how such a ball-less wonder had ever gotten chosen to be a *Righ* to begin with. Where every other Irishman he had met in this world was seemingly hung up on wars and fighting, this one could think of little save planning feasts and entertainments. He was damned lucky that he had an old warhorse like the *Ard-Righ* for patron; otherwise he would not have lasted any longer as a *Righ* than a wet snowball in hell.

He nodded once. "All right, Your Majesty, forget your fucking feast. Me and mine will only be here long enough to collect our baggage still in Ard Macha and march on south, toward Tara.

"Your Ulaid border now is safe; *Righ* Roberto seems to have no designs upon any portions of Airgialla. *Ard-Righ* Brian's orders to you—yes, I unsealed and read that letter, then resealed it, call me and my action what you wish— were to supply all the needs of me and my troops, make good any losses of horses, and pay us, upon completion of our service to you, at the rate of one ounce of gold per trooper, five ounces per officer, and ten ounces per belted knight, plus twenty ounces for me, their captain. I'll expect payment in full of your treasurer, this day, Your Majesty.

"Don't even consider trying to stiff me in some way, Your Majesty. As ill-defended as this place is, I own sufficient force to raze both your palace and your capital to the ground . . . and I am just sufficiently angry and disgusted with you to do just that given even the slightest of incentive or motive.

"Another thing. As much as I worried and sweated in your absence, I think I deserve a bonus atop the twenty ounces of gold. No, I don't want more of your bullion, I'll be taking the girl, Ita, with me." He pointed a thumb over his shoulder at the seated girl.

"But . . . but . . ." stuttered *Righ* Ronan. "But she is a most valuable slave. She's thirteen, almost fourteen years old, a well-trained concubine for either men or women and, before you took her flower, a virgin. I had intended to soon send her for sale in Spain or in Egypt; so fair a girl will bring a very high price in such markets, even more if I have her first revirginized."

Bass fought to control a rage that might well end in him striking the *Righ*'s too-pretty face with the knife-sharp edge of his Tara-Steel sword a few times, and the fat would really be in the fire should he do that; he might well then just have to sack and burn this place after all, in order to get him and his squadron out alive.

His jaws clenched so tightly together that he half feared his teeth might crack under the pressure, he grated, "You sad excuse for a man, you! You sent a helpless slave girl, a thirteen-year-old child, to bed with a barely known foreign mercenary almost four times her age, not even caring for her terror or for what he might do to her? My Turkish seamen have told me of one of Sultan Omar's favored means of execution, and I had never before this moment imagined any crime deserving of so horribly protracted a death . . . but, now, you *Righ* of pimps and slavers, I think I have; if any living man or woman fully deserves impalement upon a dulled oaken stake, it is assuredly you!

"*Nugai!*" The tone of his voice brought the half-armored Kalmyk to his side in an eyeblink of time. "Nugai, take Ita out of this palace immediately. You and Yueh take her into the town and see that she has all that she needs for a journey down to Tara with us. Should anyone ask to be paid for the goods, tell them that *Righ* Ronan will pay. The same applies to a horse and a horse car of sufficient size to carry her, a driver, and her effects. Have Sir Conn there explain to her that she no longer is the property of this thing who calls himself a man or anyone else, that she may stay with me as long as she wishes to do so and that I will provide her needs, but that I do not own her. Now, take her and get out of this den of slavers!"

They moved out of Ard Macha just after the noon hour, all waggons groaning with heavy loads of supplies, several new waggons loaded with munitions from the royal armory, twenty-three head of spare troop horses, eight head of decently bred coursers, one of Bass's warchests now heavier by nearly a hundred pounds of gold. Screaming, gesticulating, cursing merchants of many sorts and stand-ings, some of them in tears at the thought of lost profits and of having to try to collect from *Righ* Ronan, flanked and trailed the column as it wound through the narrow, crooked streets. But none of them got or stayed too close, for—sensing the current mood of their captain—the grim *galloglaiches* and black-faced Kalymks had already and publicly done painful violence upon more than one merchant who had committed the cardinal error of protesting too much the otherwise-bloodless near-sacking of Ard Macha.

They camped that night only ten miles from Ard Macha and, not sure just what *Righ* Ronan might essay, maintained tight security. But they were already again on the march the next morning before a guardsman on a well-bred black courser gelding overtook them. A curt order to halt and the sight of some drawn pistols allowed Bass to relieve the same young knight who had offered, through Nugai, to bed with him of a folded, waxed, and sealed—*and* heavily perfumed—missive addressed to *Ard-Righ* Brian VIII. It was written in French, and so Barón Melchoro translated it.

"Bass, my friend, that puling wretch back there has herein laid at your door the blame for every crime save only regicide, incest, and public sodomy . . . but then, seeing him, this messenger girl of his, and some others I well recall of his court, I would imagine that sodomy, either public or private, is no crime at all within his domains.

"He seems unusually anxious to get back that slave girl of his; indeed, he mentions her thrice and the gold only twice."

"Well." Bass smiled as he shredded the vellum with his dagger. "I think we need not see the *Ard-Righ* waste his valuable time reading such fantasies."

"What of him?" growled Sir Conn, hooking a thumb at the wide-eyed, sputtering Airgialla knight. "May I kill him, Your Grace?"

"No," said Bass, "from what little I know of him and his habits, you'd dishonor your steel with his blood. Tell your *galloglaiches* to take his horse and anything else of his they fancy and to chase him well away from the road.''

A second galloper, bearing an even more slanderous message, overtook them during the next day's march and was afforded equal treatment. That gave Bass two more decent coursers to add to his remuda and some of his *galloglaiches* a few bits of unexpected loot.

Bass was not exactly sure just what he could or would do with Ita. Since learning her true, very tender age, his guilt at having used her to his gratification and pleasure that night had so affected him that sex was now the farthest thing from his mind when he looked at or conversed with her through a translator. But one thing that he did know was that there was no way in hell or creation that he would see her ever taken back to her shameful enslavement in Airgialla, not if he had to kill half the adult male population of Ireland to keep her free.

"But how to be certain that she does stay free, that is the most pressing question," he thought to himself as his courser maintained the slow, unhurried pace of the southbound column. "Brian is tricky, sneaky, sly, and set on his own ends, and anything that will advance those ends. I assume that he will next send me back north to see the Ui Neills and get their Jewel away from them by hook or by crook or by main force, if need be. I've stopped two of Ronan's messengers, but another one is bound to get through to Brian eventually, and then Brian just might decide, with me in the field, to ship Ita back to his bunghole buddy in Airgialla.

"I could take her down to Dublin and put her aboard *Revenge*—she'd be safe from Brian and Ronan there—but a warship that might go into action at any minute is simply no place for a young girl to live for who knows how long.

"No, I think the only thing to do is to send her over to England. That's it, I'll send her to Hal, along with a letter detailing some of her story and asking him to care for her until I get back from here. Now, who to send with her? Hmmm . . . Nugai . . . but I can't send him alone. An Englishman would be best. I know, that man I knighted and gave a ship command recently. Sir John Starkley? No, Stakeley, that's it, Nugai and Sir John Stakeley. That'll kill two birds with one stone, so to speak; his dispatch lugger can sail them over to Liverpool, then he and Nugai can disembark and take Ita up to York. Ronan will play pure hell laying his slimy hands on her again in York, under the full protection of Archbishop Harold.''

Bass then little knew the surprises in store for him . . . and Ita.

When the *Ard-Righ* had told him of his plan to hire a condotta of foot from *Righ* Roberto, he asked Bass, "All right, Your Grace, you've met all three of those captains, served alongside two of them against the third. Now which one of them do you think you best could work with, depend upon, and command in battle?''

That was why the cavalry camp, in the lands of the Slaine Clan, between Tara and Lagore, was enlarged just in time to begin to house some four hundred *galloglaiches* out of the Scottish Western Isles—an identical breed to Bass's original squadron, but these newcomers fighting afoot, with matchlock calivers, pikes, axes, and greatswords. That was also why a day dawned that saw His Grace of Norfolk in conference in his headquarters with Sir Ringean Mac Iomhair, who once had served and fought in the lands of the northern Ui Neills and thus knew something of them from a soldier's viewpoint.

Widely traveled, like many another professional mercenary officer, and also owning a middling if informal education, as well as the ear for languages and dialects which was the natural endowment of not a few Celts, Sir Ringean spoke a reasonable English, plus all of the Scots dialects, Irish Gaelic, Norse, Danish, French, Flemish, Welsh, some German, and stray words, phrases, and obscenities in a number of other tongues, so Bass had no trouble at all in conversing with this newest of his captains.

While awaiting the arrival of Sir Fingean and his condotta, Bass had ridden down to Dublin and personally seen Ita and Nugai aboard Sir John Stakeley's sturdy, swift-winged little lugger, *Cassius*. He had given the loyal Kalmyk a generous purse of gold and specific oral instructions to him, Sir John, and the bilingual Irish serving woman he had hired in Slaine to attend the girl. He also had given Nugai a handful of letters—two for the Archbishop, one of which the churchman was to send on to King Arthur, one for Sir Peter Fairley, one each for the bailiffs of all three of his English holdings, one for the Lord Admiral of Arthur's navy, Sir Paul Bigod, one for the nobleman who was fostering his son, Joe Foster, and one for his wife, Krystal.

However, when he made to depart the deck of the lugger, Ita clung frantically to him, both her slender arms about his neck, showering him with a flood of teary kisses and Gaelic words.

Uasal, the middle-aged serving woman, translated: "Ita says that she should not be so sent away to an alien land, to dwell among strangers, but should rightly remain here to serve Your Grace in all ways so long as he lives. She says that His Grace was the very first freeman who ever was kind to her, since the slavers took her as a very little child from the homeland she cannot remember. She fears that she never again will be able to see and serve and comfort His Grace. She says that this should not be, for she is his now more fully than she has ever been any other master's, bound to him not just of the body but of her soul. She avows her love for His Grace with all of her heart, swears by the Sacred Heart of Our Lord that this be truth, and she once again beseeches him to not send her away."

Disentangling himself from the girl's arms, Bass took her small head between his two palms and kissed her softly upon her forehead and her two damp eyelids, then said, "Uasal, please tell Ita that I am not sending her to my friend in England because I dislike her or the sight of her, but because there is no other way that I can keep her free, protect her from reseizure by the folk to whom she was for so long in bondage in Airgialla. In England, under the shield of the powerful man to whom I am sending her, she will remain safe and comfortable and well cared for until my work here is done and I can myself return to England."

But even after the tiring-woman had finished her translations of his words, still did Ita furiously fling herself upon him, holding to him so very stubbornly that it required the efforts of both Uasal and Nugai to pry her loose and allow Bass to quit the ship.

For several days after, he wondered if he had done the right thing for the little sometime slave girl, then he was summoned by the *Ard-Righ* to his official residence complex near the Hill of Tara. Brian received him quite formally in a small but plain audience chamber lacking any furnishings save carpets, a single cathedra chair, and a silver wine table beside it to hold the monarch's potables. Brian himself held a bared ceremonial sword and looked grim as Bass was ushered in by well-armed foot guards, who had disarmed him beforehand.

Without any greeting or preamble, the *Ard-Righ* said, "Your Grace of Norfolk, I have received word from *Righ* Ronan of Airgialla, my client and ally. He writes that, among other heinous acts, you saw fit while there to insult him, humiliate him, and even offer violence to his sacred royal person. He goes on to write that you intimidated him with your raw force of arms and thereby extorted over a hundred pounds of gold from him, then proceeded to loose your troops upon Ard Macha to loot almost that much again in goods, horses, and rolling stock with which to bear all your booty away. He continues, writing that at very sword points you took from his palace a very valuable female slave, whose services and person he had loaned you out of the goodness of his heart while you had been his honored guest in his palace. He further writes that you intercepted two noble messengers he dispatched to me, opened, read, and then destroyed the letters they bore, robbed them of all they owned down to their naked skins, had them well striped, then chivvied out into the countryside and woodlands by your troopers. He does not ask for your head, though he does, it would seem, have sufficient grounds; rather, he prays that I forthwith force you to relinquish and return to him his slave, his gold, the lifted horses, and such goods as remain available and unspoiled. I stand inclined to honor his requests at this minute, but I first would hear your side of the matter, Your Grace. Just what is your answer to this plethora of serious charges?''

"Your Majesty," said Bass, being every bit as cool and as formal as the *Ard-Righ*, "you gave me a copy of the letter which I bore to *Righ* Ronan when first I was sent to Airgialla, and in it it was stated that you expected him to render me all needed assistance of a supply or a military nature whilst I was up in Ulaid, yet when I asked foot troops of him before I marched, he swore that all he had were with your army in Connachta, and when I asked for aid and supplies and guns to be brought up to the siege of Oentreib, none of the three ever came; *Righ* Ronan never so much as left his palace and his feast hall.

"As regard the gold, well, Your Majesty's letter spelled out the amount of specie *Righ* Ronan was to pay me for the services of me and my condotta, and that is the exact amount I took from his treasury, no more than that.

"Insofar as robbing Ard Macha is concerned, I had my men take from the merchants there the supplies owed them and me from the campaign in Ulaid, some few remounts, and a couple of waggons, leaving behind some unsound but curable horses and some damaged but repairable waggons in exchange.

"As for the messengers, Your Majesty, I by then considered *Righ* Ronan to be my bitter enemy and I dealt with his guardsmen gallopers as such. However, if it is Your Majesty's wish, I will collect the horses, weapons, gear, and clothing of those two carpet-knights and send them back to Ard Macha."

In a marginally friendlier tone, Brian demanded, "And this so valuable slave girl, Your Grace, what of her? Why did you steal her away without paying *Righ* Ronan, her legal owner, at least a part of her worth? Slave stealing is a capital offense, you know. Turn the chit over to me, Your Grace—I'll send her back to Ard Macha and then smooth things over, you'll see. If you want a slave girl, take your pick of mine, more than one, if you wish.''

Bass told Brian exactly why he had taken Ita from Ronan and Ard Macha, leaving out nothing. Then he said, ''I thank Your Majesty for his kind, well-meant offer, but I cannot deliver the girl, Ita, up to him, for she by now is in England, in the care of His Grace Harold, Archbishop of York.''

The *Ard-Righ* sighed and leaned back in his cathedra, letting the burnished, bejeweled sword clatter down at his feet. ''Yet an other quick-witted, prescient man of intelligence you are, Your Grace. It's no wonder that my cousin Arthur so treasures you. All right, I'll send sweet Ronan the horses and whatnot you took from his two pegboys, along with a purse of twelve ounces of gold—no slave girl, no matter how well trained, is worth more than that, I trow! I'll also send along a letter earnestly advising him to let the entire matter drop at this point and charge it all off to securing his Ulaid border.

''Immediately after the new condotta has arrived in Mide and is well amalgamated with your horse, I'll be expecting you to move north and into the lands of my northern cousins.

''Draw whatever you need from my quartermasters, they're expecting you, but be not overburdened, for you'll be living off the country. I don't think you'll ever have to go into real battle up there, but I want them to think that you mean to rob, rape, pillage, and burn until they have been stung enough to face you . . . and me, off. All us Ui Neills used to be fierce, proud, doughty warriors, and we of the southern branch still are, but my northern cousins, alas, are mostly become near as decadent as my client and ally *Righ* Ronan.

''But Your Grace, the present *Righ*, in Dun Given, will be easy enough to deal with, I neither want nor need another in his stead, so please try not to replace him, eh? Above all, please try not to yourself become a *Righ*. I shudder at the mere thought of having the old Northern Fifth of *Eireann*, the entire Fifth, controlled by Your Grace and one of the di Bolgia ilk; in such case, *Eireann* would very shortly be united, I venture to guess, but not under me as *Ard-Righ*."

Brian stood up. "And now I must ask you to leave. Sir Ugo has ridden in a half hour agone with an urgent message from Corcaigh. He refuses to give it to any save me, personally and privately."

Brian was deeply shocked when he laid eyes to Sir Ugo and quickly arose to press the tottering Italian knight into his own chair, while loudly roaring for another, a table, and brandy to be brought immediately.

Sir Ugo's face was pale and drawn with pain and strain. His bridle arm was roughly, hastily bandaged with torn strips of linen in two places—between shoulder and elbow and between elbow and wrist—and both the wrappings were showing old and more recent bloodstains. His forehead looked burned and blistered, and the hair above it had been singed off, in some way, almost back to the crown of his head. A cut and a wide patch of bruised flesh were over his left cheekbone, and there was blood crust in his black mustache, which also showed traces of singeing.

The battered knight's lips were cracked and the lower one looked to have been bitten clear through . . . and more than just once, too. He collapsed into the cathedra and gratefully gulped the entire pint of ale proffered by the *Ard-Righ*, though the monarch had to help to hold the tankard steady.

"You bear a letter for me, Sir Ugo?" Brian inquired softly.

The knight shook his head, wincing and gasping despite himself at the movement, which brought tears into his bloodshot eyes and a fresh trickle of red blood from both his nostrils. "No, Your Ma . . . jesty, message. *Righ* Sean . . . dead, murdered. The Ifriqan condotta . . . broke oaths, killed their captain . . . officers . . . joined FitzGeralds, who slew FitzRobert just as he was about to be made *Ri* of FitzGerald.

"With *Righ* Sean's head on . . . spear . . . attacked palace, all of them. *Il Duce*, I, guards, servants, fought, held . . . until condotta could be summoned, arm get to palace. I . . . had to hack way out of city. All my men, squires . . . killed there or in fights on road to border.

"*Il Duce*, condotta, palace guards, Venetian gunners hold palace, fortress, inner city, port. Fleet safe but unable to do much except fire shells into concentration they see to form. *Il Duce* begs aid, relief."

Then, even as the additional furnishings and the brandy ordered were being borne through the doorway, Sir Ugo slipped from the chair, unconscious.

"Take him to my suite," ordered the *Ard-Righ*. "Let my personal physicians be summoned to see to his wounds. Tell the physicians that this knight *must* recover, for I feel—have long felt—that he bears destiny upon his shoulders.

"You, there, have His Grace of Norfolk sent to me at once. And you, Sir Baetan, collect my squires and arming men. They are to meet me in the palace armory. Then present my compliments to Sir Artgal and tell him I order him to mount my guard, ready for an immediate departure for Munster. I mean to leave before nightfall."

EPILOGUE

Manus Mac Dhomhnuill, Bishop of the Isles, was younger brother of Sir Aonghas Dubh Mac Dhomhnuill, Regulus of the Isles, Earl of Ross, and a man with whom to reckon, only King James having more power in Scotland, and there were those who said that James had less than the fierce, dour Mac Dhomhnuill of Mac Dhomhnuill.

Despite his savage antecedents and ilk, Harold of York had found the man of late-middle years to be courteous, cultured, well educated, and widely traveled, an excellent conversationalist with a near-brilliant, surprisingly open mind. They first had met and conferred during the time that Harold had been arranging the treaty of alliance with nobles and high clergy representing King James, at Whyffler Hall. They had since met twice more, at York, and Harold had been most pleased when he heard that the influential bishop was once more bound for England and York.

After day-long conferences, Harold took great pleasure in sitting before a warm fire on the hearth of his smallest parlor and chatting on a wide variety of subjects with so witty and well read a companion. Often, on this visit, he had brought in Rupen Ademian as well, that he might overhear and thus learn more about his strange new world from the lips of a man who had seen much of it, far more than had the Archbishop, bound down as he had been for so many years with not only churchly duties but affairs of the kingdom.

On an evening, Bishop Manus drained off the remainder of his jack of ale and said, "While ale be a true sovereign for thirst, your grace, would you not pefer a bit of mulled wine on so damp a night as this?"

Harold smiled and nodded. "An excellent suggestion, friend Manus. Rupen, please go out and tell Alfred to fetch up the necessaries . . . oh, and see if little Ita be not yet abed. She owns a true talent for mulling wine just so."

While the girl knelt before the hearth, watching the mulling irons heat and mixing spices with rare, dear white sugar in a brazen mortar, the Bishop of the Isles grinned slyly and winked at Harold, remarking, "Your 'ward' indeed, old friend. She's a bit young and skinny for mine own tastes, but I doubt not that she can warm a bed nicely, for all. Are we two not become close enough to speak truth one to the other, Harold?"

"I have spoken nothing but truth, Manus," said the Archbishop gravely. "This poor child here was delivered out of most odious bondage to a wicked king in Ireland by His Grace Sir Bass Foster, Duke of Norfolk. Fearful that she might be retaken and returned to him who had held and abused her, His Grace sent her to me here, bidding me keep her until he return from King's business oversea. She seems a sweet girl, though she speaks no English or French, so I cannot talk with her and learn more of her history."

"Irish, is she, then?" asked the bishop. "Then let me try, eh?"

To the kneeling girl, he held out his right hand, saying in the Gaelic of the Western Isles, which was not too dissimilar from some of the more northerly Irish variants of that widespred tongue, "Child, come here."

Hesitantly, the slim girl arose from before the hearth and took the few steps necessary to stand before the Scot, ceasing to tremble when she saw the gentleness of his dark-blue eyes. Dropping her gaze by chance, for a moment, she saw the odd-shaped purplish mark on the palm of his hand, bearing a vague similarity to the head of a bull with one cursive horn.

Suddenly smiling, she said in Gaelic, "Master . . . master, Ita has a mark like that, too. See?" she held up her own opened right hand.

Harold and Rupen, comprehending none of the guttural language, both sprang up in alarm, certain that the Scot was suffering some sort of seizure, for he had stared, bug-eyed, at Ita's tiny hand, first paling to ashiness, then going red as fire.

Grasping both her wrists in a crushing grip, Manus demanded of the once more terrified girl, "*Who are you, child?*" Who was your sire? Your mother? *Damn you, tell me!*" Furiously, he shook her. Trembling and gasping like a spent horse, she spoke no more words, but rather began to cry.

"Manus . . . ?" said Harold of York softly, then, when he did not thus get the Scot's attention, his voice took on the timbre and snap of the military leader he had perforce been in years past.

"Bishop Manus Mac Dhomhnuill, you will at once release the child and cease to abuse her and shout at her! What has she done to offend you, anyway?"

After Rupen and Harold had dried Ita's tears, comforted and calmed her to the point of only an occasional burping sob, and she sat at Harold's side upon the carpet, her head against his knee, the Bishop of the Isles began to speak.

"Harold, you must know that between the vicissitudes that befall folk of all ranks and stations on the Isles, very few of us make old bones, least of all the men and women and even bairns of mine own house and clan. My poor brother, the regulus, sired no daughters, only sons, eleven of them. Of those sons, three died at birth or near to it, two more were taken to God while still children, one was lost with the most of his ship's company in a great tempest at sea, two fell in battle here in England during the late ill-starred Crusade, and yet another was so badly maimed on the retreat back to Scotland that he died shortly after he had been brought back to his home. Another fell, foully murdered by a coward out of the Stillbhard ilk, in the very midst of a sacred truce. The last, my poor brother's long-chosen heir, though the youngest of all eleven, died with all his retainers when pirates—presumed to be Irish slavers—attacked his island home, took away all the common folk, and laid siege to his tower. Unable to take it against such fierce resistance, they finally fired the roof, and my nephew then sallied out with his gillies and so wrought upon the attackers that they neither stripped nor mutilated his corpse, leaving it even his sword and armor, lest his indomitable spirit, living on in his arms and blade, do them all to death, in time.

"Those who were next to land on that island say that they believe that that brave young man's wife took her own life lest she be enslaved and dishonored. Her ten-year-old son lay beside her, they said, having fought so hard and well, despite his tender years, that at last they had slain him, too. But no one ever found the body of their daughter, then a child of about four years . . . until now, here, in this room and on this blessed night."

He half-rose and drew his chair closer to Harold's. Whimpering, Ita shrank from him, cringing closer to the Archbishop, who softly patted her head with a blue-veined, bony hand.

Bishop Manus held out his own right hand, palm upward and held in such a way that both firelight and candle-light illuminated it and its vivid red-purple birthmark.

"You see this mark, Harold, Sir Rupen? It is known as the Bull from the Sea, and so far as is known, it never has appeared on any bairn save one sired by a Mac Dhomhnuill . . . and not all of them. My brother has the Bull, I do, and that valiant prince who died defending his own, Iain Mac Dhomhnuill, bore it as well. His brave little son did not, but . . . *but his tiny daughter did!*

"Now, Harold, take that girl's right hand and look well at what is upon the flesh of *her* palm."

Rupen stood up to see the better as Harold held the opened hands of Ita and Manus close together in the bright firelight, scrutinizing them from several distances and angles. Then he shook his white-haired head in amazement, saying, "Save only for the disparity of sizes, they are almost identical, in shape and in coloring, as well."

Bishop Manus nodded. "Just so, Harold. Now you know why I became so agitated. This Ita can be of no ilk save that of Mac Dhomhnuill. And she looks of just about the right age to be the little grandniece for the repose of whose innocent soul I have for so long prayed. Nor can any of you imagine how my poor bereft brother will rejoice at this blessed occurrence. His Grace of Norfolk will know well the gratitude of Clan Mac Dhomhnuill, ere long, and you, too, my dear friends."

And so, a month later, down the road from the north came such a cavalcade that the citizens and garrison of that city once called Jorvik brought in their kine and barred their gates, thinking that the thrice-damned Scots once more were sending an invading army into England. Beneath a crested banner of finest silk, it bearing a motto in Latin—*Per Mare per Terras*—and borne high aloft on a gilded ashwood lance shaft, rode a richly dressed man. Although his face bore the marks of age and war and sorrow, his body looked muscular and firm and he easily handled the reins of a tall, prancing stallion.

Behind him, his banner, and a score of bodyguards rode above two hundred knights and noblemen, their squires, sergeants, and attendants. Two hundred mounted axemen preceded and flanked a long and rich train of waggons, a herd of spare horses, and a larger herd of skinny cattle of the long-horned and -haired breed of western and northern Scotland.

To the inestimable and very evident relief of the folk of York, this host of Scots camped on the site of the old Royal Army camp, well outside the walls. Only the old man and some of his guards, nobles, and knights actually entered the city, riding straight to Yorkminster and the archepiscopal palace.

Thanks to the efforts of Harold, Rupen, and Jenny Bostwick, the girl who was brought into the room, wherein were assembled Aonghas Dubh and his principal vassals,

along with Bishop Manus and a selection of the Scottish
clergy just then in York, Archbishop Harold, and Sir
Rupen, looked far less the part of a recently freed slave
concubine and far more like a young maiden of good
breeding.

Rumbling in a basso voice that sounded not in the least
aged, the fearsome Lord of the Isles said in his native
language, with tones that none of his many enemies ever
had heard or would, "Come you to me." Stripping off
his doeskin-and-gold-thread riding glove, he held out to
her a scarred and sinewy hand the palm of which bore the
same red-purple mark as did her own and that of the
bishop.

Now, at Bishop Manus's firm insistence, Ita had been
kept completely ignorant of the fact that this great lord was
coming, and this day had been held secluded and alone in
a distant part of the palace, so that she might have no
inkling of the identity of the man she was being taken to
meet. Therefore, the near-miracle that followed came as a
shocking surprise to all who saw and heard it, those who
could understand Gaelic, that is.

His hand still extended, Aonghas rumbled yet again, "I
say, come you to me, little fair one."

Then, it happened. Ita's forehead wrinkled briefly, while
her lips shaped soundless syllables, and then she said,
questioningly, "*Seanair? Seanair tarbh?*"

Bishop Manus, among others of the Scots, paled and
gasped, then he grasped his pectoral cross while his lips
moved. But his brother roared out a wordless cry and in
two long strides was upon Ita, his powerful arms crushing
her frail form to him, while unashamed tears of joy cas-
caded down his lined, scarred old face and his thick,
massive body shook to the intensity of his sobs, as he
gasped out her true name over and over again, "Eibhlin,
my little Eibhlin, joy of my heart, Eibhlin, yes, you are
back where you belong, Eibhlin, with your Grandfather
Bull, Eibhlin, and no foul Irish pigs will ever take my little
Eibhlin from me again, Eibhlin."

Fully spanning her waist with both his hands, he rasied her above his head and turned about so that both of them faced his amazed vassals. "Look upon her fairness, clansmen," he said in a voice that rattled the leaded panes in the windows, "for she is of our ilk. Look upon my dear little granddaughter, Eibhlin Mac Dhomhnuill, restored to us by God and a *Sassenach* Duke, assuredly our Lord's implement. Look upon her! Now, down on your knees, all of you, and afford her her due homage, for she is Princess of the Isles and from out her loins will come your next chief and regulus!"

Sitting at meat later that day, the two brothers flanking the Archbishop and Ita-Eibhlin beside her grandfather, the old regulus explained, "*Seanair tarbh*, Your Grace of York, means Grandfather Bull. Before she was stolen from us, it was her chief pet name for me, as it had been her poor young murdered brother's before her. It was only some eight or nine years ago she was taken, and we of the Mac Dhomhnuill ilk are noted for our memories. I wore today those clothes I wore when last she saw me . . . or as close to them as I could find, hoping that her Mac Dhomhnuill memory might cause her to recall them and recognize me. And, as you all saw and heard this day, she did. She can be naught save what I proclaimed here before my clansmen, Eibhlin Mac Dhomnhnuill, Princess of the Isles, her husband to be the sire of the next chief and regulus."

Livid with rage, Kogh Ademian, president and chairman of the board of the Ademian Enterprises conglomerate— the ultrasensitive nature of the defense equipment manufactured by some of the companies within that conglomerate giving him a great deal of power with certain governmental agencies and persons—glared at the three men standing before his monstrous desk and snarled, "And I say, bullshit, damn you! It ain't no way on God's green earth that none you fuckin' college boys can get me to believe that my oldest son, my own fuckin' older brother, two of my nephews, and *nine* other people can just flat, *poof*, disappear off a fuckin' lawn of a fuckin' lit-up river place with a half a hundred fuckin' Ay-rabs watchin' them! It's just fuckin' impossible, and if you three fuckers can't see that, then you all of you is got shit for brains. Hear me?''

State Police Lieutenant Marty Gear, who had come along to see the big-shot Armenian at the request of the two federal agents who had come up just as dry as had he and his investigative staff in the search for even a trace of the missing musicians and dancers, had not liked the loud, arrogant, and abusive swell from first meeting, and he liked him even less now. He had never taken kindly to being cussed at and called dirty names by anybody—man or woman or punk kid, black or white or whatnot, rich or poor, American or foreigner. When the two federals said not a word, looking down at their Corfam shoes and moving not a muscle, Gear decided it was up to him.

Clearing his throat, he asked, ''Mr. Ademian, has it been any letters or calls you've got from anybody as might've snatched your kinfolks and the rest?''

''Well, thank God for good old-fashioned honest-to-pete cops,'' snorted Kogh Ademian. ''Lootenant, that's the least dumb-ass thing I've heard since you three stooges come in here. Naw, it ain't been a fuckin' word from no fuckin' body. I done put feelers out all over the whole fuckin' world, checkin' up on anybody we can think of might of had a reason or thought they had a reason for to try and hold my fuckin' feet to the fire for somethin'—the goddam Russkies, of course, them and the Chinks and that fucker Castro. Then too, we got feelers out at all the damn fuckin' nitwit groups—the PLO, the IRA, all them fuckin' Commie nigger groups in Africa, the SDS and SNCC and CORE and RAM, them bomb-happy Basques with the ETA, the TPLA, and I don't know whatall. I even got a fucker checkin' out the fuckin' Cosa Nostra, fer God's sake! I've done ever' last thing I can. Now what're you three fuckers doin', huh?''

Lieutenant Gear held his piece this time, figuring that it was now the turn of the feds in the barrel. But neither of them spoke for long moments.

"Goddam you, you dumb cocksuckers, I asked you a fuckin' question!" Ademian urgently prompted. "Is one of you gonna answer me or have I gotta start makin' fuckin' phone calls to some fuckers who will *make* you answer me?"

The senior of the two agents took the ball and tried to run with it. "Mr. Ademian, sir, every square centimeter of that estate on the Potomac has been gone over extensively and repeatedly by different teams, each one starting out from scratch, and nothing of any value or significance has been turned up. All the servants, the caterer and all his people, every man, woman, and child who was a guest at that party has been questioned exhaustively, most of them more than once, and exactly the same story has been gotten from all of them."

"Exhaustively?" growled Kogh Ademian. "Until who was exhausted, you or them Ay-rab fuckers? And what the fuckin' shit you bastards expect them to say? That they had my boy and my brother and my nephews and all them took off by somebody?

"Shit, you candy-ass motherfuckers sound dumber and dumber ever' time you open your friggin' mouths! Them Ay-rabs ain't gonna tell you what really went down out there long as you all is nice and polite to them. Ay-rabs and Turks, they got no respect for folks what's polite. What you gotta do is take them fuckers down in a basement someplace and beat the holy livin' shit out of them till they comes to tell you the fuckin' truth. You ain't got the guts to do it, I got some men that will! Just give me the word."

"Mr. Ademian," said the senior agent in evident alarm, "what you, ahhh . . . suggest is completely illegal by federal statutes and by those of every state. We cannot and would not ever perpetrate such horrible interrogative practices. As for you and your men, you were well advised to leave well enough alone. Some of those people have diplomatic immunity, you know, and I think—"

"*You think*!" snapped Kogh scornfully. "Mr. shithead, you don't know how to think nothin's not in a fuckin' lawbook somewheres. So, okay, I won't take my men Ay-rab huntin' . . . for a while, yet. But you take diplomatic immunity and shove it straight up your fuckin' asshole, mister. You get the truth out them fuckin' Ay-rabs fuckin'-A quick, or you all gonna be out panhandlin' down around the bus depot in D.C. after your fuckin' unemployment has run out. And mister, you ask anybody knows Kogh Ademian and they'll tell you I don't threaten nuthin' I ain't prepared to fuckin' do!

"You find out what happened to my boy, Arsen, and my brother, Rupen, and all and you find out goddam fast or I'll nail your fuckin' hides to the fuckin' wall. Now, get the fuck out of my office and get to work!"

ABOUT THE AUTHOR

Robert Adams lives in Seminole County, Florida. Like the characters in his books, he is partial to fencing and fancy swordplay, hunting and riding, good food and drink. At one time Robert could be found slaving over a hot forge, making a new sword or busily reconstructing a historically accurate military costume, but, unfortunately, he no longer has time for this as he's far too busy writing.

For more information about Robert Adams and his books, contact the National Horseclans Society, P.O. Box 1770, Apopka, FL 32704-1770.